THE MON... INVESTIGATION

Claude Izner

Claude Izner is the pen-name of two sisters, Liliane Korb and Laurence Lefèvre. Both booksellers on the banks of the Seine, they are experts on nineteenth-century Paris.

Lorenza Garcia

Lorenza Garcia translates from French and Spanish. Her two most recent translations are *The Père-Lachaise Mystery* by Claude Izner, which she co-translated with Isabel Reid, and *Trouble in My Head* by Mathilde Monaque. She lives in London.

Isabel Reid

Isabel Reid studied History and French at Oxford University and has lived in France and Geneva. Her most recent translations are *Wolf Hunt* by Armand Cabasson and *The Père-Lachaise Mystery* (with Lorenza Garcia) by Claude Izner.

VICTOR LEGRIS MYSTERIES BY CLAUDE IZNER:

Murder on the Eiffel Tower
The Père-Lachaise Mystery

Praise for *The Père-Lachaise Mystery*:

'. . . brilliantly evokes 1890s Paris, a smoky, sinister world full
of predatory mediums and a ghoulish public, in a cracking,
highly satisfying yarn'
Guardian

'. . . briskly plotted, intriguing second outing for Legris'
Financial Times

'A charming journey through the life and intellectual times of
an era'
Le Monde

'. . . top Gallic hokum'
Observer

'. . . an extremely enjoyable, witty and creepy affair'
Independent on Sunday

THE
MONTMARTRE
INVESTIGATION

THE
MONTMARTRE
INVESTIGATION

CLAUDE IZNER

Translated by Lorenza Garcia and Isabel Reid

GALLIC BOOKS
London

A Gallic Book

First published in France as *Le carrefour des Écrasés* by Éditions 10/18

Copyright © Éditions 10/18, Département d'Univers Poche, 2003
English translation copyright © Gallic Books 2008

First published in Great Britain in 2008 by Gallic Books,
134 Lots Road, London SW10 0RJ

A CIP record for this book is available from the British Library

ISBN 978-1-906040-05-5

Typeset in Fournier MT by SX Composing DTP, Rayleigh, Essex
Printed and bound by Norhaven A/S, Denmark

2 4 6 8 10 9 7 5 3

As always, to our dear ones!
And to Andrée Millet, child of Montmartre,
Elena Arseneva, Kumiko Kohiki, Solvej Crévelier.
Warm thanks to Jan Madd.

Dans les plix sinueux des vieilles capitales,
Où tout, même l'horreur, tourne aux enchantements,
Je guette, obèissant á mes humeurs fatales . . .

In sinuous folds of cities old and grim,
Where all things, even horror, turn to grace,
I follow, in obedience to my whim . . .

Charles Baudelaire

Les Petites Vieilles – Dedicated to Victor Hugo
from *Les Fleurs du mal*, 1857

CONTENTS

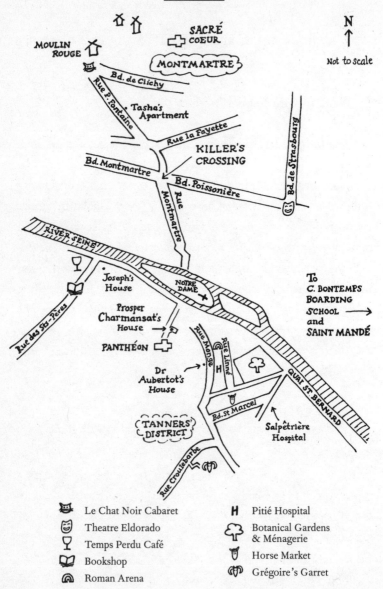

PARIS

N ↑
Not to scale

MOULIN
ROUGE

SACRÉ
COEUR

MONTMARTRE

Bd. de Clichy

Rue P. Fontaine

Tasha's
Apartment

Rue la Fayette

KILLER'S
CROSSING

Bd. Montmartre

Rue Montmartre

Bd. Poissonière

Bd. de Strasbourg

RIVER SEINE

Joseph's
House

NOTRE
DAME

Prosper
Charmansat's
House

PANTHÉON

Rue des Sts-Pères

Rue Monge

Rue Linné

To
C. BONTEMPS
BOARDING
SCHOOL →
and
SAINT MANDÉ

Dr
Aubertot's
House

H

QUAI ST BERNARD

Bd. St Marcel

Salpêtrière
Hospital

TANNERS'
DISTRICT

Rue Croulebarbe

🐱 Le Chat Noir Cabaret
😀 Theatre Eldorado
🍷 Temps Perdu Café
📖 Bookshop
🏛 Roman Arena

H Pitié Hospital
🌳 Botanical Gardens
   & Ménagerie
🐴 Horse Market
🐸 Grégoire's Garret

CHAPTER 1

Saint-Mandé, Sunday 26 July 1891

Quick! She had to rinse her hands and remove the traces of jam.

Mademoiselle Bontemps hastily dried her hands and cast a longing look at the plate piled with strawberry biscuits, mocha cakes, éclairs and meringues. Resisting temptation, she shut the plate away in the bottom of the cupboard. 'I'll have them this evening when everyone's gone to bed . . .' She smoothed her dress over the crinoline she persisted in wearing as if she were still only twenty, and rustled back into the salon, where her visitor was putting on his gloves.

'Excuse me for taking so long, Monsieur Mori,' she simpered. 'I thought I heard a tap dripping.'

'Yes, I distinctly heard running water too,' replied the immaculately turned out Japanese man.

He adjusted his black silk top hat, which complemented his double-breasted blazer and pinstriped trousers, and attempted to extricate his cane from an umbrella stand decorated with a profusion of frills. The entire salon was overrun with flounces and furbelows: they embellished the curtains, the seat covers, the shelves laden with knick-knacks and even the hostess's dress. They ran all over the décor, their rippling little waves forming an unceasing tide, and indeed the elegant Asiatic seemed to be suffering from seasickness as he wrestled with the swirls of material. Finally managing to reclaim his stick, he let out a sigh.

'And where is your goddaughter?' asked Mademoiselle Bontemps.

'Iris has gone off to the fête with her friends. I don't approve of these popular outings.'

'The young must have their entertainment.'

'Pleasure heralds regret, just as sleep heralds death.'

'Oh, Monsieur Mori, that's beautiful, but very sad.'

'Well, I don't feel light-hearted at the moment. I don't like separations.'

He pretended to examine the tip of his cane, which he had been nervously tapping on the carpet.

'I do understand,' murmured Mademoiselle Bontemps, discreetly rearranging the pleats of the umbrella stand. 'Don't worry, Monsieur Mori, two months will pass quickly.'

'I'll have her bathing suit and sunhat delivered by Thursday. Are you still leaving next Monday?'

'God willing, Monsieur Mori. Lord Jesus what an expedition! It will be the first time I've taken the young ladies to the seaside. They're beside themselves with excitement. I've had to reserve four compartments. What with the cook and the two chambermaids we're a party of sixteen. The journey is costing an arm and a leg! And when you're away for more than six weeks, you're not entitled to the cheap excursion rate. In previous years, we've made do with Saint-Cyr-sur—'

'Morin, yes, yes, I know,' finished the Japanese man, clearly exasperated.

'But what can you do? Times change; now all people talk about is tourism, beaches and bathing!'

'Make sure Iris never goes into the water without supervision.'

'Of course! The young ladies will not stray by so much as an inch from the roped-off area. I've engaged a swimming teacher.'

'Keep an eye on him, especially if he's attractive.'

'Monsieur Mori, I watch over my girls like a cat—'

'Over her kittens, I know, I know. Would you be able to call me a cab?'

'At once, Monsieur Mori. Colas! Colas! Where has that rascal got to? He's the gardener's son, a good-for-nothing,' she explained, casting a smug glance at herself in a mirror adorned with plump cherubs, and delicately adjusting the two looped coils of dyed black hair on either side of her moon-shaped face. A youth appeared, sullenly chewing a straw.

'What on earth is he wearing? You'd think he'd been dragged through a hedge backwards. Go and find a cab and be quick about it – Monsieur is waiting.'

As soon as he was out on Chaussée de l'Étang, the youth stuck his tongue out at the heavy bourgeois building behind the iron gates on which a brass plate read:

C. BONTEMPS BOARDING SCHOOL
Private Establishment for Young Ladies

Then he set off, following the sound of the fête's music to the square in front of the town hall.

A handsome, rather feline young man of about twenty pulled himself from the chestnut tree on which he'd been lounging and fell into step behind him. Colas was about to cross over to the line of cabs in front of Gare Saint-Mandé when a hand grabbed his shoulder.

'Oh, it's you, Monsieur Gaston! You gave me a fright.'

'You took your time!'

'Well, I couldn't get away from the Boss.'

'Here, take this to you know who,' said the man, handing him a note.

'How will I find her? They're all at the fête – have you seen the crowds?'

'That's your problem. Go on, kid, get on with it.'

'Look at that one with the gold braid on his uniform and all the medals – isn't he handsome!'

'If you like all that metal. He's so red in the face he looks as though he might burst! I prefer the chap with the trumpet; look how serious he is, with his great fat neck and that stomach like a big drum!'

A dozen young girls in light-coloured dresses were lined up at the foot of a podium, admiring the brass band of the municipal fire brigade. The girl who had admired the uniform was a gawky girl in a hat weighed down with cherries. She turned to her companion, a dumpy little person as crimped as a freshly groomed poodle, and gave her a severe look.

'You're so vulgar, Aglaé, just like a shop girl! And out with no hat into the bargain!'

'Well, I can't help it if my father's only a shopkeeper. We can't all be the niece of a rich marquis!'

'Oh, go to the devil!'

Oohs and *aahs* greeted the strains of '*L'Alsace et Lorraine*', and the enthusiastic crowd joined in:

> *You Germans can take our plains*
> *But you'll never put our hearts in chains*

'That's enough, you two; stop bickering!'

Fed up with their squabbling, the pair's friends separated them with blows of their parasols. Two of the girls, a slim brunette dressed in blue and a plump blonde in bright red, took advantage of the general scrimmage to slip off into the crowd. They stopped, out of breath, by the swing-boats.

'They're loathsome,' declared the blonde. 'Squabbling in public, like fishwives!'

'Will you come on with me, Élisa?' asked the dark-haired girl, fascinated by the motion of the swings.

'Iris, you're completely mad! We've just had lunch! And why they served us split peas in this heat, I can't imagine! The old frump must have bought a job lot on the cheap.'

'As you like, but I'm going on,' declared Iris, moving resolutely towards one of the newly vacated swings.

Before Élisa could stop her, a boy in shirtsleeves was installing Iris on the bench of the swing and setting it vigorously in motion. Iris sat rigid as he pushed her harder; she held on to her hat with one hand, while with the other she clung to the side.

Élisa tried to watch her friend in motion, but when Iris stood up and bent her knees to increase her speed, she grew dizzy and turned away, pretending to take an interest in a strongman who was lifting a dumbbell bearing two cheerful midgets.

'Mam'zelle Lisa!'

She jumped. Colas put his finger to his lips and slipped her a piece of paper.

'It's from the man who wrote to you before,' he whispered. 'He says you've got to hurry – it's a unique opportunity, and won't happen again. I had trouble finding you. I was late to begin with – the cabs were all taken – and the Chinaman and the Boss are going to be furious, that's for sure.'

'Where is he?'

She noticed his outstretched palm and gave him a coin.

'He's hiding,' the youth blurted out, and took to his heels.

Élisa checked that Iris was still swinging and retreated under the awning of a stall selling marshmallows, where a man with his sleeves rolled up dangled thick glossy skeins of green and red paste. A group of children, noses pressed against the counter, were following his every move, intoxicated by the smell of melted sugar. Élisa unfolded the message. She immediately recognised the cramped handwriting and glanced up at the sweet-seller, her face radiant. She had longed for this to happen. For as far back as she could remember, she'd had a strange sense that she was destined for something special, but she had begun to lose patience of late. She was seventeen years old and the routine of Bontemps Boarding School was far from exciting. If this goes on much longer I shall die of boredom, she thought to herself each morning.

It had been just over a month since the stranger had burst into her life. Although she had never spoken to him, he was always in her thoughts, and she had even begun to dream about him. At first he had been just another ordinary fellow who appeared when Mademoiselle Bontemps and her girls took their walk along the lake. He would pass by with an indifferent air, never looking at any girl in particular – although after a while each of them believed that he had come just to see her. None of the girls confided their secret desire to be noticed by him – who would admit to an attraction towards the extravagantly dressed bohemian? Then, one evening in June, he had sent her a note. After lights out Élisa had taken the note over to the window and read it by the light of the street lamp:

You is the most beautiful. I love you.

Gaston

Twenty-three equally laconic, misspelt messages had followed that declaration. She had kept them all, meticulously hidden beneath the mantelpiece. Gaston scarcely had the makings of a great romantic letter-writer; his prose was limited to the most elementary construction: subject, verb, a compliment sometimes qualified by a superlative, and above all love, always, always love. She was bowled over by his persistence, but she had never dared to reply. This time he had surpassed himself, quite a feat for a man normally so concise!

Leave your friends, make up a xcuse, and join me at the botom of the slope behind Pont de la Tourelle. I love you,

Gaston

Did she dare abandon Iris and go to the rendezvous? Iris would worry, and tell Mademoiselle Bontemps. She would have to invent something – and quickly. Dizziness? . . . She could tell them she felt ill. It was almost true. She felt hot all of a sudden – her head was spinning; she was seeing herself anew, as Gaston saw her. He found her beautiful; he loved her!

Darkness was falling and all around the fête Chinese lanterns were being lit. The showmen were haranguing the passers-by.

'Ten centimes! Only five for soldiers!'

The whistling trombones punctuated the sonorous tone of the barrel organs and the rhythmic drum rolls. A clown in stockings was perched on a barrel, calling out that the best attraction was Nounou the famous flea master. A few yards further on, two exhausted ballerinas in sequinned costumes jiggled about in a poor imitation of belly dancing.

'Come and see the headless man talk!'

'Waffles, who would like my waffles, come and taste the delights of Pantruche!'

'Toffee apple, mademoiselle? For the apple of my eye!'

Élisa wandered among the excited throng crowding the stalls and almost bumped into Aglaé, her mouth stuffed with dough-nut. The fête had freed her to behave as she liked. On the opposite pavement, plump Mademoiselle Bontemps, decked out like a ship in full sail, tottered towards a merry-go-round on which three of her girls were perched.

'Edmée, Berthe, Aspasie! It's late, where are the others?' she shrieked.

Élisa melted into the stream of people heading back to Paris. Near Gare Saint-Mandé a crowd had gathered round a busker who was singing a popular song to the accompaniment of a fiddle.

Mademoiselle! Pray listen to me
I want to offer you a glass of Madeira

She went round the side of the railway station, darted out on to the platform and stopped short, almost under the wheels of a train. She recognised Monsieur Kenji Mori, Iris's godfather, leaning out of the carriage. She fled, staying close to the station wall.

She had finally reached the embankment. She took a good look around, but saw only amorous couples and marauding dogs. Which direction would he come from? What would he say to her? Suddenly she was frightened. She remembered her mother's advice:

'Don't fight it, my dear; fear is good – it helps us to avoid all manner of disagreeable things.'

When she thought of her mother, Élisa was torn between anger and pity. Now aged thirty-five, the poor woman had had a series of lovers without ever finding true passion. Her love life had begun badly, and nothing had turned out as she'd hoped. Élisa was certain that she was not like her mother. Even as a young child in a London boarding school, she had boasted to her friends: 'One day my father will come and take me to his estate in Kent. I'll marry a lord – he'll be madly in love with me!'

Her father, whose name she did not even know, had never appeared.

The railway ran along a trench between two embankments –

in one direction to Paris, in the other towards the eastern suburbs and the banks of the Marne, to Nogent, Joinville and Saint-Maur. Élisa leant over a hedge running along the fence and took in the view. She had always been keen on trains; they conjured up far-off places, glamorous encounters, luxury and freedom . . . But the dark platforms below her were reminiscent of an ant hill; she wondered with detached curiosity what would happen if she were to bombard the people with stones.

Like a mechanical toy, a train wrapped in a cloud of steam arrived from Vincennes. It had barely come to a halt when the human tide surged towards the carriages, but to the irritation of the waiting throng, most of the doors opened on to crammed carriages. The people ran about looking for spaces, but in vain, and there were altercations and shouts of protest. Disappointed, the ants resigned themselves to wait for the next train. One man with a top hat and cane who had got on to the train was now leaving it, followed by his wife rigged out in a purple dress and his *antlet* in short breeches. (Élisa was pretty sure that word did not exist and decided that she had just invented it). Amused by the absurdity of the turmoil below, she forgot about her rendezvous as she stood on tiptoe to drink in the scene.

Hidden behind an overgrown hedge, Gaston smoked a cigarette and watched the young girl. He had had his fair share of wenches and normally had no hesitation in undoing a bodice or ruffling up a petticoat, but this time he was wary. The girl seemed to come with a warning: 'Careful, fragile.' He had known such a delicate flower before, carefully reared in the best society, pale-skinned, with exquisite undergarments, and he could recognise one from afar. How should he approach her?

Bow and kiss her hand; then compliment her on her pretty face and fine ankles? That would be beyond him. He knew only one way of expressing his desire and that was to fling a girl on the ground and smother her with the rather rough kisses to which wenches of his milieu seemed partial. He lit a second cigarette from the end of the first, giving himself a moment longer before he made his advance.

The ant with the top hat was searching the carriages for a free seat. Élisa looked to the right, her attention caught by a serpentine movement. She could foresee the disaster about to unfold. Unable to pull out because of the comings and goings of the top-hatted man, the train from Vincennes was about to be rammed by another train, which had been hooked up to a locomotive and was being pulled backwards into the station.

The noise was terrifying. The blind train, its back to its victim, slammed into the stationary train, crumpling it with an appalling crunching sound and crushing it under its weight. It seemed to devour the last three coaches. Mounted on a heap of iron, its funnel brushing the vault of the Pont de la Tourelle, the engine, mangled into an inextricable tangle of pipe and axle, breathed its last. It had all happened in a few minutes. The noise reverberated interminably and when it ceased, screams could be heard.[1]

Staring in horrified fascination at the dislocated bodies of the driver and engine stoker, her ears ringing with heart-rending cries, Élisa was dimly aware of the swarms of people scrabbling up the sides of the embankment, away from the darkened railway line. She stumbled, feeling as if she were soaring over the clouds on a swing that had cut loose from its moorings. She drifted in tumultuous currents, and then . . . total darkness. Some of the people fleeing had already reached the top of the embankment and were in danger of stepping on her. Arms lifted her, pulling her out of the way.

'Clarissa! Clarissa, where are you?'

'Maman!'

Élisa opened her eyes. There were shouts and groans; figures moved around in the night, lit by lamps and torches. She was lying on the ground and someone was shaking her. Her vision gradually cleared, her befuddled mind took in snippets of information. How she would have loved to go to sleep, to relax. But she must not – she tried to stand but was unable to muster the strength. A man was holding her by the wrists.

'What happened?' she murmured.

Her voice seemed to come from a long way away.

'Don't worry, I'm here,' said the stranger kneeling by her side. 'It's me, Gaston.'

The accident, she thought. That's why I'm lying on the grass . . .

'Gaston? . . . Was it a long time ago?'

She freed herself from him and stood. Her legs gave way but he caught her, leaning her against a parapet of the bridge. The laments of the survivors mingled with the wails of the injured as the fire brigade and volunteers busied themselves around the locomotive. The wooden carriages burned and crackled, spilling sparks on to the platforms, which were strewn with bloody debris and puddles. People were still desperately trying to escape, clinging to the shrubs on the slope, trying to keep their balance, but more often than not sliding back and falling to the bottom of the embankment.

'Come, Mademoiselle,' insisted Gaston, 'I'm going to help you; we must leave the rescuers to do their work.'

They stepped over men and women collapsed on the pavement, forced their way through the incessant coming and going of ambulances and reached Chaussée de l'Étang where lights shone in the windows. Suddenly Gaston dragged her into the trees on the edge of the Bois de Vincennes. She tried to resist, overcome with panic. Without a word, he pushed her against the trunk of a chestnut tree, crushing her mouth with his, forcing her lips painfully apart. There was no tenderness in his kiss or in his grasp; it was not like her dreams. He was holding her so tightly she could not move. Filled with anguish and anger, she wanted to push him away, but the catastrophe she had witnessed had weakened her defences. Gradually her disgust changed to a growing wonder, then a sense of euphoria. He drew back, and fear and guilt rushed over her.

'Gaston, I beg you, please don't; it's wicked.'

He raised her chin, forcing her to look at him. He whispered: 'No, it's not wicked, because I love you.'

Those words swept away her last defences. She flung herself against him, ready this time and responsive to his kisses. The clamour from the station ebbed with the slow rhythm of the man's hands as he caressed her body, releasing in her waves of pleasure.

'Can we see each other soon?' he breathed into her ear.

'Yes, I . . . Oh! I forgot – we're going away.'

'We?'

'Mademoiselle Bontemps, the other boarders . . . to Trouville, we'll be back in the middle of September.'

'What's the address?'

'Villa Georgina.'

'I'll come, and we'll find a way of seeing each other. You'll have to go back now or your friends will worry. It's our secret, isn't it? You do love me a little?'

'Oh, Gaston!'

He kissed her forehead. She teetered across the street, unable to stop herself from turning back several times. He did not take his eyes off her, his lips frozen in a smile.

As soon as Élisa had closed the gate, Gaston's smile vanished. He lit a cigarette and inhaled deeply.

That was a stroke of luck, he thought as he headed towards the lake. The accident made it easy for me to bamboozle the romantic little ninny.

He did not yet know exactly how he would manage, but one thing was for certain, a trip to Trouville was on the cards. The Boss would be pleased: in November he would complete his assignment and hand over the wench. He picked up some stones and amused himself by skimming them across the black lake.

CHAPTER 2

Paris, Thursday 12 November 1891

Paris slumbered under a waxing moon. As the Seine flowed calmly round Île Saint-Louis, patterned with diffuse light, a carriage appeared on Quai Bernard, drove up Rue Cuivier and parked on Rue Lacépède. The driver jumped down and, making sure no one was watching, removed his oilskin top hat and cape and tossed them into the back of his cab.

Just before midnight, Gaston Molina opened the ground-floor window of 4 Rue Linné and emptied a carafe on to the pavement. He closed the shutters and went over to the dressing table where a candle burned, smoothed his hair and reshaped his bowler hat. He cast a quick glance at the young blonde girl who lay asleep, fully dressed, in the hollow of the bed. She had sunk into a deep slumber as soon as she swallowed the magic potion. Mission accomplished. What happened to her next was of no concern to him. He stole out of the apartment, careful not to attract the attention of the concierge. One of the tenants was leaning out of an upstairs window. Gaston Molina hugged the wall, lighting a cigarette, and passed the Cuvier fountain before diving down the street of the same name.

A man in a grey overcoat lying in wait on Rue Geoffroy-Saint-Hilaire gave Gaston a head start before setting off behind him.

Gaston Molina walked alongside the Botanical Gardens. He froze, his senses alert, when something growled to his right. Then he smiled and shrugged. Calm down, my friend, he thought, no need to panic; it's coming from the menagerie.

He set off again. The silence was broken by the coming and going of the heavy sewer trucks, with their overpowering, nauseating smell. Going unobtrusively about their business through the sleeping city, the trucks rattled as far as the quayside at Saint-Bernard port and emptied their waste into the tankers.

Gaston Molina was almost at the quay when he thought he heard the crunch of a shoe. He swung round: no one there.

'I must be cracking up; I need a night's sleep.'

He arrived at the wine market.[2] Sometimes tramps in search of shelter broke in and took refuge in the market. Beyond the railings, the barrels, casks and vats perfumed the air with an overpowering odour of alcohol.

I'm thirsty, thought Gaston. Ah, what I wouldn't do for a drink!

Something skimmed past his neck, and a silhouette appeared beside him. Instinctively he tried to parry the blow he sensed coming. An atrocious pain ripped through his stomach and his fingers closed round the handle of a knife. The moon turned black; he collapsed.

As always, Victor Legris reflected on the soothing effect of half-light.

He had woken in an ill temper in anticipation of the stories his business associate would invent to avoid taking Dr Reynaud's prescriptions.

'Kenji! I know you're awake,' he had shouted. 'Don't forget the doctor is coming later this morning!'

Receiving nothing in reply but the slamming of a door, Victor had gone resignedly down to the bookshop, where Joseph the bookshop assistant was perched precariously at the top of a ladder, dusting the bookshelves with a feather duster and belting out a song by a popular young singer.

> *I'm the green sorrel*
> *With egg I've no quarrel*
> *In soup I'm a marvel*
> *My success is unrivalled*
> *I am the green sor-rel!*

His nerves on edge, Victor had failed to perform the ritual with which he began each day: tapping the head of Molière's bust as he passed. Instead he had gone swiftly through the bookshop and hurried down the basement stairs to closet himself in his darkroom.

He had been here for an hour, savouring the silence and dim light. No one disturbed him in this sanctuary where he could forget his worries and give himself over to his passion: photography. His collection of pictures of the old districts of Paris, started the previous April, was growing. He had initially devoted himself to the 20th arrondissement and particularly to Belleville, but recently he had started on Faubourg Saint-Antoine, cataloguing the streets, monuments, buildings and studios. Although he had already accumulated a hundred negatives, the result left him profoundly frustrated. It was not for lack of all the best equipment; it was more because there was nothing of his own personal vision in his work.

All I have here is the objective view of a reporter, he thought.

Was he relying on technique at the expense of creativity? Did he lack inspiration? That often happened to painters and writers.

The meaning of the pictures should transcend the appearance of the places I photograph.

He knew that a solution lurked somewhere in his mind. He turned up the gas lamp and examined the picture he had just developed: two skinny urchins bent double, struggling with a sawing machine that was cutting out marble tablets. The image of a frightened little boy stammering out one of Chaucer's *Canterbury Tales* under the watchful eye of an imposing man in a dark frock coat sprang to mind. Those poor brats reminded him of the terrorised child he had been faced with his domineering father's displeasure. And suddenly he had an inspiration:

'Children! Children at work!'

Finally he had his theme!

He put his negatives away in a cardboard box with renewed energy, smiling as he glimpsed a large picture of two interlaced bronze hands above an epitaph:

My wife, I await you
5 February 1843

My husband, I am here
5 December 1877

A photograph slipped out of the packet and drifted slowly down to land on the floor. He picked it up: Tasha. He frowned. Why was this portrait of her hidden among views of the Père-Lachaise cemetery? He'd taken it at the Universal Exhibition two years earlier. The young woman, unaware she was being photographed, wore a charming and provocative expression. The beginning of their affair, recorded in that image, re-awakened his sense of their growing love. It was wonderful to know a woman who interested him more with each encounter and with whom he felt an unceasing need to talk and laugh, to make love, to hatch plans . . . He was again overcome by the bitter-sweet feeling that Tasha's attitude provoked in him. Since he had succeeded in wooing her away from her bohemian life and installing her in a vast studio, she had devoted herself body and soul to her painting. Her creative passion made him uneasy, although he was happy that he had been able to help her. He had hoped that after the show at which she had exhibited three still lifes, she would slow down. But the sale of one of her paintings to the Boussod & Valadon gallery had so spurred her on that some nights she would tear herself from his arms to finish a canvas by gaslight. Victor sought to prolong every moment spent with her, and was saddened that she did not have the same desire. He was becoming jealous of her painting, even more than of the artists with whom she consorted.

He paced about the room. Why was he unable to resolve this contradiction? He was attracted to Tasha precisely because she was independent and opinionated, yet he would secretly have liked to keep her in a cage.

Miserable imbecile! That would be the quickest way to lose her! Stop tormenting yourself. Would you rather be with someone dull, preoccupied with her appearance, her house and her make-up?

Where did his unreasonable jealousy and desire for certainty and stability come from? With the death of his overbearing father, Victor had felt a great weight lift, but that feeling had quickly been succeeded by the fear that his mother loved another man. This threat had haunted him throughout his adolescence. When his mother Daphné had died in a carriage accident, he had decided to stand on his own two feet, but Kenji had joined him in Paris and, without knowing it, had limited Victor's choices. Through affection for him, Victor had submitted to an ordered existence, his time shared between the bookshop, the adjoining apartment, the sale rooms and passing affairs. As the years had drifted down he had grown used to this routine.

He looked at the photo of Tasha. She had a hold over him that no other woman had ever exercised. No, I don't want to lose her, he thought. The memory of their first encounter plunged him into a state of feverish anticipation. He would see her soon. He extinguished the lamp and went back upstairs.

An elderly scholar, taking a break from the Collège de France, was reading aloud softly to himself from Humboldt's *Cosmos*, while a balding, bearded man struggled to translate Virgil.

Indifferent to these potential customers, Joseph was massacring a melody from *Lohengrin* while working at his favourite hobby: sorting and classifying the articles he clipped from newspapers. He had been behaving unpredictably of late, lurching from forced gaiety to long bouts of moroseness punctuated by sighs and incoherent ramblings. Victor put these changes of mood down to Kenji's illness, but since he too was rather troubled, he found it hard to bear his assistant's capricious behaviour.

'Can't you put those damned scissors down and keep an eye on what's going on?'

'Nothing's going on,' muttered Joseph, continuing his cutting.

'Well, I suppose you're right, it is pretty quiet. Has the doctor been?'

'He's just left. He recommended a tonic; he called it robot . . .'

'Roborant.'

'That's it, with camomile, birch and blackcurrant, sweetened with lactose. Germaine has gone to the herbalist.'

'All right then, I'm going out.'

'What about lunch? Germaine will be upset and then who will have to eat it? I will! She's made you pork brains in noisette butter with onions. Delicious, she says.'

Victor looked disgusted. 'Well, I make you a present of it – treat yourself.'

'Ugh! I'll have to force it down.'

As soon as Victor had climbed the stairs to the apartment, Joseph went back to his cutting out, still whistling Wagner.

'For pity's sake, Joseph! Spare us the German lesson,' shouted Victor from the top of the stairs.

'*Jawohl*, Boss!' growled Joseph, rolling his eyes. 'There's no pleasing him . . . he's never happy . . . if I sing "Little Jack Horner sat in a corner", he complains. If I serve up some opera, he complains! I'm not going to put up with it much longer, it's starting to wear me down, and I'm fed up! One Boss moping in quarantine, the other gadding about!' he said, addressing the scholar clutching the Humboldt.

Victor went softly through his apartment to his bedroom. He put on a jacket and a soft fedora, his preferred headgear, and crammed his gloves into his pocket. I'll go round by Rue des Mathurins before I go to Tasha's, he thought to himself. He was about to leave when he heard a faint tinkling sound.

The noise came from the kitchen. Victor appeared in the doorway, surprising Kenji in the act of loading a tray with bread, sausage and cheese.

'Kenji! Are you delirious? Dr Reynaud forbade you . . .'

'Dr Reynaud is an ass! He's been dosing me with sulphate of quinine and broth with no salt for weeks. He's inflicted enough cold baths on me to give me an attack of pleurisy! I stink of camphor and I'm going round and round in circles like a goldfish in a bowl! If a man is dying of hunger, what does he do? He eats!'

In his slippers and flannel nightshirt Kenji looked like a little boy caught stealing the jam. Victor made an effort to keep a straight face.

'Blame it on the scarlet fever, not the devoted doctor who's working hard to get you back on your feet. Have a glass of sake or cognac, that's allowed, but hang it all, spare a thought for us! You can't leave your room until your quarantine is over.'

'All right, since all the world is intent on bullying me, I'll return to my cell. At least ensure that I have a grand funeral when I die of starvation,' retorted Kenji furiously, abandoning his tray.

Suppressing a chuckle, Victor left, one of Kenji's Japanese proverbs on the tip of his tongue: 'Of the thirty-six options, flight is the best.'

'Berlaud! Where have you scarpered to, you miserable mongrel?'

A tall rangy man with a cloak of coarse cloth draped across his shoulders was driving six goats in front of him. At the entrance to the Botanical Gardens, he struggled to keep them together. Cursing his dog for having run off, he used the thongs attached to their collars to draw them in.

The little flock went off up Quai Saint-Bernard, crossed Rue Buffon without incident and went down Boulevard de l'Hôpital as far as Gare d'Orléans,[3] where the man stopped to light a short clay pipe. The silvery hair escaping from under his dented hat and his trusting, artless face gave him the look of child aged suddenly by a magic spell. Even his voice was childlike, with an uncertain catch to it.

'Saints alive! I'm toiling in vain while that wretched mutt is off chasing something to mount.'

He put two fingers in his mouth and gave a long whistle. A large dog with matted fur, half briard, half griffon, bounded out from behind an omnibus.

'So there you are, you miscreant. You're off pilfering, leaving me yelling for you and working myself to death with the goats. What you lookin' like that for? What you got in your mouth? Oh, I see, you went off to steal a bone from the lions while I was chatting to Père Popèche. That's why we heard roaring. But you know dogs aren't allowed in the Botanical Gardens, even muzzled and on the leash. Do you want to get us into trouble?'

Berlaud, his tail between his legs and teeth clamped round his prize, ran back to his post at the back of the herd, which trotted past the Hospice de la Salpêtrière, before turning towards Boulevard Saint-Marcel and into the horse market.

Each Thursday and Saturday the neighbourhood of the Botanical Gardens witnessed a procession of miserable worn out horses, lame and exhausted but decked out with yellow or red ribbons to trick the buyers. They were kicking their heels in resigned fashion, attached to girders under tents held up with cast iron poles where the horse dealers rented stalls. Ignoring the auctioneers proffering broken-down old carriages just outside the gates, the goatherd pushed his flock in among the groups of rag and bone men and furniture removers in search of hacks still capable of performing simple tasks. Each time he visited, the goatherd found it heart-rending to see the dealers with their emaciated nags, whose every rib could be seen, making them trot about to display their rump, their face and their flanks to possible buyers.

'Savages! Tormenting to death these poor beasts worn out by pulling the bourgeois along the streets of Paris! My brave horses, you certainly know what it is to work hard. And the day you're of no use you'll be sent to the knackers' yard or to the abattoir at Villejuif! Dirty swindling dealers!'

'So, here comes our friend Grégoire Mercier, the purveyor of milk direct to your home, the saviour of consumptives, the ailing and the chlorotic! Well, Grégoire, still heaping invective on the world? I'm the one who should grumble – you're late, my fine fellow!'

'I couldn't help it, Monsieur Noël. I had so much to do,' replied the goatherd to a horse dealer who was impatiently waving a household bottle at him. 'First, at dawn I had to take the she-kids to graze on the grass on some wasteland at the Maison-Blanche. Then I had to visit a customer on Quai de la Tournelle with a liver complaint; she has to have milk from Nini Moricaude – I feed her carrots. After that it was straight off to do some business at the menagerie at the Botanical Gardens.'

'You're curing the chimpanzees with goat's milk?'

'Don't be silly, Monsieur Noël! No, I had to speak to someone and . . .'

'All right, all right, I don't need your whole life story.'

Grégoire Mercier knelt down beside a white goat and milked it, then held out a bowl of creamy milk to the horse dealer, who sniffed it suspiciously.

'It smells sour. Are you sure it's fresh?'

'Of course! As soon as she wakes up Mélie Pecfin gets a double ration of hay fortified with iodine; it's the best thing for strengthening depleted blood.'

'Depleted, depleted, my wife is not depleted! I'd like to see how you'd be if you'd just given birth to twins! I'll take it to her while it's still warm.'

The man dropped a coin into the goatherd's hand and snatched up the bowl.

'Tomorrow, do you want me to deliver to your house on Rue Poliveau?'

The horse dealer turned his back without even bothering to say thank you.

'That's right, run off to your missus. You may treat her better than you do your horses, but you don't cherish her the way I cherish my goats when they have kids! Isn't that right, my beauties? Papa Grégoire gives you sugar every morning and he nourishes your babies with hot wine. Come on, Berlaud, let's go!'

As he reached Rue Croulebarbe, Grégoire Mercier regained his good humour. Now he was back on home turf, the borders of which were the River Bièvre[4] to one side and to the other the orchards where the drying racks of the leather-dressers were lined up.

Freed from the strap holding them prisoner, the goats gambolled between the poplar trees bordering the narrow river, its brown water specked with foam. The Bièvre snaked its way along by tumbledown houses and dye-works whose chimneys belched out thick smoke. Although he was used to the sweetish steam of the cleaning tubs and the fumes from the scalding vats where the colours were mixed, Grégoire Mercier wrinkled his nose. Piled up under the hangars, hundreds of skins stained with blood lay hardening, waiting to be plunged in buckets of softening agent. After a long soaking, they would be hung out and beaten by apprentices, releasing clouds of dust that covered the countryside like snow.

Determined not to drop his find, Berlaud guided the goats on to the riverbank where tomatoes, petits pois and green beans grew. He hurried past the wickerwork trays of the peat sellers and the coaching-shed of Madame Guédon who leased hand-carts for use on Ruelle des Reculettes, which opened out just beyond the crumbling wall behind the lilac hedge.

Old buildings with exposed beams housed the families of the curriers. Blackened twisted vines ran over their packed earth façades. The sound of pistons, and the occasional shriek of a strident whistle, served as a reminder that this was the town and not the countryside.

Letting his dog and beasts trot ahead, Grégoire Mercier stopped to greet Monsieur Vrétot, who combined work as a concierge with his trade as a shoemaker and cobbler to make ends meet. Then the goatherd started up the stairs, whistling on every landing. Thirty years earlier he had left his native Beauce for Paris, and settled at the heart of this unhealthy neigh-bourhood, ruled by the misery and stench of the tanneries. A delivery boy for the cotton factory by Pont d'Austerlitz, he had fallen in love with a laundress, and they had married and had two little boys. Three happy years were brutally cut short by the death from tuberculosis of Jeanette Mercier. Moved by the plight of the little motherless boys, public assistance had given them a goat to provide nourishment, until consumption carried the little boys off in their turn. When he had overcome his grief, Grégoire decided to keep the goat and take in others as well. He had never remarried.

He reached the fifth floor, where his flock were massed before a door at the end of a dark corridor. As soon as he closed the door of his garret, the goats went into the boxes set up along the wall. He went into a second room, furnished with a camp bed, a table, two stools and a rickety sideboard, shrugged off his cloak and hurried to prepare the warm water and bran that his goats expected on returning from their travels. He also had to feed Mémère the doyenne a bottle of oats mixed with mint, before opening the cubby hole where Rocambole the billy goat was languishing. Finally he heated up some coffee for himself and took it to drink beside Mélie Pecfin, his favourite. It was then that he noticed Berlaud. He was sitting on his blanket, wagging his tail, his find from the Botanical Gardens still between his paws, but with his eyes fixed on the sugar bowl. Grégoire pretended not to know what his dog was after and Berlaud growled meaningfully.

'Lie down!'

Instead of obeying, the dog adopted an attitude of absolute servility, flattened his ears, raised his rump and crept stealthily forward, begging for his master's attention. Grégoire distracted him by throwing him a sugar cube and grabbed the dog's spoils.

'What's that? That's not a bone, that's . . . that's a . . . How can anyone mislay something like that? Oh, there's something inside . . .'

Grégoire was so puzzled he forgot to drink his coffee.

Lying back with his hands under his head, the man reflected on the enormity of what he had done. He had returned exhausted at dawn and sprawled on top of the rumpled sheet under his overcoat, going over the events of the previous night. The journey to the wine market on Rue Linné had barely taken him ten minutes. The blonde girl had slept deeply under the effect of the sleeping draught and he had carried her to the carriage without difficulty. No mistakes, no witnesses. And then? Child's play; she had not suffered.

He put a coffee pot on the still warm stove, went over to the window and looked down into the street. It was an autumn day like any other. He had managed everything to perfection. It would take the police a while to identify the blonde and by then he would have had his vengeance. As for the young thug he had hired, there was no risk that he would give him away or try to blackmail him – when they found his body they would imagine it had been a settling of accounts. No one would link the two murders. He let the curtain fall. A detail was troubling him. That fellow at the first floor window . . . had he spotted him? He would have to reassure himself, find out who the man was and perhaps . . .

'You're mad,' he said out loud.

But he let this thought go, and instead gloated over his plan, which he considered ingenious, cunning, brilliant – it had come off without a hitch, except that when he'd arrived at Killer's Crossing[5] he had noticed that the blonde was only wearing one shoe. It would have been much too risky to return to Rue Linné. At first he had panicked – that kind of error could be fatal. Then the solution had presented itself: all he had to do was remove the other shoe.

He poured himself a cup of coffee.

'The *flics* will easily trace the owner of the stolen carriage but so what! Where will that get them, the fools?'

As he hunted in the pocket of his overcoat for some cigarettes, three little stains on the grey material caught his eye. Blood? It was an alpaca coat; it would be costly to get rid of it.

'Just wine,' he decided.

He inspected his trousers and shoes: spotless. He sat down at the table and regarded the red silk shoe sitting beside a flask of sulphuric acid.

'The police will think it was a crime of passion.'

It was an amusing idea, and it soothed him.

'In fact, I can make use of the shoe.'

He opened a drawer, took out some writing paper, a pen and an inkwell and wrote out an address:

Mademoiselle C. Bontemps
15 Chaussée de l'Étang
Saint-Mandé. Seine

Victor sat on a bench outside a building on Rue des Mathurins, leafing through *Paris Photographie*, a review to which he had just subscribed. He looked half-heartedly at an article by Paul Nadar and a collection of portraits of Sarah Bernhardt. His mind was elsewhere; he had not warned Tasha he was coming as he planned to surprise her. He consulted the pneumatic clock and decided to wander slowly to Tasha's apartment. Making a detour to avoid Boulevard Haussmann, which stirred up unhappy memories, he turned off down Rue Auber and walked along Rue Laffitte.

As he passed 60 Rue Notre-Dame-de-Lorette he felt a sudden wave of nostalgia. He pictured Tasha's miniscule loft, and the memory of the early days of their affair produced an ardent longing to share his life with her.

On Rue Fontaine he noted with satisfaction that the little notice was still up in the hairdresser's window:

Shop and Apartment to Let
For information contact the concierge at 36b

He had made up his mind. He went in under the porch.

On Thursdays the courtyard overlooked by Tasha's studio became the domain of the joiner's little girls, who were energetically playing hopscotch using a wooden quoit. A washing line stretched from a second floor window to the acacia tree in the middle of the courtyard. On windy days Victor loved to watch the washing billow like the sails of a boat. He circled the water pump splashed white with bird droppings and made his way over to the back room of the hairdresser. He shaded his eyes to make out the layout of the room through the dirty window: it was a well-proportioned space. Once done up it would make a splendid photographic studio! . . . Yes, it was the ideal solution; he would only have a few yards to cross . . .

Tasha was leaning over a pedestal table mixing colours on her palette. Lemon yellow, Veronese green and Prussian blue echoed the tones of the canvas she was working on, which depicted a laurel branch and two ears of corn emerging from an iridescent vase. The slanting rays of sunshine caught the brilliant copper lights of her hair, which hung loose. On impulse Victor buried his face in the magnificent mane of red hair.

'Victor! You gave me a fright!' cried the young woman. 'I should wipe my brush on your shirt! Oh, it doesn't matter, I wasn't getting anywhere anyway.'

She threw the corn and the laurel down beside a potted palm. 'I'm sick of still lifes!'

Victor, sitting in a Tudor chair, watched her put the vase away in a sideboard, then turn back to her easel.

'Tasha, am I preventing you from fulfilling your potential?'

'Of course not, idiot, I'm just not up to it, that's all! I'm incapable of distinguishing the incidental from the essential.'

'You're overworking! Sometimes less is more; take a step back. What are you trying to prove?'

'Maurice Laumier says that . . .'

'Oh please! For pity's sake! Forget about him! He has no originality; he thinks theory obviates the need for creation. Theory, theory, that's all he talks about!'

'You really do hate him.'

'I despise what your Laumier stands for; there's a difference. He paints by numbers and he calls that art. What he's really interested in is making a sale.'

'First of all, he's not *my* Laumier, secondly . . .'

'I'm right and you know it. Good grief! You don't have to bow to fashion! Explore your interior universe, search what Kenji calls "the chambers of the soul" . . . Excuse me, I'm getting carried away, but perhaps you should take more interest in other aspects of life, in people.'

'Do you think so? That's what Henri advocated . . . Come

on, don't look like that. You have no reason to be jealous; he's just a kind friend, and he's talented. I met him at the Salon des Indépendents[6] and . . .'

'I demand nothing of you, you are free.'

'Oh, stop it, Victor. Please don't be childish; it's becoming tiresome.'

She knelt down before him, slid her fingers under his collar and caressed his neck. He relaxed, ecstatic to feel her so close.

'Isn't it hot in here?' she murmured, unbuttoning his shirt. 'There now, I need to see the only male model that inspires me.'

'Now?'

'Just a quick drawing, there, on the sofa. Come on, take everything off.'

She picked up a sketchbook.

'I'll call it *Monsieur Récamier in the Nude*. Stay still.'

She adjusted the position of his right arm across his chest. He embraced her, pulling her towards him, fumbling to unfasten her dress. The sketchbook slipped to the floor.

'Oh well, the light isn't very good,' she said.

He kissed her on the nose, the forehead, the hair as she helped him to slip off her dress.

'Tasha, marry me; it would make everything so simple.'

'It's too soon,' she whispered. 'I'm not ready; I don't want children . . . Have you got any . . . ?'

He looked at her intensely, propped on one elbow, patted the pocket of his frock coat and pulled out a box of condoms.

'Victor, are you angry with me?'

'You know perfectly well that I always make an effort to be careful, even without protection.'

He pushed a lock of hair back from her cheek.

'We'll have to wait a little before we move on to the serious business and I advise you not to laugh,' he murmured, clasping her to him.

A little later, as they lay together on the narrow sofa, he came close to confessing that he had rented the hairdressers' shop.

'Tasha, I . . .'

But she silenced him with a kiss. Everything ceased to exist, except her. He no longer felt the need to explain. Ideas, the future; nothing mattered. She stretched; she was happy. Her eyes were shining. Her breasts rose and fell with her quickened breathing.

'I adore you. But my back hurts. We'll have to move to the bed!' she said over her shoulder, already making for the alcove.

Grégoire Mercier's sciatica was troubling him. How long had he been sheltering under the porch of this building under the suspicious eye of the concierge? Twenty, thirty minutes? And when would those two chatterboxes finally clear off?

He clutched his iron-tipped staff, anxious about his flock, left at home in the care of Berlaud. Angry that his find had been confiscated, the dog had registered his disgust by lying down and growling in Rocambole's cubby hole. That was a bad sign, a very bad sign. Grégoire hoped he would not take it out on the kids. The dog was becoming unpredictable in his old age.

Grégoire Mercier went over to the window and turned his

gaze on the woman nearest him, as if he could force her to leave by a simple exercise of will.

Unaware of the thought waves aimed at her, Mathilde de Flavignol refused to comply. Oppressed by a grief she felt unable to contain, she had come to the bookshop hoping to be comforted by the bookseller. The seductive young Monsieur Legris aroused a strange excitement in her. But she was out of luck; he was absent, no doubt off paying court to that Russian hussy. The slightly hunchbacked blond shop assistant was there on his own, munching an apple as he read the newspaper. Still, she preferred him to the other one, the Oriental with the inscrutable expression.

She had scarcely begun to explain that her mourning sash marked the suicide of poor General Boulanger in Belgium, driven to shoot himself on the grave of his lover Marguerite de Bonnemain, when a woman in a fine wool suit, her grey hair braided under a ridiculous Tyrolean hat, had come in.

'It's not my day; here's the Valkyrie,' muttered Joseph. Then, out loud, 'Mademoiselle Becker, what a lovely surprise!'

'*Guten Tag*, Monsieur Pignot. You're going to help me out, I know!'

Madame de Flavignol learned that this German lady was passionate about cycling and that she had come to look for works on the celeripede and the dandy horse, ancestors of the bicycle.

'You see, Monsieur Pignot, I would like to give our national hero Charles Terront a present for winning.'

'Who's Charles Terront?' demanded Mathilde de Flavignol.

'I can't believe that you haven't heard of him! He's the winner of the Paris to Brest race – held last September, on the sixth. One thousand miles there and back in seventy-two hours! He pedalled day and night without stopping to sleep! What an outstanding man. And he's going to be giving cycling lessons at Bullier.'

'Perhaps that would take my mind off my misery . . . You see I worshipped the General, a passionate man who could not bear the death of his Dulcinea. I made the journey to Ixelles to attend his funeral. What a magnificent ceremony! He still had many friends – that was clear from the crowd of French who went to his obsequies. Oh, I'll never get over it . . . Bullier . . . Isn't that a dance hall of ill-repute? It's said that La Goulue[7] danced the cancan there . . . I'm so miserable. Do you think that bicycling would . . . ?'

'Assuredly, Madame. The sport has two advantages: it has a very calming effect but it is also wonderful for firming up the calves!'

'I'm too frightened to get in the saddle . . .'

'Do you have a good sense of balance? Can you walk in a straight line?'

'Well . . . I rarely drink too much.'

'In that case you will certainly be able to master the bicycle, take my word for it.'

Joseph Pignot was not the only one to breathe a sigh of relief as the two women went off arm in arm, allowing him to settle down to his newspaper again. Hurrying out from his shelter and escaping the venomous eye of the concierge, Grégoire Mercier made his entrance.

What now? Jojo thought, his nostrils assailed by a pungent odour.

A strangely attired, snub-nosed fellow advanced towards him, pulled a woman's shoe from his cloak and laid it on the counter.

'There you are. Berlaud found it this morning; he loves to pick up whatever's been left behind. Mind you I let him do it; nothing is more important than freedom and independence. When we got home again, I took a good look at what he'd found. Well, I said to myself, a lady's slipper. The lass who left behind that trinket must be furious, especially since it's beautifully made. I'm giving it to you; it just needs a bit of work from the cobbler. He'll be able to fix the holes; my dog bit it a little too hard.'

Stupefied, Jojo looked first at the embroidered red slipper, decorated with pearls, and then back at the strange man.

'Why are you giving it to me?'

'Because it has the name and address of your shop fitted inside, like an inner sole.'

He held the folded sheet of headed notepaper out to Jojo, who opened it out and read:

ELZÉVIR BOOKSHOP
V. LEGRIS – K. MORI,
Established in 1835. Antiquarian and New Books.
First Editions. Catalogue by Request.
18 Rue des Saints-Pères, Paris VI

'Well that's truly bizarre!' he exclaimed. 'Perhaps it belongs to a client.'

'One who's not short of a penny? Who could afford to have precious stones on their shoes?'

Guessing that the visitor was fishing for a tip, Jojo opened the till and proffered two francs, but the strange fellow recoiled, offended.

'Grégoire Mercier does not accept payment, other than for the produce of his goats. Naturally if the owner of the shoe wants to thank me with a little something I won't say no.'

He touched two fingers to his hat and turned to go.

'Wait! Where did you unearth this shoe?'

'In the middle of my rounds, after having delivered a bowl of milk from Nini Moricaude, who I feed on carrots, to Quai de la Tournelle . . .'

'So your dog . . . ?'

'Berlaud scampered off. I heard lions roaring and I thought he'd pilfered a piece of their meat; he's old but intrepid. I whistled for him, he didn't come back, so . . .'

'Right, well I'll do my best to return this shoe to the correct foot,' said Jojo nasally; he was breathing through his mouth to avoid the overpowering stench of goat. 'Where can we find you if there's a reward?'

'Ruelle des Reculettes, in the Croulebarbe quarter. Over there everyone knows Grégoire Mercier.'

When the man had gone Jojo examined the slipper carefully.

'Yup, there's something odd about this shoe business. I'll have to put it in my notebook.'

'Joseph! Who was that?'

'Boss! Are you up? That's not allowed! What will become of us if you give the customers scarlet fever?'

'I'm recovered. My quarantine expired thirty-four minutes

and eighteen seconds ago. Show me that,' said Kenji, leaning over the banister.

Murmuring, 'The Boss has put himself on Paris time,'[8] Jojo held out the shoe against his better judgement. Kenji studied it carefully, and his expression suddenly changed as if something terrible had happened. He let the slipper clatter to the floor. Jojo put it back on the counter.

'Go and fetch me a cab, this instant!' commanded Kenji, in a husky voice.

'A cab! You're joking! If he finds out, Monsieur Legris will slaughter me!'

'It's an order!' shouted Kenji.

The afternoon was dull. The only visitors to the bookshop were a Paul Bourget enthusiast, a woman in pince-nez anxious to buy the latest book by Edmond de Goncourt on the painter Outamaro and two young men seeking travel books. At each tinkle of the doorbell, Jojo looked up hopefully, but neither of his bosses deigned to appear. At seven o'clock, neglected by everyone, he closed the shutters and abandoned ship. On the way out he picked up the red slipper and, not knowing what else to do with it, stuffed it into his pocket.

Rue Visconti, where Madame Pignot and her son lived, had been transformed by a fine and persistent autumn rain into a dark tunnel. Joseph bounded over the threshold and took refuge in the study his father, during his too-short life, had transformed into a bookseller's treasure trove. Euphrosine Pignot had finished her costermonger's rounds and was stirring her pots on the stone sink of their narrow lodgings. Joseph lit a match and adjusted the wick of the petrol lamp. The shelves, weighed down with books and newspapers, acted as a balm to his soul. He hung his soaking jacket on the back of a chair and hummed the disparaged couplet that had incurred Victor's displeasure:

> *Do you know her, Lohengrin,*
> *Lohengrin, Lohengrin,*
> *A woman divine*
> *But full of venom . . .*

The word 'venom' revived his despair, reminding him of Valentine de Salignac, his lost treasure. Last May the niece of the Comtesse had married the nephew of the Duc de Frioul, a pretentious, drunken young rake named Boni de Pont-Joubert. Ever since their marriage, celebrated in the Église Saint-Roch the day after the shooting at Fourmies,[9] Jojo had been prey to those changes of mood that so annoyed Victor. The pain was gradually abating, but was reawakened by the merest trifle. Deep down he had known that his love for Valentine could never lead anywhere, and that the young girl had been forced into her alliance despite her own feelings for Joseph. But this had not stopped him from shelving his great literary project, destined to outdo the mysteries of Émile Gaboriau: *Blood and Love*.

'Women! First they inspire you and then, because of them, the muse deserts you! So, what am I going to do this evening? Perhaps I should go back to writing *The Life and Times of Rue Visconti*. I was at the chapter describing the attempted murder of Louis-Philippe by Louis Alibaud, resident of number 3, with a rifle-cane . . .'

Taking up a manuscript and a pencil he settled himself in a rickety armchair.

A chubby face topped with a chignon appeared round the door connecting the study to the rest of the apartment.

'So, you are there, my pet? I thought I heard singing. You might have let me know you were here! Are you going to tuck into some lovely cabbage soup?'

'Not hungry.'

'You've got to eat! You're as white as a sheet and your arms are like lollipop sticks! You're wearing yourself out; I might have something to say to your bosses. And for heaven's sake, how many times over could Monsieur Mori have given you scarlet fever? That would have taken the biscuit! He's better at least?'

'No, yes, I don't know. I'm writing in case you're interested . . .'

'He should have taken my advice. Cupping is what draws the illness out from under the skin or leeches; it's six of one and half a dozen of the other. Writing or not, you've five minutes to come through for dinner.'

She wrinkled her nose and sniffed, looking about suspiciously.

'There's a strange smell, and it's not my soup! Is it you, by any chance?'

'Me? What does it smell of?' asked Jojo, flaring his nostrils.

Madame Pignot studied her son dispassionately; when had he stopped shaving?

'It smells of goat. Right, five minutes!' she finished in a threatening tone as she went out.

Jojo sniffed his jacket. His mother had a keen sense of smell. The shoe! He pulled it from his pocket, took it over to the lamp and let the light play on it, the pearls shimmering. A fairy tale slipper, a Cinderella slipper . . . '*The girl who fits this slipper shall be my betrothed . . .*'

He imagined Valentine slowly removing her corset, her underskirts and her blouse . . . but his fantasy was ruined by the extremely disagreeable smell emanating from the red silk. What had that bizarre character been telling him? He'd mentioned a sheepfold, a street called 'croule' something or other, a dog, goats, lions, a real muddle, but that smell . . . There was no doubt, it was the smell of goat. And the headed notepaper from the shop – was that just a coincidence? And why had Monsieur Mori run off like that at the sight of the shoe, as if he had had the devil at his heels?

'Say what you like, it's not normal. I'll note it all down; it might come in handy . . .'

Just as he picked up his notebook, a ferocious voice thundered: 'My pet! The five minutes are up! Your soup is getting cold!'

CHAPTER 3

Friday 13 November

THE bookshop was still slumbering, bathed in a gloomy half-light. A wisp of steam rose from a cup that had been left beside the bust of Molière. Kenji had spread a green cloth over the centre table and was busily arranging the wicker chairs that Jojo had fetched from the back of the shop. The silence was broken by the occasional rumble of a carriage on Rue des Saints-Pères.

'I can't see a thing. Turn the lights up, will you, Joseph,' said Victor, yawning.

He tottered down the stairs. He should have resisted the urge to go back to bed after returning from Tasha's at dawn. He felt about as refreshed as a drunk nursing a hangover. He narrowly avoided colliding with Kenji.

'What are you doing here? What about the quarantine?'

'The ship is ready to weigh anchor. Dr Reynaud has given me a clean bill of health.'

'And you have organised a party to celebrate this new freedom?'

'May I remind you that we are receiving the Friends of Old Paris? Monsieur Anatole France said he would be coming. Why are you waving your arms about like that, Joseph?'

'It's the battleaxe, Boss! I mean . . . the Comtesse de Salignac.'

Joseph indicated a haughty woman wrapped in a large, floral cape and wearing a stern expression who was standing outside the shop, waiting for someone to deign to let her in, which Kenji hurriedly did.

'Not a moment too soon. I was beginning to believe you intended leaving me out there to freeze. It would appear you are opening late today. I see you have returned from your travels, Monsieur Mori.'

'Yes, I . . . How may we be of service, my dear lady?'

The sound of the telephone ringing took Victor away.

'I want three copies of Georges de Peyrebrune's latest book, *Giselle*, which Charpentier and Fasquelle are about to bring out. First editions, if possible.'

While Kenji went over to his desk, Joseph turned his back on the Comtesse and picked up the newspaper he had bought on his way to work.

'If you had a modicum of manners, young man, you would offer me a seat on one of those numerous chairs. Unless of course they are merely for show,' said the Comtesse.

Jojo dropped the newspaper with a start, and it fell open on the floor. Victor, having hung up the receiver, was hurriedly pulling up a chair for the Comtesse. Ignoring his gesture, she extracted a lorgnette from her reticule, bent down and began reading an article out loud:

'Macabre dawn discovery. A young woman was found strangled, her face disfigured by acid, lying at Killer's Crossing, between Boulevard Montmartre and Boulevard Poissonière. She was wearing . . .'

'These rags are sickening!' cried the Comtesse, standing bolt upright. 'Gore is all that interests them! If it isn't train crashes and executions, it's murder! And it is contaminating our literature. This article is as grotesque as the latest novel of Monsieur Huysmans!'

'Are you referring to *The Damned?*' Victor asked.

'I am indeed. Monsieur Huysmans might one day regret having written it. Many of his admirers, Monsieur Legris, already regret having read it. Poor France!'

She exited imperiously before Kenji, who had stood to attention, had a chance to say goodbye.

'Was she referring to Monsieur Anatole?'

'She was lamenting the moral state of the country,' Victor replied wearily. 'Would you go and buy me a cigar, Joseph?'

Jojo grabbed his newspaper, relieved to have an excuse to slip away. Kenji watched him leave and then went upstairs under the pretext of writing a letter. He stood at his desk, fiddling with the corner of his blotter and idly contemplating a very fine ink-on-silk drawing of Mount Fuji by Kanō Tanyu,[10] which he planned to frame. Through his clouded vision, the volcano took on the form of an enormous, snow-capped shoe. What had he done with the shoe that had given him such a fright? He seemed to recall having dropped it in the bookshop, or had he left it in the carriage? He had nearly asked Joseph, but stopped himself just in time, for that would have meant mentioning Iris. The events of the previous evening had been so confused! His panic when he had recognised the shoe Joseph had proffered as one he had bought in London; his frantic race to the Bontemps Boarding School, expecting to learn some tragic piece of news; his dread of revealing his secret to Victor; his relief when Iris came running towards him, overjoyed at his surprise visit, and the explanation she had given for the lost shoe. He had been awake all night rehearsing the conversation he had now resolved to have with Victor, which he had put off for so long.

He shut himself in the bathroom, and after holding his hands under the hot-water tap for a moment placed them over his face. He looked at a photograph in an ornate frame that stood on a marble shelf above the washbasin: *Daphné and Victor, London 1872*. A young, dark-haired woman was lovingly embracing a boy of around twelve and staring at the camera with a dreamy expression. Kenji picked up the portrait and pressed it to his lips.

Joseph walked, reading his newspaper so avidly that he narrowly avoided colliding with a passer-by.

'Well, I'll be damned!' he muttered.

He hurried back, racing through the bookshop to where Victor stood, holding a leather-bound volume.

'I thought you were never coming back. Where's my cigar?' asked Victor.

'Just listen to this, Boss! The dead woman at Killer's Crossing had no shoes on! And guess what? She was dressed in red.'

'Joseph, when will you get over your morbid interest in murders?' groaned Victor.

'But, Boss, it's astonishing, because yesterday this strange fellow came in here with a red shoe and you'll never guess what he'd found in it: a piece of the bookshop's headed notepaper, and when Monsieur Mori saw it he turned so crimson I thought he was ill again!'

'When Monsieur Mori saw what?' Victor asked, exasperated.

'The shoe! He sent me out to hail a cab while he got dressed quick as a flash. He was in a right old panic!'

'And you let him go! Well done!'

'Confound it! Am I a shop assistant or a nursemaid?'

'Just calm down and tell me exactly what happened.'

'Very well, I shall speak clearly to avoid confusion. The chap with the shoe reeked of goats and looked like a peasant. He talked so loudly that Monsieur Mori overheard him. I had no choice but to show him the shoe. He looked as if he'd seen a ghost!'

'Do you know where he went?'

'Saint-Mandé; 15 Chausée de l'Étang. That's the address he shouted to the cabby.'

'Where is this shoe?'

Victor carefully examined the slipper Joseph took from his pocket. On the inside he noticed the name of the manufacturer printed in gold lettering:

Dickins & Jones, Regent Street, London W1

'Blimey! Made in England,' Jojo breathed, leaning over his shoulder. 'Do you think Monsieur Mori . . . ? I mean he's often been to London.'

'Don't talk such rubbish. Go and serve that lady. I'll be back shortly,' Victor said, pocketing the shoe.

47

'Morbid interest, eh! People should practice what they preach,' Joseph muttered, making his way over to the customer.

The cab dropped Victor in Rue de la République. He walked away from the Bastille-La Varenne railway line, the recent site of an appalling accident, and past the Saint-Mandé town hall. The rhythmic tapping of his cane on the pavement punctuated his thoughts.

This really is the limit! There's no earthly reason for poking my nose into Kenji's affairs. Naturally, anything that affects him concerns me, and I do find his peculiar behaviour worrying, but anxiety does not justify indiscretion. Admit it, Victor, you've once again fallen prey to your fondness for mysteries!

As he strolled past the fine villas, whose gardens stood in a row overlooking the lake and the Bois de Vincennes, he had a sudden urge to bring Tasha to this place. He recalled a line from a poem by Victor Hugo:

Connaître un pas qu'on aime et que jaloux on suit . . .

Did not the remains of the poet's great love, Juliette Drouet, lie in the Saint-Mandé graveyard?

He read the brass plate on the railings of number 15:

C. BONTEMPS BOARDING SCHOOL
Private Establishment for Young Ladies

'This is a strange place to keep a mistress,' he muttered.

A plump, moon-faced woman of about forty greeted him. She was dressed in the style of the Empress Eugenie and wore her hair parted in the middle and drawn into a bun.

'My respects, Madame; I am here on behalf of Monsieur Mori, my business associate.'

'Oh! Are you a bookseller too? What an honour. Please come in. Dear Monsieur Mori! He seemed so upset yesterday. Mademoiselle Iris realised only a few moments after her godfather's departure that he had left his cane behind. Your visit couldn't be better timed; you will be able to return the precious object to him.'

Victor stood in front of a mantelpiece adorned with flounces and porcelain statues, desperately trying to gather his thoughts. Iris! Was he finally to meet the mysterious woman who had aroused his curiosity these past two years; the woman Kenji visited regularly in London but kept hidden from him? It had been months since Kenji had last ventured across the Channel and Victor had assumed their romance was over. Iris was the very young girl once glimpsed in a photograph taken at the Universal Exhibition, but whose face he simply could not remember.

Her godfather my eye! So this is where he keeps her locked up! Victor thought to himself.

'Please take a seat,' said Mademoiselle Bontemps, pointing to an ottoman. Monsieur . . .'

'Legris. I should like to speak to Mademoiselle Iris. Here is my card.'

'Oh! Well, I did not wish to appear suspicious, but . . .'

'It is only natural.'

'I am glad to hear you say so. You see I have my instructions. Of course, our boarders are free to walk about town; they watch over one another and report on each others' deeds and conduct, but as far as conversing with strangers is concerned . . . Monsieur Mori never mentioned an associate. Have you worked together for long?'

'I was three years old when my father first employed Monsieur Mori.'

Mademoiselle Bontemps lifted a plump hand to her mouth to suppress a nervous giggle.

'Goodness, how extraordinary that he never once mentioned your name!'

'He is a reserved gentleman.'

'Such reserve is comparable with deceit! That said; judge not that you be not judged. Would you care for a macaroon?'

She held out a plate to him, which he declined with a smile. She helped herself generously before going to find Iris.

Victor was astonished to see a young girl, not more than seventeen, walk towards him. Her childlike features brought back the faded image of the photograph he had glimpsed without Kenji's knowledge. She was pretty, possessed of an exotic beauty: olive skin, almond eyes and a dainty, delicately curved nose. Her dark hair, worn in braids tied with a ribbon at her neck, made her look even younger.

Surely it's rather lecherous of Kenji, who's fifty-two, to have such a young girl for a lover! I'd never have guessed. And he is attracted to women of an entirely different type: mature, shapely, provocative. His last lover, Ninon Delarme,[11] would have turned the head of a saint . . . Who is this girl? Might she really be his goddaughter? Or even his daughter? If so, then her mother must be a European. His daughter! Impossible! He would have told me!

He felt uneasy, afraid of committing an indiscretion. It seemed best to go straight to the point.

'Good day, Mademoiselle. Allow me to introduce myself. I am Victor Legris, an associate of . . .'

'What a pleasure to meet you, Monsieur Legris. Godfather has often spoken of you!' cried Iris.

'Oh! I assumed . . . Mademoiselle Bontemps did not know of my existence.'

'My godfather doesn't tell everybody everything! He loves to shroud himself in mystery. I'm sure it's because he reads so many novels. I rarely read them myself; I avoid filling my head with fantasies. The day I leave this boarding school, I shall start to look after him, bring him down to earth a little! Nothing bad has happened to him, I hope?'

'He is in perfect health. He is concerned about you, that is all.'

'Why? I explained to him about the shoes.'

Victor handed her the single slipper that had been stuffed in his pocket. Iris took it, trying to conceal the flicker of emotion that crossed her face. She fingered the marks Berlaud's fangs had made.

'Yes, I lent them to Élisa, a schoolmate. She insisted – even though they were too wide for her. It's odd that she should have lost one. How featherbrained she is!'

'This piece of paper was inside.'

'I know. My idea was to make an inner sole to stop her foot from slipping out. She wanted to look elegant and . . . If I had known it would create such trouble . . .'

She blushed as she handed the shoe back to Victor, who sensed that she was lying.

'And where is your friend?'

'At her mother's house.'

'Are you sure?'

He started at her so intently that she began to lose her nerve.

'Oh! Monsieur Legris, please don't mention it to anybody! Élisa trusts me. She begged me to help her, so I told Mademoiselle Bontemps that while she was out Élisa's mother had telephoned to say that she was unwell and asked that her daughter go to her immediately. Mademoiselle Bontemps believed me.'

'What is the man's name?'

She looked at him, aghast.

'What is her lover's name?' Victor repeated.

'Gaston. He's very nice. He came secretly to Trouville with us.'

'Where does he live?'

'Élisa hasn't told me his address. But she said she likes his place because she can hear the wolves howling from his bedroom.'

'What wolves?'

'That's all she told me. Please, Monsieur Legris, my godfather must not find out about this. He would be terribly angry.'

'Is this the first time you have covered for her?'

'The second; she promised she'd be back on Saturday.'

'Saturday – that's tomorrow. I will be discreet, but if your friend doesn't return tomorrow . . . Do your parents live abroad?'

Before Iris could reply, there was a knock at the door and Mademoiselle Bontemps bustled in carrying a tea tray.

'It is time for your piano lesson, Iris. Mademoiselle Pluchard is waiting for you. Monsieur Legris, I thought that with this damp weather you might enjoy a cup of Earl Grey tea. Monsieur Mori orders it for us from London.'

As Iris took her leave she filled the teacups with the steaming brew and stacked a second saucer with biscuits. To his horror, Victor found himself, hands laden and mouth full, sitting next to the mistress of the house, who had planted herself demurely on the ottoman.

'Are you acquainted with Élisa's background? Monsieur Mori wonders whether it is appropriate for his goddaughter to keep her company,' he managed to ask through a mouthful of biscuit.

'The little Fourchon girl!' exclaimed Mademoiselle Bontemps. 'I do not see why not. She's a charming girl, and well-liked. Yes, I grant the mother sings, but . . .'

Victor recalled one of Kenji's proverbs: 'When the monkey is ignorant he feigns understanding and soon knows everything', and nodded knowingly as he made an effort to swallow a last mouthful.

'Yes, the singer.'

Mademoiselle Bontemps chortled.

'A singer? Don't make me laugh! L'Eldorado is hardly an

opera house, Monsieur Legris; you might as well compare chalk with cheese! She sings those Andalusian popular songs.'

'What songs are they?'

'You know, those rather soppy love songs filled with blue skies and dark-haired beauties with flashing eyes, with lovers called Pedro and heroines Paquita.'

'Does she use the name Fourchon when she performs?'

'Of course she doesn't. She uses a stage name, which I have promised not to reveal. It's a professional secret,' whispered Mademoiselle Bontemps, who having closed the gap with a surreptitious sideways shuffle was now pressing up against Victor. 'Would you care for an almond biscuit? Here, try these delicious mint-flavoured wafers. I do love sugar! I can't resist sweet things. I need tying up! There I go again, giving in!' she said, and gobbled down three wafers in quick succession. 'I can't tell you Madame Fourchon's stage name, but I might let you guess at my own first name. Aren't you curious to know what the 'C' on my brass plate stands for, Monsieur Legris? What is the mystery contained therein? Camille? Charlotte? Celestine? Do you give up? Corymbe! Do you like it?'

'Oh indeed!' said Victor, shifting imperceptibly away from her. 'It is worthy of a tragic actor. I'll wager Madame Fourchon's is far more commonplace.'

'It cannot hope to compete with mine. Though it is certainly flowery and eye-catching,' she added, with a beguiling smile. 'It is curious that we should be discussing this lady and her daughter! I am about to lose a boarder; Élisa is leaving us. Her mother has decided to take her away. I received a letter announcing the bad news this morning. Ah, life does not spare us women on our own, Monsieur Legris. We must struggle to make ends meet!'

She puffed up like a balloon and let out a deep sigh. This was too much for Victor, who rose to his feet. Mademoiselle Bontemps, saddened by the abrupt nature of his departure, followed him outside. He had already reached the railings around the garden when she came waddling after him.

'Monsieur Mori's cane! You were about to leave without it!'

Hampered by the two canes, Victor made his way in the direction of the town hall, feeling a mixture of relief and disappointment. If Élisa were at her mother's, Joseph's theory about the dead woman found at Killer's Crossing didn't hold up. He chuckled at the boy's penchant for fiction, and paused for a moment in the middle of the road: the woman with the disfigured face had been wearing no shoes, yet the paper said nothing about her age. Élisa had lost one of her shoes. It could be a simple coincidence . . . Iris had mentioned this fellow Gaston. But could he trust her after she had confessed to lying? Above all else, what intrigued Victor the most was Kenji's behaviour. Why was he keeping his supposed goddaughter locked away in Saint-Mandé?

Back at the bookshop, Victor rearranged the chairs left out by the Friends of Old Paris, who had gone with Kenji to whet their whistles at the Temps Perdu. He was obliged to wait until Joseph had concluded the sale of ten duodecimo volumes of Boccace's *Fables*, published in London in 1779, before he could satisfy his curiosity.

'What were the exact words of the man who came here yesterday to return the famous shoe?'

'Do you mean that strange fellow? Well, you're in luck, Boss, because after he'd gone I jotted down a few things in my notebook. Here we are: his dog had stolen a hunk of meat from some lions – in my opinion lions mean a circus. I asked where he lived and he said Ruelle des Culettes, round the corner from Rue Croule-something.'

'Brilliant! Clear as day! Total gibberish!'

'Well, it's not my fault if Monsieur Mori interrupted me to get him a cab and I lost the thread! As for the man's identity, I am certain his name is Grégoire Mercier and he was well known around Rue Croule-something.'

'The dog had stolen a hunk of meat from some lions . . .' echoed Victor, recalling Iris's words: 'You can hear the wolves howling from his bedroom.' Could the two things be connected?

'Did you discover anything about the shoe, Boss?'

'Nothing of any importance,' Victor called down from the stairs.

'That's right, don't be grateful. Just squeeze the facts out of me so you can play the sleuth! Fine then, you asked for it, from now on my lips are sealed!' muttered Jojo, and then broke his word the moment Victor called out to him.

'You haven't by any chance seen the Paris street directory?'

'It's upstairs on Monsieur Mori's desk!'

Victor easily found Rue Croulebarbe, Ruelle des Reculettes, in the Bièvre district, the 13th arrondissement, and came back down, whistling jauntily. He ignored the sullen look on

Joseph's face and enquired kindly how he was getting along with his book, *Love and Blood*.

'I already told you, but I guess I'll have to say it again because you clearly weren't listening: I have abandoned the project.'

'That seems a shame. You should have seen it through.'

'That's right, tell me I'm lazy! Well, I chose to give it up and I have my reasons, and I don't see why I should share them with you since you're not in the habit of sharing!'

Victor was about to ask whether his lack of inspiration was related to Valentine de Salignac's marriage when Kenji walked into the bookshop. He nodded briefly at Victor, reminded Joseph he had a delivery to make and went to sit at his desk, which was stacked with index cards ready for making up a new catalogue. Victor lit a cigar and exhaled a puff of bluish smoke. What was in Joseph's notes? he asked himself Ah, yes! A dog that stole meat from some lions; lions and howling wolves . . .

'Where might one find lions and wolves in Paris?'

'In the Botanical Gardens,' replied Kenji, burying his nose in his handkerchief. 'You aren't considering breeding them, are you? If you show the same enthusiasm as you do for running a bookshop, the enterprise is doomed to failure. Would you mind smoking that outside?'

'What have I done to make you and Joseph gripe at me so? Well, if that's the way you want it, I shall leave you in peace.'

Victor buttoned up his frock coat to protect his *Photo-Secret* from the spitting rain. He had brought it with him to give the impression of self-assurance. He passed Hôtel de la Reine-Blanche and went down a flight of dilapidated steps. At the beginning of Rue Gobelins he paused, overcome by ammoniacal fumes. He held his breath until he reached a narrow quay where he leant on a parapet wall overlooking the River Bièvre, realm of the tanners and dyers. Shades of yellow, green and red mingled in its waters, producing a brownish-looking soup that formed here and there into a muddy froth. The water glistened with golden-brown flecks like the fish oil floating on the surface of the murky broth served up at Maubert's cheap eateries. Victor, feeling nauseous, turned round to face a building whose ill-repaired façade was covered in inscriptions scored by knives. A heart with an arrow through it appeared to be telling him to go left.

He obeyed without demur, turning down Passage Moret, where an incongruent cluster of rickety dwellings with wooden balconies faintly evoked Spain. People were busy at work under the hangars where the flayed hides of animals hung on ropes to dry. Scrawny-looking dogs and cats prowled the wet cobblestones observing the arrival of carts and groups of curriers.

All along the winding river bank, washerwomen had set down their tubs by the water's edge and were singing as they pounded their shirts. Children played at skimming stones, and one held a stick with a piece of string attached to the end, as though fishing. Victor wondered what a fish that had managed to survive in that foul water might look like. Instinctively he took out his camera to photograph the children, but he felt awkward, and so instead turned his attention to the young fisherman. He was filthy and ragged and looked no older than six. The baggy clothes he wore made him appear even scrawnier.

'Are the fish biting today?'

'Not a whole lot. But I did catch this,' said the child, holding up a smoked herring.

'Are you sure you caught it?' Victor asked, amused.

'Shh! I pinched it from old Mère Guédon while she was stuffing her mattress. I climbed through her kitchen window. She won't miss it.'

A one-eyed tomcat meowed as it came over to beg.

'Get lost, Gambetta; this ain't for no cats – it's for Gustin.'

'Is that your name? Tell me, Gustin, how would you like to earn a franc?'

'Wouldn't I half!' cried the boy, stealing a glance at the washerwomen.

'Do you know of a goatherd who lives around here?'

'I certainly do. Old Père Mercier! He dosses round the corner from here.'

'Show me the way.'

They left a trail of footprints in the reddish dust as they walked through warehouses where the hide and leather goods were stored, past steaming vats and piles of acrid-smelling tanbark. Here and there, a weeping willow formed a shady corner, allowing Victor a moment's respite from the dismal surroundings. They arrived at Rue Reculettes, where he was relieved to discover what looked almost like country cottages alongside the workers' hovels.

'That's it, over there where it says "cobbler". I've got to

look sharp. If I'm late helping my brothers tan that hide I'll be the one getting the tanning from my dad – he's on the booze today.'

'Take this.' Victor handed him a coin, which the boy snatched greedily.

'Blimey! A whole franc!'

He wanted to ask the man if he had made a mistake, but Victor had already disappeared inside.

Each new smell eclipses the next, thought Victor as he lowered himself on to the stool Grégoire Mercier had offered him. The man looked distinctly un-Parisian in a smock, trousers tucked into leather leggings and clogs. As he watched the goats standing meekly in a row while they were being mucked out, Victor felt as though he'd been magically transported to the heart of the Beauce region to the south of Paris.

'I'll be with you in a minute, Monsieur. There we are. It's a rotten job. I toil like a slave all the livelong day. Thanks to these little goats and their milk, I earn my crust. Lie down, Berlaud! So you're the owner of the bookshop? I thought you'd come about the reward. I can't tell you any more than I told your assistant.'

'There's just one thing I wanted to clarify. Did your dog find the shoe in the Botanical Gardens?'

Grégoire Mercier frowned, his honest brow creasing into furrows.

'I don't like to admit it, as dogs aren't allowed,' he murmured, stroking Berlaud's head roughly.

'Don't worry, I shan't tell a soul.'

'Well, all right. My rounds take me there. It's my cousin Basile from back home, Basile Popêche; he's got kidney stones. I give him Pulchérie's milk. She's that one over there, second from the right, the white one with a black goatee. She's all blown up like a balloon because she's expecting. I mix the sapwood of a lime tree with her hay to make her milk into a diuretic.'

'Oh! So your animals are a sort of walking pharmacy. Are these remedies effective?' Victor enquired sceptically.

'Ask around and you'll find out. In any case no one must know about Basile being poorly or he'll lose his job, which only pays a pittance anyway. He looks after the wild animals. People don't appreciate what hard work it is, Monsieur. My goats are a piece of cake in comparison. Poor Popêche and his partner have to muck out sixty-five pens containing a hundred carnivores, plus the three bear pits. Holy Virgin, the racket is deafening! It's back-breaking work to scrub down those floors every day. And it breaks my heart to see those poor animals caged up like that until the end of their days. At least my nanny goats go into town, and when the cold weather comes I wrap a blanket around . . .'

'What time were you at the Botanical Gardens?'

'That was yesterday, on my way from Quai de la Tournelle, so it must have been about ten or eleven o'clock. Oh, I work all hours, Monsieur! It beats being in the army, but I've got to keep moving if I'm to keep my customers happy. Money doesn't grow on trees, does it? Berlaud must have found the shoe near the Botanical Gardens. That dog's so good with my goats I put up with his fancies. When he has a yearning to run off, he won't come to heel, no matter how much I yawl.'

'Yawl?'

'You know, whistle. Ah, you fickle beast, you give me the run around, but I'll miss you when you're gone!' he muttered, scratching the backs of Berlaud's ears as the dog closed its eyes with contentment.

After he had left, it occurred to Victor that he should have given the goatherd a coin, but he did not have the energy to climb back up all those stairs. On a piece of paper he jotted down the words:

Basile Popêche, lion house at Botanical Gardens, Grègoire Mercier's cousin.

He could question the man later if necessary.

The rain had stopped. As he walked back through Rue Croulebarbe he searched in vain for little Gustin. All he could see were groups of apprentices busy plunging hides into vats of alum or scraping skins stretched over trestle tables. If he was serious about his project of documenting child labour, he would have to come back one morning when the light was good.

The River Bièvre disappeared under Boulevard Arago. Victor walked up Avenue des Gobelins and turned off into Rue Monge. A sign caught his eye: 'Impasse de la Photographie'. Was this an omen? And if so was it a good or a bad one? He chose to smile at it, and yet he felt a lingering anxiety about the young woman found strangled at the crossroads, and about little

Élisa. He jotted something else down on the piece of paper where he'd noted Basile Popêche's name:

L'Eldorado: Madame Fourchon sings there, under a flowery name that catches the eye.

CHAPTER 4

Saturday 14 November

'Sulphuric acid is a formidable substance, crucial to the advance of science and industry, without which chemistry as we know it would not exist. It is also a terrible means of vengeance, and the chosen method of cowards. Why it was used on the woman whose unidentified corpse was found strangled at the crossroads remains a mystery. Was this a crime of passion? As usual Inspector Lecacheur's investigation is advancing slowly but surely. Yet there are questions that still need asking. What, for example, was an abandoned cab doing close to where the body was found lying on the road?'

Jojo stopped reading aloud from the article in *Le Passe-partout* to speculate as to the identity of the author.

'I wonder which journalist uses the pseudonym "The Virus". Could it be Monsieur Isidore Gouvier?'

Victor was only half listening. He was busy ticking off from a catalogue the books he intended buying at auction. At the same time an inner voice was telling him that Élisa was sure to be at her mother's house, although there was no way of verifying this. Just then his cab arrived.

Victor walked out of the auction room after the sale of the

library of Hilaire de Kermarec, cousin to the well-known antiques dealer of Rue de Tournon, carrying a parcel under one arm. He passed through the first floor, reserved for the more valuable items, and crossed the ground floor reserved for deceased estates and the auction of shop stock. The courtyard was filled with an assortment of objects. He wandered among the piles of artisans' tools and the battered possessions of impoverished labourers, over which dealers from Temple Market and scrap merchants from Rue de Lappe were haggling: cheap chests of drawers, twenty-sou lots of crockery, men and women's clothing, sheets, eiderdowns, blankets, pillows and old bric-a-brac, the pitiful sight of which moved Victor.

He paused when he reached Rue Drouet. If he walked fast, it would take him between fifteen and twenty minutes to get to Boulevard de Strasbourg. That would give him time for a quick snack. Should he ring Kenji from a telephone box and tell him he had bought the Montaigne?

'No! Let him stew! It'll serve him right for keeping his gorgeous goddaughter locked away at the edge of the Bois de Vincennes and giving me sulky looks for the past two days!'

Victor let himself be swept along by the tide of bank clerks and insurance-company employees surging down Rue Provence and Rue Grange-Batelière, until he reached a cheap eating house on the outskirts of Montmartre. Inside, amid the coming and going of diners that created a continual breeze, he sat at a marble-topped table strewn with grains of sugar and breadcrumbs that were quickly swept to the floor by the flick of a waiter's cloth. A grease-stained menu offered him a set meal for one franc twenty-five, and he bolted down veal Marengo, followed by camembert and prunes, barely touching the sharp table wine. He took his coffee at a bar where the owner stood filling row upon row of cups from the spout of a copper kettle. Crowds of people filed past outside the steamy windows.

How many of the shadowy figures drifting about this city are potential criminals? Victor wondered.

He paused before the narrow offices of *Le Figaro*, not far from the town hall of the ninth arrondissement, and walked in. He wandered through the dispatch room where portraits of famous people, the daily Bourse prices, important political events and gory news items were on view. He had no difficulty finding a reconstruction of the drama next to an image of General Boulanger, prone on his mistress's grave after committing suicide.

VILE MURDER AT CROSSROADS

A group of onlookers had gathered round a very lifelike drawing of the disfigured woman, and was discussing the affair in an extremely distasteful way, putting Victor in mind of the spectators at the morgue. He left in a hurry.

He paused at Boulevard Poissonière after crossing Boulevard Montmartre. Perhaps the crossroads had been baptised 'Killer's Crossing' because a combination of cabmen's incompetence and pedestrians' recklessness had led to more fatalities here than at other junctions? In any event, the morbid name had taken on a new significance since the previous evening. Victor noticed a row of cabs lined up by the pavement. The horses were taking advantage of the halt in proceedings to chomp on feed in the nosebags hanging from their halters while the cabmen exchanged vulgar stories.

'Do you know where the body was found?' Victor asked one of them.

'You're at least the thirtieth person who's asked me that since this morning. If this continues, I shall have to start charging! You see that paunchy copper standing guard on the corner over there outside the cobbler's – the one who looks like a dog watching over his bone? Well, it was there. But I can tell you now they've cleaned up the whole area; there's not a trace of acid!'

Victor moved away to the sound of the cabmen's guffaws, telling himself that given his own passion for unsolved murders he had no right to sneer at the public's bloodthirstiness.

Two huge pintos, their nostrils steaming, struggled to pull the Madeleine-Bastille omnibus up Boulevard Bonne-Nouvelle. The hammer of hooves, the clatter of wheels and the cries of card-sharps rattled in Victor's ears. He feigned interest in the window display of an English hat shop, then, moving on a few paces, stopped in front of a Morris Column plastered with posters: brightly coloured advertisements for Papillon bicycles, Soleil washing powder and Mariani wine vied with theatre notices. But the yellow, red, black and white Moulin-Rouge poster eclipsed all the others with its eye-catching simplicity, reminiscent of a Japanese painting, and its exuberant style. It was signed by someone called Hautrec or Lautrec. The profile of a very angular man with a prominent nose and hooked chin wearing a top hat was in monochrome in the foreground, and behind him a blonde woman in a spotted bodice lifted her skirts in a frenzied motion, revealing black-stockinged legs. 'La Goulue' it said. In the background were the silhouetted shapes of men and women. Victor was struck by the uncanny similarity between those faceless onlookers and the anonymous passers-by he had watched earlier through the window of the café.

'What a fine illustration,' a young man exclaimed, mesmerised by the dancer's legs.

Victor moved on. On the raised terrace of the Théâtre du Gymnase, nursemaids in ruched hats rocked perambulators with moleskin hoods containing restless infants. In an instant Victor pictured Tasha coddling a baby, then shrugged his shoulders and smiled.

You have plenty of time to burden yourself with a family! he thought, as he turned the corner into Boulevard de Strasbourg.

With its mullioned windows flanked by columns, L'Eldorado was trying to hang on to its Second Empire splendour, the era when the singer Thérésa, who wrote *Never Trust a Sapper!* was the star attraction. Competition was stiff in this neighbourhood where there was an abundance of *café-concerts*. Victor studied the poster advertising the programme:

Seats:	75 centimes
	1 franc
Boxes:	2.50 francs

Introducing:	
Messieurs	Kam-Hill
	Vanel
	Plébins

Mesdames	Bonnaire
	Duffay
	Holda

NOÉMI GERFLEUR

The name certainly was eye-catching, and flowery! Satisfied, he decided to return later that evening.

Jojo was leaning on the counter, taking advantage of a quiet moment to fill a page of his notebook with a hasty scrawl. He'd had one of those ideas, those flashes of genius he must put into writing immediately for fear they might be quickly forgotten. He was planning to write a serial entitled *Blood and Treason*, which began with the discovery of a woman in red, found strangled on the Boulevards, her face disfigured by acid. However, no sooner had he outlined the atmosphere of the story than his inspiration dried up – no matter how much he wet his pencil lead.

Kenji looked up from his papers when he heard the doorbell, muttering, 'About time!' as Victor walked in.

'Forgive the delay, I had lunch out.'

'Did you get it?'

Victor handed him the package. Kenji opened it and took out *The Essays of Michel, Seigneur de Montaigne*, a 1588 in-quarto fifth edition, bound in yellow morocco-leather.

'How much?'

'Four thousand, nine hundred francs.'

'A little pricey, although the Duc de Frioul is not known for his thriftiness. What about the Clément Marot?'

'It's coming up this afternoon. With any luck I might get it for three thousand francs. Is that all right?'

'You have a free hand.'

Kenji's relaxed face and the hint of a smile on his lips conveyed a cheerfulness that had been markedly absent in the past few weeks.

'Are you pleased with your associate?' enquired Victor.

'Quite pleased.'

'Only quite!'

'A single nod of approval is better than a thousand words of flattery. Joseph, serve us some sake.'

The sky was like a liquid veil shrouding the city. The room was like a cave, its barely perceptible shadows obscuring the furniture and blurring the lined wallpaper. The man lay on the bed listening to the murmur of voices half-drowned out by the rattle of omnibuses and carriages. He lit the petrol lamp. Prompted by a baby's cry coming through the partition wall, he went into the bathroom and emerged carrying a bottle of rum and a tumbler. This was what he needed to steady his nerves, to enable him to separate the real from the imagined. The first slug burnt in his throat; the second warmed his insides and invigorated him. The alcohol calmed his rage, allowing him to see exactly what must happen next. He found it so hard to control himself, to rein in his hatred, his impatience! But he had finally succeeded, and soon he would reap the rewards. He was nearing his goal and he would not stop before he attained it. He emptied the glass and stared for a long time at the bottle. No, he must keep a clear head.

He went to rinse his mouth out with a menthol solution, trimmed his moustache and smoothed down his greying sideburns. He felt as if he were about to emerge from a long sleep. To the devil with inertia! He sat down at the table. Soon it would all be over; she would have paid for the five years of pain and loneliness she had inflicted on him. He had taken great care not to incriminate himself; no one would ever suspect him. The sole witness was pickling in a vat of cheap wine, the alcoholic content of which he would never know.

'My life is beginning anew,' he murmured.

He looked at the box of cards and the envelopes and smiled.

'I must follow my plan to the letter. I'm a lucky devil; everything has gone smoothly. If the police have an ounce of intuition and common sense, they'll follow the clues I've left for them.'

Spurred on by these words, he opened a map of Paris, smoothing out the fifth, ninth and thirteenth arrondissements, all marked with crosses denoting the various florists' shops from which he had ordered eight roses to be sent each day for the last eight days. 16 November 1886 was the day she had betrayed, dismissed and humiliated him – the bitch! The day after tomorrow, he would wish her a happy anniversary. He had placed each order with a different florist before losing himself in the crowd of a thousand nameless faces. Who would remember him? Today he would send the flowers from Rue Auber. She would receive them as she made her exit from the stage and, flattered, would lift them to her nose to smell their scent. Then she would see the note.

He dressed and picked up the cards and envelopes. He was not sure exactly what to write, but it would come to him on his way there. He looked at his watch; it was a quarter past six. He glanced about the street. A couple of servants were chattering beside a carriage entrance, and a little girl hopped along the gutter clutching a small loaf of bread to her chest. It was drizzling. He pulled his hat down over his forehead, and turned up the collar of his grey overcoat. He must remember to remove the stains from the sleeve. He walked down the street, unaware of a chubby little man with a bushy beard, in a threadbare frock coat and shabby bowler hat who was standing on the corner next to the dairy.

The city's cosmopolitan neighbourhood around Rue Auber, with its English tailor, American optician, telegraph and cable office and travel agent, was alive and bustling. Shop girls, purveyors of the latest fashions, and accountants were all racing for a seat on the omnibus. The man in the grey overcoat strode through the revolving door of the travel agent. Inside, well-dressed customers sat at green-topped desks in leather chairs writing letters to loved ones abroad under a bluish lamplight. At the far end of the room the model of an ocean liner was an invitation to travel. The man went over to a display counter and flicked through one of the shipping company's catalogues until a chair became free. Then he sat down at a desk with a metal inkpot, put down the cards and envelopes, nibbled the end of his pen and proceeded to dash off the following message:

To the Jewel Queen, Baroness of Saint-Meslin, a gift of ruby red roses in fond memory of Lyon – from an old friend.

He signed himself in careful, rounded letters: A. Prévost, slipped the card into an envelope and addressed it to the recipient:

Madame Noémi Gerfleur
Théâtre L'Eldorado
Boulevard de Strasbourg

Indifferent to the rain, the chubby little man stood pressed up against the window of the travel agent's, pretending to peruse the price lists of the brightly coloured brochures. His dull protruding eyes gave an impression of blindness, and yet they were fixed on the back of the man in the grey overcoat as he sealed the envelope. The man rose and headed towards Rue Caumartin, followed at a distance by the little man who hopped about like a sparrow through the crowd. They walked past a brightly lit tea room, where Singhalese waiters in traditional dress moved deftly between the rattan tables occupied by elegant ladies. The figure in the grey overcoat stepped into a florist. The little man leant against a Wallace fountain[12] and watched as the man pointed out some red roses to the shop assistant and handed her an envelope and some money before leaving. He waited until the man was far enough away from the shop and went in.

*

The edition of Marot safely tucked in his pocket, Victor dined at a smoky brasserie decorated with stained-glass windows. As he left that shrine to the consumption of tough meat and bad wine he noticed the hands on the shiny face of the pneumatic clock were pointing to seven thirty. The show started at eight o'clock.

The busy boulevard was lined with brightly lit pleasure palaces and shimmering signs: a foaming beer glass; a silvery fork, green and red billiard balls. Thousands of shoes clattered over cobblestones glistening in the rain and people leant from cab windows. A coach and four stuck between an advertising vehicle and an upholsterer's cart managed to break free, spraying the passers-by with dirty water from the gutter.

The façade of L'Eldorado, lit up in blaze of electricity, held the night at bay. The audience, a mélange of middle-class families, shop girls, workers and students had gathered on the promenade. As he approached the ticket office, Victor spotted Stanislas and Blanche de Cambrésis – he tall and potbellied in a tailcoat, she larger than life in her furs – who had come to rub elbows with the masses. Victor arrived just in time to climb up to the gods where, not without a struggle, he found a seat in the second row.

A few moments earlier he had been soaked through by the fine rain and shivering, but now as the theatre began filling with people he felt suffocated. He looked down towards the ground floor, where the boxes overlooked the stalls. The first row was taken up by well-dressed people. Behind them in the second row the dress code was already more casual, and in the gods all formality had been left behind; the men in berets or cloth caps removed their jackets and rolled up their shirtsleeves.

A stout woman with a rosy-cheeked infant plonked herself down on Victor's right and to his left a young girl wearing a flannelette top, embroidered dress and no hat, sat down and began making eyes at him.

'I've never been to a music hall before,' she whispered, excitedly. 'It's just bad luck that my friend who was supposed to come with me had to return to his barracks. Do you have a programme?'

He shook his head, frowning. The combined smell of cigar smoke, gas and perspiration was overpowering, and the lily of the valley perfume the girl had smothered herself in did not improve matters. He had a sudden urge to leave, but could not face pushing past rows of people.

'I've got one if you want,' said the woman with the little baby, handing her a cheap brochure.

The girl thanked her. Out of the corner of his eye Victor glimpsed an advertisement extolling the curative virtues of Samo-coca-Kola, and next to it in a box framed by arabesques the name: Noémi Gerfleur.

'I'm here mostly because of La Gerfleur; they call her the darling of the people. Still, it's a shame Jeanne Bloch isn't here, they say she's a scream as Colonel Ronchonot!' The girl was addressing the woman, who replied:

'I've seen her! She's the queen of the *café-concert*, always ready to hold court. Seventeen stone she weighs, but that doesn't stop her from playing the parts of young girls. The Galleon they call her, because she's as broad as she is long. On one occasion her co-star couldn't get his arms round her and some wag from the audience yelled out: "You'll have to make two trips!"'

Down in the stalls the spectators hailed young boys clad in black serving glasses of beer and cherry brandy. These were set down on small ledges fixed to the backs of chairs, occasionally spilling on to people trying to reach their seats and causing insults to fly and the general level of excitement to intensify.

'Start the show! Start the show!' voices chanted to a rhythmical tapping of feet on the floor.

'Get that bloody curtain up!' shouted a youngster from the gods.

As if this were the signal they had been waiting for, the gas lights went down and the curtain rose on a stage where a clown-like soldier in a comic uniform comprised of a greenish-yellow hussars jacket, a pair of red trousers and a shako appeared to the sound of a clarion call. He planted himself centre stage by the prompter's pit and delivered 'The Godillots of Tringlot' in a muffled voice. The audience was quick to show its disapproval and pelted the wretched singer with cherry stones as he wisely beat a retreat into the wings. He was briskly replaced by a man in a diminutive peasant's outfit and a huge bowtie who broke into a popular song, the chorus of which the audience joined in:

> *Who loves a little chocolate?*
> *It's Papa!*
> *And who loves a wee tipple?*
> *It's Mama!*

By the time they'd sung their way through the little boy's cheese and the girl's butter biscuits, Victor was bitterly regretting not having some cotton wool to stick in his ears. He was relieved when a Romeo with a handsome moustache appeared and in a warbling voice delivered a repertoire that was entirely devoted to that most ineffable of all mysteries: love. The audience was treated to 'The Chimes of Love' and then 'Love's First Call'.

The man spouting verse would almost certainly have sent Victor to sleep if his neighbours had not felt a sudden, irresistible urge to eat and drink, probably in order to quell an excess of emotion from the poetry.

And so two new smells were added to the fug of tobacco and perspiration: garlic and verjuice. The bare-headed girl pulled a cured sausage from her bag and offered a slice to Victor, who politely refused. The wet nurse provided wine, and everybody chomped in time to the mournful and disjointed delivery of bad rhyming couplets.

'Do you know what?' said the girl, her mouth full of food, 'that fellow has so much blacking in his hair he could be advertising shoe polish!'

'Sh! It's Kam-Hill!' said the woman with the baby. A man in red coat-tails, a flannel waistcoat, silk culottes and stockings, white gloves and an opera hat, had made his entrance to loud applause. The spectators stamped their feet – those in the stalls banging their spoons against their glasses, and the pianist pounded the keys. Victor tested his powers of concentration by closing his eyes and imagining he was in a concert hall, lulled by the melancholy harmonies of Schumann. But it was no use, 'One-legged Man's Jig' triumphed, and he suffered until the interval, when he was able to take a breath of tepid air outside on the promenade. When he returned, the girl with no hat, who had removed her jacket to reveal a plunging neckline, had occupied his seat next to the wet nurse, with whom she was exchanging artistic observations. Victor insisted she should not get up.

'You see that skinny lout in the orchestra pit? They call him the Guide to the Tarts of Paris!' cried the girl.

'And that other one who looks like an epileptic is a pickpocket – a right show-off, he is, and he'll pinch your wallet before you can say "strumpet",' said the woman with the baby.

Victor slumped down in his seat, determined to nap, but the bellicose tones of a singer of patriotic songs from Alsace with her hair in two thick coils woke the baby, who wailed indignantly as she belted out the words:

> *Be on your way for this nipple is French,*
> *No German'll taste the milk of this wench*

The wet nurse promptly unbuttoned her bodice, exposing an opulent bosom, the mere sight of which silenced the baby.

At last, Noémi Gerfleur, the star of the show, for whom everyone was clamouring, appeared on stage.

'She looks like a *demi-mondaine*,' the girl with no hat observed.

'More like a courtesan,' corrected the wet nurse.

La Gerfleur had a penchant for pseudo-Spanish costumes. Beneath her enormous hat she sported a curly black wig and rather violent make-up. Her pendants and bracelets sparkled with each step, and as she sashayed across the stage, or tossed an occasional rose from a basket into the front row, her mantilla slipped off her shoulders. The rest of the time she stood, her gloved hand furiously waving a black lace fan that matched her black-stockinged legs – more and more of which appeared with each new verse and with every sway of her hips.

'Higher, higher!' the crowd cried.

'Give us a gander at those silk stockings!' shouted a boy sitting near Victor.

'Get your knickerbockers off!' bellowed another.

La Gerfleur signalled to the orchestra to stop playing and walked downstage to scold the audience:

'For God's sake shut up, will you! Put some oomph into your catcalls or belt up! Do you really think I'm going to strain my vocal chords for a bunch of idiots like you?'

The theatre fell silent, the conductor raised his baton and the piano began a syncopated tune.

'And now I shall sing for you "Crime of Passion",' La Gerfleur announced.

> *D'you see that gentleman scurrying?*
> *Where d'you think he's ahurrying?*
> *He's going to where his lover dwells*
> *To sweet young Sophie he loves so well*

'They say she owns a coach and two and diamonds as big as a bottle stopper given to her by . . .' the girl with no hat began.

'Sh!' interrupted the wet nurse.

> But why does he look so dismayed?
> His eyes are filled with dread;
> Oh misery! He's been betrayed
> Another's in her bed.

'. . . one of her lovers was a Russian Grand Duke,' the bare-headed girl continued, turning to Victor. 'She combs the Monte Carlo casinos and . . .'

> Up the umpteen flights of stairs,
> Up he runs and then he's there!
> Outside the room he knocks, no answer,
> Then in he bursts and shoots the bounder.
> But it is she, his beauty who falls
> And now he's rolling on the floor.
> Ha Ha Ha!

'Is it true that she is called Noémi Fourchon?' Victor asked.
　'Whatever gave you that idea? What an ugly name!'

> D'you see that gentleman scurrying?
> Where do you think he's ahurrying?
> Terrified, he's going to confess
> To the commissioner himself, no less,
> Rue Buci, 'Yes, sir,
> I was mad about her, intoxicated,
> I loved her more than I could a wife.
> I killed her and my rage abated;
> Now I will pay for it with my life.

With one hand over her heart and the other holding her fan up high, La Gerfleur kept her audience spellbound. Eyes staring, pupils dilated, it was as though she sought to hypnotise her spectators, who sat motionless.

> *Arrest me for I am the killer;*
> *A bullet I fired at her breast.*
> *The commissioner turned whiter,*
> *Said he: I loved Sophie the best!*
> *And slumped in a heap on his desk.*
> *Well, well, what a jolly old mess!*

La Gerfleur raised her arms, allowing her mantilla to slip from her shoulders, and the men in the audience gaped at her armpits and at her bosom spilling out of her shimmering dress.

> *D'you see . . .*
> *D'you see that gentleman scurrying?*
> *Where do you think he's ahurrying?*
> *Oh Lord! He's hung himself from a rafter,*
> *Thus ends this tale of the sweet hereafter.*[13]

A deep sigh followed the final note. There was a moment of silence before the audience awoke from its trance. People began banging their beer glasses on the little wooden ledges in a frenetic rallying cry and erupting into loud cheers. La Gerfleur hiked up her skirts, curtsied and blew kisses to her public. She was about to leave the stage, exhausted, but the applause and cries of encore obliged her to take another curtain call. She forced a smile, her brow covered in beads of sweat and the kohl round her eyes running. The curtain went down.

'Well! The *café-concert*'s not a patch on this. La Gerfleur was unforgettable!' exclaimed the girl with no hat, turning to Victor, but he had already left.

Victor wandered towards the box office, but instead of walking out he went down a gloomy passage that opened off the auditorium and was strewn with pasteboard props and wicker chairs. To his right a steep staircase led down to the dressing rooms below stage. He let himself be guided by the smell of grease paint and patchouli oil and the rank smell emanating from the row of slop buckets at the far end of a narrow corridor. As he passed a door he heard a woman's rasping voice cry out:

'Well, you can't claim to have earned your wage tonight! You were sloppy. Take your money and clean yourself up – you're covered in blacking!'

Through the crack of another door he glimpsed Romeo busy rehearsing a scene of jealousy with the soldier, while the comedian nonchalantly grilled a herring on the iron frame of a gas lamp.

'Hey! You're smoking us out! Do you want to get us sacked?' yelled the soldier.

Victor cleared his throat and carried on towards the ladies' dressing rooms, where he was greeted by a small commotion.

A dresser was energetically pushing back a group of five or six male admirers blocking the doorway to La Gerfleur's dressing room.

'She told you she's changing. Are you deaf? Go on, get out!'

Just as the men were about to beat a retreat, a bellboy arrived with an enormous bouquet of roses. Through the door, Victor glimpsed a haggard woman in a petticoat and camisole, her blonde hair flattened against her head, tearing open a tiny envelope. She read the card inside, a horrified look on her face; then she cried out before falling to the floor in a faint. The men crowding the doorway didn't move, assuming it to be an act. But when the dresser cried out: 'Madame! Madame! What's wrong with you?' they rushed forward as one.

Victor managed to slip in behind them and saw that he had no hope of reaching La Gerfleur, who was now laid out on the settee and completely surrounded. He glanced around the dressing room, taking in pots of cold cream, clothes draped over a screen, the floor strewn with pieces of cotton wool caked in grease paint, a fan, a black silk stocking and a card, which he retrieved.

To the Jewel Queen, Baroness of Saint-Meslin, a gift of ruby red roses in fond memory of Lyon – from an old friend.

He read the note without understanding its meaning and slipped it in his pocket. Suddenly the dresser lost her temper and began pushing everybody out, shouting:

'You'll be the death of her!'

Back outside, amid the hubbub of the boulevard, Victor felt as though he had woken from a strange dream. He ambled past cafés, where artists and revellers celebrated their common victory over ennui with vast quantities of beer and absinthe. He strolled for a long while, unaware that he was exhausted and soaked to the skin, the copy of Marot in one hard, and La Gerfleur's card in the other.

CHAPTER 5

A RAT, disturbed by the noise of footsteps, scurried between the casks piled up on the pier of the wine port at Quai Saint-Bernard. It hesitated, worried, at the edge of the dark water, and then scurried as far as a row of trees. Its long tail, illuminated in the trembling flame of a street lamp, narrowly missed the trajectory of a stone. The rat fled.

'Dirty rodent,' muttered Basile Popêche, continuing on his way towards a clock tower, 'any minute now, Paris will be overrun with rats!'

A lion in the Botanical Gardens roared as if in agreement.

'Ah, that must be Tiberius; he's sleeping badly at the moment. I think his teeth are bothering him.'

Basile Popêche turned off into one of the five roads leading down to the river, all bearing the names of wine-growing regions – Burgundy, Champagne, Bordeaux, Languedoc, Touraine – whose low buildings divided into wine cellars marked the edge of the wine market. Gripped by fear and cold at the sight of the deserted market, shrouded in darkness, he stamped his feet as he passed a warehouse where a storm lantern burned, giving off a light that was almost friendly.

'What time must it be? Five o'clock? Five thirty? This is where we usually meet . . . Polyte is late!'

He started at the sound of muffled footsteps, and made out the shadow of a cart crossing one of the alleys on its way to a wine cellar. The noise of the horses' shoes on the road was equally muffled and ghostly. Head thrown back and eyes closed, Basile savoured the heady bouquet of alcohol. He cried out when someone tapped him briskly on the shoulder.

'Only me, don't panic!'

He recognised the figure of his friend Polyte Gorgerin, hat pulled down low, his breath in a steaming cloud before him.

'Sorry I'm late, had to deliver some Beaujolais. Come on, let's go. Be careful where you put your trotters – there's red wine spilled everywhere and it's as slippery as glass!'

As he did each Sunday at dawn, Basile Popêche advanced cautiously over the scantily lit avenues bordering what looked like a military camp, where casks emitting a sour odour stood. He came to collect his weekly ration of cheap wine courtesy of Polyte, an old regiment mate, and he returned the favour each week with a side of meat diverted from the rations of the wild animals. His doctor had forbidden him to drink, given the poor state of his kidneys, but he paid no heed to that, convinced that wine was not only necessary for his happiness, but would also dissolve his kidney stones.

Barrels of wine, shaken up in transport and gone mouldy, stood to one side in an enclosure surrounded by bushes. Polyte had set up a little trade that permitted him to pad out his monthly takings. He sold this mediocre plonk cheaply to the owners of the drinking dens of the Latin Quarter who, for a modest price, would dole it out to their loyal customers when they came to drink a jar at the counter.

This Sunday morning several bar owners, cans in hand, were waiting to profit from the windfall. Polyte was greeted with exclamations:

'So, are we going to get it or not, this grape juice?'

Polyte pushed his way impatiently through the group to reach a yellow cask with iron bands sitting beneath a street lamp.

'Don't fret, it's good stuff. You'll be able to wet your whistle, and tell me what it's like!'

He put a quart jug under the copper spout and opened the tap. Red liquid started to flow, tinkling against the metal, then faltered, diminished to a dribble and gurgled to a halt.

'For God's sake!' he complained, fiddling with the spout.

'Looks like the frogs have got into your barrel,' bawled a crone with flaxen hair.

The bar owners laughed amongst themselves as they watched Polyte trying to extract a few drops from the tap.

'Confound it! What's going on here! It can't have emptied itself all on its own. Unless some joker siphoned it out in the night!'

He struck the side of the barrel violently.

'It sounds full. We'll have to find out what it's got in its belly!'

He bent down, seized an iron lever and prepared to prise open the lid, expecting to have to use considerable force. But the lid came off easily, and Polyte toppled backwards against the ample bosom of the crone.

'Watch out there, love! Are you trying to have your wicked way with me? Cos I warn you, I'm spoken for.'

Sniggering, Polyte leant into the barrel then hastily turned away, nauseated. The others looked in.

'Good God Almighty,' exclaimed a large fellow in a grey smock.

He made way for Basile Popêche, who had forgotten his glasses, and had to squint in an effort to see exactly what was in the barrel. An icy terror gripped him by the throat as he made out the horrifying sight. It was like something floating in a specimen jar at a museum: hair undulating on the surface of the vermilion liquid, mottled yellow in the light of the street lamp, staring eyes with dilated pupils, mouth twisted in a mute cry. Transfixed, he leant further over. He recognised the drowned man. Although he had only passed him twice, he was sure it was the ground floor tenant from his building.

'We'll have to tell the coppers,' murmured the giant.

Everyone recoiled. No one wanted to get involved in this sordid affair. Embarrassed, they avoided looking at each other. As if with one mind, they scattered to the four corners of the market.

'Oy! Wait for me!' yelped Polyte. 'Basile, where are you going?'

Basile Popêche, sweating profusely, was walking fast up Rue de Champagne towards the Seine. That man from his building, he had seen him the other evening, when he was taking a breath of fresh air at his window; it must have been about midnight. And there had been another man, a strapping fellow in a grey overcoat who had appeared from Rue Geoffroy-Saint-Hilaire. He had glimpsed Monsieur Grey Overcoat for long enough to remember his face, and to notice that he seemed to be following the fellow from the ground floor.

'But it's nothing to do with me. I've got enough of my own worries; best to leave them to sort it out without me. I know nothing; I saw nothing!'

A ray of sunlight pierced the milky daylight that filtered through the window and found its way into the alcove, dragging Victor from sleep. He was astonished to find himself lying on his stomach. He sat up so quickly he felt slightly dizzy. Tasha was painting. Apart from her bare feet and her tousled chignon, she was entirely hidden behind her easel. The stove was purring like a contented cat. Victor leaned back against the pillows, yawning, and flattened his rumpled hair.

'Can't you stop doing that?' he complained. 'It's Sunday – come back to bed!'

'No, I'm determined to finish this sketch while it's fresh in my memory. You go back to sleep.'

Annoyed, he threw back the eiderdown. Go back to sleep! What he wanted was to laze in bed with her, nibbling the lobes of her ears and her breasts, caressing her body tenderly and yielding slowly to his desire.

But she wants to finish her drawing! Why did I have to fall in love with an artist?

Just for a moment, he wished she was one of those women obsessed with nothing but her appearance and attire.

'Are you sulking?' she teased him. 'Victor, this picture is important to me, and you know how obsessive I am.'

He knew it well. He watched her as he dressed. What he saw was familiar, soothing. She seemed to him extremely vulnerable, and yet he knew she was possessed of a stronger character than his.

'I understand,' he said. 'I'll leave you to concentrate.'

His words were totally insincere; he felt ashamed.

'Shall we have dinner together? Oh bother, I have to go and see someone. I'll be home late.'

'I have to see someone too,' he replied, quick as a flash.

She tossed a cotton sheet over her canvas, and ran over to him, putting her arms round his neck.

'A woman?'

'And you, a man?'

'Of course not, idiot!'

They kissed lingeringly. By the time she pulled away he felt reassured. Those beautiful green eyes – surely they would not lie to him? But then even if she were lying he would still be besotted with her.

'What are you hiding under there?' he asked, indicating the easel.

'I'll show you when it's finished,'

'One of your rooftops? A nude? A still life?'

'It's a secret.'

As soon as he was outside, his obsessive jealousy came flooding back. He imagined lifting the cotton cover to discover a drawing of another man, of having his suspicions confirmed with his own eyes. To take his mind off his anguish, he forced himself to think about Élisa Fourchon. Had she left the Bontemps Boarding School dressed in red, like the girl found murdered at Killer's Crossing? He would have to find out. He reflected, not without bitterness, that he would rather frolic in the woods with Tasha; they could have picnicked on the banks of the Saint-Mandé lake.

'In this weather, you imbecile? That would be a sure way to contract pneumonia. You'll see her this evening, and then you will hold her in your arms and tell her that it can't go on like this. Until then, concentrate on this new mystery. Go to Chaussée de l'Étang and see what you can discover. Take your photographic equipment; Mademoiselle Corymbe Bontemps will surely be delighted to have her photograph taken . . .'

'Monsieur Legris, what a wonderful surprise! The young ladies and I were about to set off on our walk. Oh, you're a photographer!'

Caught in the middle of the pavement of Chaussée de l'Étang, encumbered with his concertina camera and the satchel containing his plates, Victor recoiled in the face of Mademoiselle Bontemps's ebullience.

'Would it be taking advantage if I were to ask you to take a group picture of us?' she cried excitedly.

'Well, I had in fact come to ask your help. You see I'm looking for models.'

Victor felt perfectly ridiculous, standing there surrounded by a knot of girls decked out in their Sunday best. As for Mademoiselle Bontemps, she resembled an enormous, belligerent parakeet under the green feathers of her huge hat.

'I'm not sure I'm looking my best,' she cooed, fidgeting.

'Yes, yes, you are ravishing; people will think you're one of the girls. Let's go down to the lake.'

Iris, very chic in a grey coat with a fur collar, slipped over to him and whispered, 'That's going a bit far! She looks hideous. Did Godfather send you?'

'Come along, girls, behave nicely. It's not every day that an artist takes an interest in us! Berthe, Aspasie, you tall girls stand behind. Iris, stand here in the front beside Henriette and Aglaé. The others . . .'

'That's not fair; I'm an inch shorter than them,' muttered Aspasie.

'It's a pity Élisa's not here!' said Berthe.

'She's gone home to her mother,' said Mademoiselle Bontemps, who added in an aggrieved tone to Victor: 'That mother, she has no idea how to behave. She hasn't paid me for this term; if she thinks I'm just going to overlook it . . .'

'The Fourchon girl? Noémi Gerfleur's daughter?' asked Victor innocently.

'So you solved the enigma of the flowery name; what perspicacity, Monsieur Legris! Girls, girls, calm down, stay in your places. I'll leave you to your work, Monsieur Legris.'

Victor set up his camera, adjusted the pose of the girls and disappeared under a black cloth. There were suppressed giggles, elbowing and mutterings of, 'How long must we stand like statues?'

When he'd finished, the girls scattered, chased by a furious Mademoiselle Bontemps, clutching her plumed hat with one hand. Iris came over to Victor.

'You didn't say anything to Godfather?'

'Not a word . . . How was Élisa dressed when she went to meet her lover; what colour were her clothes?'

'Why? . . . Oh, I see, my godfather has asked you to keep an eye on the people I associate with and . . .'

'You're on the wrong track, Mademoiselle Iris; be kind – enlighten me.'

She looked at him quizzically.

'You're hiding something, but I'll find out what it is eventually,' she murmured. 'Élisa was wearing a red dress and coat, that's why I lent her my red shoes. It was a joke – her good friend Gaston was taking her dancing at Le Moulin-Rouge; it's easy for him to get in – he works there. Is it true, what they say about the naturalist quadrille?'

'What do they say?'

'That the dancers show their petticoats and their drawers.'

'If the posters are to be believed, yes it's true.'

'I would give anything to see that!'

'I very much doubt that your . . . ah . . . godfather would agree to that.'

'We wouldn't have to tell him if you agreed to chaperone me. You can keep a secret can't you, Monsieur Legris?' she said in an icy tone.

Victor was saved by the return of Mademoiselle Bontemps, who had gathered her lost flock. It was a struggle to extricate himself; the young ladies, egged on by their headmistress, insisted on his trying a sensational blend of tea accompanied by apple strudel. As he left, he could not help glancing at Iris anxiously. Was Kenji taking his responsibilities towards the young girl seriously?

*

Victor collapsed exhausted in a bistro on Avenue Victor-Hugo. Restored by a glass of vermouth, he laughed at his propensity to turn events into the plot of a novel. But it was impossible to deny that there were similarities between the circumstances of the murder and Iris's account. The red dress, the bare feet, the slipper found by Grégoire Mercier. Now that he was on the trail it was out of the question that he should abandon it.

'Le Moulin-Rouge . . . Gaston . . . Is he a musician? Dancer? Stagehand? I'll go there this evening. That way I won't have provoked Tasha for nothing, and I'll get to see the ladies show off their underwear.'

He laughed to himself. The ardent eyes, shiny black hair and sensual mouth of Eudoxie appeared before him: the beautiful Eudoxie Allard, languorous succubus who had tried to seduce him in the offices of *Le Passe-partout*, where she worked as a typist. Hadn't she given up journalism to become a dancer? He vaguely recalled Isidore Gouvier saying of her: 'She's been taken on by Zidler at Le Moulin-Rouge to kick up her pins.'

'Let's see, what did he say her stage name was? PhiPhi? . . . No . . . Fifi . . . Fifi . . . Fifi Bas-Rhin!'

Victor climbed out of the cab and stood still for a moment, mesmerised by the incessant movement of the red sails. Drawn to this flame of variegated colour, a crowd of revellers filled Boulevard de Clichy, where two years previously a Catalan named Joseph Oller and a former butcher, Charles Zidler, had built a sumptuous music hall on Place Blanche, aimed at dethroning the Élysée-Montmartre. It was an instant success, thanks to its principal attraction, the cancan, revived from its heyday in the 1830s. Now the lewd dance, which had been only accessible to habitués of the clubs and dives of Pigalle, was available to the bourgeoisie and aristocracy of Paris.

Beautiful women escorted by men in evening dress, errand girls flanked by lovers, their caps pushed back on their heads; all had come to bask in the glow of the tawdry windmill that ground out nothing but jigs, polkas and waltzes at a time when the real mills on the heights were in their death throes.

Victor paid his two francs. Passing through a lobby decorated with paintings, posters and photographs, he was surprised by the size of the interior; it resembled a station concourse furnished with tables and chairs surrounding a dance floor occupied until the start of the show by couples whirling around to the syncopated music. Charles Zidler, a shrewd innovator, had taken care to provide his clientele with an extravagant experience, a temple of pleasure designed by the illustrator Adolphe Willette. High up on a wooden balcony, supported on pillars ornamented with banners, was an orchestra of forty musicians. The vibrantly coloured décor was starkly lit by gas footlights, chandeliers and electric globes and was reflected in a wall covered with mirrors; the effect was oriental in flavour.

Victor tried to reach the bar, knocking into Englishmen in knickerbockers and tweed deerstalkers, and making way for *demi-mondaines*, genteel in their pallor and their slenderness, and showing off the latest dresses from Worth.

'Hello, handsome, what will you drink?' asked the waitress, a comely girl with a mane of red hair.

'Nothing, I'm looking . . .'

'Yes, look, look, and when you've found what you need, let me know. Just shout out: "Sarah!"'

He studied two enormous canvases hung behind the bar, evidently by the same artist. One showed a dancer doing the *chahut* before a man with a hooked nose in the midst of a crowd of people. He immediately recognised the man and woman from the poster he had spotted the night before on Boulevard Bonne-Nouvelle. The second was of a woman on a horse, prancing before a circus audience.

'You there, you're in love but you can't say so because you're too lily-livered! Suppose I serve you a cocktail?' proposed Sarah, sticking her bosom out. 'With cassis, would you like that?'

'All right then. Who's the painter?'

'A nobleman no bigger than a dwarf, but with a name to make up for it. Henri de Toulouse-Lautrec, that boozer watering himself at a table over there.'

Victor took a mouthful of his red drink and put his glass down with a grimace.

'What on earth's in there?'

'Dry white wine, cassis and a drop of vodka. It was a Rusky, Prince Troubetzkoï, who gave me the recipe.'

'That man with the beaked nose, who's that?' he asked, pointing to one of the paintings.

'The man with the big hooter? Where have you been, lovey? Don't you know Valentin le Désossé? I can point him out in the flesh. Let's see, where's he hiding, that demon of the quadrille? Got him – just to the left of La Môme Fromage and La Goulue; the beanpole there, see? I'm assuming you at least recognise the girls?'

He nodded, not wanting to appear like an idiot. So this is what it was like, the famous Moulin-Rouge! There had been strings of articles about it. Unlike Iris, he had never felt the slightest interest in the subject. He disliked large crowds and the lifting of petticoats left him cold. Tasha's gentle curves aroused him more than the black-clad calves of the girls practising in front of the mirrors.

'I'm looking for a young man called Gaston . . .'

Sarah guffawed.

'There are about twenty Gastons round here! Gaston who?'

'I don't know. And Fifi Bas-Rhin, where is she?'

'Well, I must say you've an awful lot of questions about our little world. I haven't seen Fifi yet. If I were you, I would wander over to the galleries. She likes to sup from the tankard before she goes on.'

'Sup from . . . ?'

'She likes a tipple! Strange creature, that one!'

The orchestra had just launched into a waltz. Buffeted between couples, Victor breathed in the scent of ylang-ylang, or *Cuir de Russie*, mixed with sweat and tobacco. In spite of the enthusiastic brass band and the stamping of feet, he caught snippets of conversation.

'Look at them all at the mirror this evening!'

'She's a looker, that little one.'

'If she comes over here, I'll tell her what I think!'

He passed Valentin le Désossé who, impassive and rigid, was dancing with the voluptuous La Goulue. Part-laundress, part-bourgeoise, her red hair with its square-cut fringe was piled on top of her head and she wore a ribbon of watered silk around her neck. Aware that Victor was looking at her curvaceous figure and plunging neckline, she stopped, stared at him, hands on hips, and bellowed:

'These fops, don't they have birds at home?'

Mortified not so much by the vulgarity of her words as by the harshness of her tone, Victor hurried towards the gallery, desperate to find Eudoxie Allard amidst the forest of penguins in stovepipe hats and courtesans sprouting plumes, among whom the waiters scurried.

'A bowl of mulled wine!' called a man in a crooked boater flanked by two adoring young girls; Victor recognised him as Alfred Stevens the society painter.

Then he spotted her, tightly laced into a red and white striped dress and weighed down by a hat made all the taller by its giant bows. He made to retreat, suddenly reluctant to suffer her advances. Too late!

'Look, it's Monsieur Legris! Over here! Come and join us!

She was seated at a table with three drinkers, a swarthy lothario, his sombrero tilted over one ear, an elegant bon-viveur with a long face and a morose expression, and a blond young man sporting a monocle and chewing on a cigar. She made the introductions.

'Monsieur Legris, an old friend. He's a bookseller. We became friendly at *Le Passe-partout*.[14] Louis Dolbreuse, poet and songwriter, based at the moment at Le Chat-Noir.' She indicated the lothario who smiled, dreamily stroking his goatee beard. 'And Alphonse Allais, writer and entertainer, he's just published . . .'

'Yes, I know, with Ollendorff, *Stories to Make you Laugh: Tales of Le Chat-Noir*. I adored that book,' said Victor to the morose bon-viveur.

'And this is Alcide Bonvoisin, Paris's future best chronicler, after his friend Aurélian Scholl,'[15] concluded Eudoxie Allard, tapping the shoulder of the blond young man. 'Sit there, Monsieur Legris.'

Victor shook everyone's hands and settled himself between Eudoxie and Louis Dolbreuse who was pouring champagne, and offered him a glass.

'Are you still writing? Alcide, you have a rival here. I forgot to mention that Victor – may I call you Victor? – pens highly regarded articles.'

'I've stopped. There was too much competition. Now I'm . . .' Victor began.

'He has other fish to fry!' exclaimed Eudoxie. 'You should know that this gentleman has hidden depths – he's a detective in his spare time, and delights in trumping the efforts of the cops at headquarters. He's untangled two knotty crimes already! It's true, Victor, don't be modest!'

'At Le Moulin, you'll have to make do with inspecting the women for decency, although we do have on site our very own "moral policeman",' joked Louis Dolbreuse.

'Speak of the devil,' whispered Alcide Bonvoisin, indicating a chap in a dark suit with a white tie, a steel watch chain across his chest, who was lurking behind a pillar. 'That strange fellow leads a double life, policeman of the club's moral standards by night, photographer by day.'

'What a coincidence! My friend is a bookseller, but he's also a photographer,' exclaimed Eudoxie, pressing her knee against Victor's.

'Aha, a man of many parts,' declared Louis Dolbreuse. 'And who do we have here today? The bookseller, the photographer or the sleuth?'

'I'm looking for a fellow named Gaston; I was told he worked here.'

'There's your answer, Louis; it's the detective we have here tonight,' murmured Alcide Bonvoisin.

'Gaston? Musician? Stagehand?'

'No idea.'

'There's one person who'll know for certain – Grille d'Égout,[16] she knows everyone. Hey! Lucienne, come and have a bevy!' Eudoxie sang out.

A coquette with sweet sad eyes came towards them languorously. She flopped down with a sigh.

'Thank you, Fifi, I could do with one. Those would-be toffs run me ragged, the cads, and not one of them bothered to offer me a tipple. They were kowtowing to me last month when I was giving *fin de siècle* dance classes to high-class ladies!'

'Waiter, a beer with a little less head,' shrieked Alphonse Allais, suddenly shaking off his torpor. 'Where is Jane Avril?'

Grille d'Égout smiled, revealing the two widely spaced incisors that had provided her nickname.

'This gentleman, Victor to his friends, wants to pin down a certain Gaston, who works here,' explained Eudoxie.

'Gaston? . . . Hang on, Arsène! Not Alsatian beer I hope?' shouted Grille d'Égout at the waiter who had brought her a tankard. 'Because I refuse to drink a drop of that stuff until Alsace and Lorraine are returned to the mother country! Gaston you say? Josette's Gaston maybe? Gaston Molina? If it's him, he's done a bunk, even though Josette's a firecracker, a volcano who'll erupt when he shows his face again.'

'Gaston Molina, is that him, Victor?' Eudoxie asked, increasing the pressure on his knee.

'Possibly,' he muttered.

'Well, he's a waiter, a serving boy. What do you want with him?'

'One of my clients asked me to contact him discreetly; he seduced his daughter. My client wants to sort things out.'

'Well, that's a fine mess! And how does he think he's going to "sort things out"? By extracting payment for the girl's virtue? Gaston's in dry dock; completely broke! As for making an honest woman of her, your client can whistle for it. That urchin's a philanderer; he's got a girl in every dive.'

Pleased with this tirade, Grille d'Égout tossed off the rest of her beer while Alphonse Allais pushed back his chair roughly and ran after a slim, graceful woman with red hair and a black hat.

'Poor Alphonse, she drives him wild.'

'Who is she?' asked Victor.

'Jane Avril. La Goulue says Avril has legs like curtain rods but she kicks them in rhythm, and she's right. She was committed when she was a kid, yes, my dear; under the care of Professor Charcot, and they say that's where she learnt to swing her hips. It's true! Apparently to entertain the inmates they'd get in dance teachers and organise parties and balls. Balls for the loonies, I ask you! Jane Avril gives us the cold shoulder; she dances alone. What do they see in her? She's nothing but skin and bone! They call her "Honey"; I would call her "Sonny". Take a squint at the painter dwarf – he's smitten!'

Grille d'Égout tilted her head towards a table separated from theirs by a pillar. A strange-looking fellow with a nasal voice was holding court to three men and a woman. It was as if his body had been screwed on to two short legs moulded into checked trousers. Victor could only see his profile; he had to wait until he turned round to see his features: a massive head with a bowler hat perched on top, pince-nez on a prominent nose, a black beard framing sensual lips like a wound. His eyes blazed with intelligence and sensitivity. He was roughly Victor's age, thirty.

'Is that him, Toulouse-Lautrec?'

'That's him. "The Little Jewel", as he likes to be known. An arrant drunkard, he tipples as much as he paints, drinks like a fish. See the cane hanging on the back of his chair? He calls it "my helpmate". Inside the handle there's a minuscule flask of cognac. When the pint-sized fellow isn't here seducing the cancan girls, he hangs out at the brothels!'

Louis Dolbreuse said all this in a detached, almost neutral tone, but it was obvious he was having difficulty concealing his aversion to the painter. Alcide Bonvoisin sat up indignantly.

'That man is a genius! A genius, do you hear? Have you looked closely at his poster for Le Moulin-Rouge? The first one by Jules Chéret was a success, but his! . . . There is more talent in that poster than in many a fashionable painting. In a few strokes Lautrec captures the spirit of the dance; he exposes the primitive instincts that we all have. That work, in the Japanese style, took weeks of labour. And his canvases . . . I tell you, he's going to be famous!'

'He should avoid putting La Goulue in the middle of his daubs!' murmured Grille d'Égout. 'She shows off the heart embroidered on the back of her drawers; I'm convinced that that Louise . . .'

'Who are the others?' interrupted Victor.

'The bearded four-eyes is a composer with a caustic sense of humour who lives in Rue Cortot, Erik Satie; we rub shoulders with him at Le Chat-Noir. The iron wire bent in two is Lautrec's cousin, another aristocrat, Gabriel Tapié de Celeyran. The bloke opposite in the battered hat, that's Henry Somm, a cartoonist and engraver whose song is often heard at Le Chat-Noir: "A staircase with no steps is not a staircase at all." The woman . . . the woman . . . I don't recall who she is,' finished Louis Dolbreuse.

They were accosted by Bibi la Purée,[17] who offered scraps dredged up from the rubbish and boasted that his shirt had been given him by his comrade Verlaine.

Victor looked at the back of the unknown woman at Lautrec's table, a redhead with her hair piled up under a simple hat with a single rose stitched on it. He would know that neck anywhere. Tasha. She was laughing, pressing the artist's wrist as he drew on a corner of the tablecloth. Eudoxie had followed his gaze and understood what was upsetting him. She smiled at him coarsely and whispered in his ear:

'He adores carrot-tops; everyone has their preference. For example, unlike most women, I am not interested in blond men. I much prefer dark-haired men; they have a certain something . . . Do you follow me?'

Blushing, Victor swung round abruptly and studied the contents of his glass.

'Mademoiselle, may I have the honour of this waltz?' begged a stout, bald man, bowing to Grille d'Égout.

'I'll dance with you when you've grown some hair, egghead!' she retorted. 'Honestly!'

'Messieurs, we must abandon you. It's time for us to prepare for the cancan. Our lace petticoats don't just appear on us as if by magic – twelve yards of insertion and broderie anglaise, can you imagine? Perhaps you would like to lend a hand?' Eudoxie said, batting her eyelashes at Victor. 'See you later, Louis, at my place.'

Louis Dolbreuse nodded. As soon as the two women had departed, Alcide Bonvoisin leapt from his seat, stammering a vague excuse about an interview with the writer Jean Lorrain.

'An etheromaniac;[18] I wish him luck. Right, we're alone now. What do you want to do about your Gaston Molina? Are you still keen to find him?' said Louis Dolbreuse.

'I'm waiting for the bill.'

'Leave it; I'll settle it. Look, here's someone who can help you.'

He clicked his fingers at an obsequious man in a dicky and cravat, carrying a tray loaded with tankards.

'Monsieur Dolbreuse?'

'Good evening, Bizard, the bill please. This is Monsieur

Legris, bookseller. Victor, this is the head waiter of Le Moulin-Rouge. Monsieur Bizard, we would like to catch a fish named Gaston Molina.'

'That scoundrel, he can go to the devil! It's been a week since he bothered to show his face. I've stopped his wages, he's dismissed.'

'Where does he live?'

'As if I should know, or care! He comes, he goes, he gets drunk, sometimes here, sometimes elsewhere.'

'Thank you, Bizard, keep the change.'

The head waiter pocketed a banknote and went off towards Lautrec's table from where there came gales of laughter.

'He calls himself an artist; he's nothing but a drunk! That Lautrec should dry out,' growled Dolbreuse. 'Listen, old chap, I'm a friend of the famous Josette. If it would be helpful, I could intercede for you.'

'Too kind.'

Victor was in a hurry to escape Tasha and the guffaws of the dauber. Dolbreuse's antipathy to Lautrec created a sort of complicity between them. They dodged in and out of the waltzing couples whirling elegantly around.

'You won't find such an eclectic group of people anywhere else. You have the Prince de Sagan, the Comte de Rochefoucauld and the Duc Élie de Talleyrand rubbing shoulders with the regulars of Le Mirliton cabaret and the ladies of the night of Place Blanche.'

'Ladies of the night?'

'Street walkers, trollops – you'll have to get used to all this, my friend. You have rich brokers chasing after milliners' girls,

English and Russians fraternising cheerfully and well-bred ladies propping up the bar. Le Moulin-Rouge is a melting pot; not just a café or a cabaret or a brothel, but all three at once, just as Zidler intended.'

'And the acme of bad taste!' remarked Victor, as they crossed the area of the hall reserved for the winter *café-concert*.

The audience was roaring with laughter at a stage where, haloed in green light, a little man in a red jacket, his hair standing up like a brush and sporting a handle-bar moustache, was performing. The programme announced him as:

THE FARTISTE
The only artist who doesn't have to pay royalties!

The incongruous sounds emitted by his posterior provoked hilarity amongst the spectators. A suspicious dandy climbed on to the stage to check that there was nothing hidden under the black velvet trousers.

Scandalised, Victor turned away.

'As Zidler says, "deep in the heart of every man vulgarity hides",' said Dolbreuse, and laughed. 'Josette kicks up her heels in the elephant; she dances under the name Sémiramis.'

In spite of the damp evening, the garden was full of people come to get a breath of fresh air. With an air of resignation, donkeys were carrying the beau monde along paths bordered with trees brightly lit by gas and electricity. There were also wooden horses, a shooting range and an outdoor *café-concert* dominated by the massive structure of an elephant brought from the Universal Exhibition of 1889. For twenty sous men could buy themselves a little excitement by watching a pretend Oriental girl perform an erotic dance.

When Victor and Dolbreuse ventured into the elephant, the show had just finished, and the audience was applauding in an effort to get the voluptuous odalisque, draped in a revealing gossamer costume, back on stage. They went to the dressing room behind the miniscule stage where she was removing her make-up.

'Hello, my darling, I've brought you an admirer.'

'Not now, I'm beat,' replied the odalisque in a strong regional accent.

'He just wants to ask you a question or two about Gaston.'

She stared at them, one eye circled with kohl, the other red from having been rubbed clean.

'Don't talk to me about that cockroach! He filched my money and the silver locket of the Blessed Virgin my father gave me! You're not from the *flics*, are you?' she said to Victor, looking worried. 'Is he in trouble?'

'Don't worry, this gentleman is after the same thing as you, he would very much like to speak to Gaston.'

'Well, I hope Gaston sinks to the bottom of the sea!' screeched Josette, turning her back on them.

'It's a beautiful thing, love,' sighed Dolbreuse.

'In case you do manage to run him to earth, I warn you straight away I cleaned up after him. If he wants to get his togs back, he'll have to go to Biffin & Co, and if he's looking for a room, I'm full up. Goodbye!'

*

Discouraged, Victor wandered back inside, forgetting about Dolbreuse, who watched him thoughtfully.

'It's very annoying. I sympathise with the daughter of your client – disgraced by a wastrel. There's one more place that might possibly give you a clue – the employees' cloakroom.'

They had to go back through the hall. Dolbreuse suddenly stopped. 'Drat! My hat. One minute, I'll be right back.'

Victor craned his neck and saw Tasha going arm-in-arm with Lautrec to the bar. He wanted to follow them, but at that moment Dolbreuse returned.

'I have it. Are you coming?'

Dolbreuse pushed open a door to reveal a narrow room with cupboards round the walls. From the one marked 'Molina' he extracted a crumpled shirt and an open packet of Turkish cigarettes. He stuck one in the corner of his mouth. A piece of paper slipped out of the packet. Without reading it, he held it out to Victor, who deciphered with difficulty a note scribbled on a flier for chocolates from the Compagnie Coloniale:

Charmansat at uncle. Aubertot, rite cour manon, sale pétriaire. Rue L., gf 1211 . . .

'Does that help?' asked Dolbreuse.

'Take a look for yourself.'

'Hmm, might as well be Chinese or a dialect, if it's not Volapük.[19] Have fun with that! I'm going to watch the quadrille – does that appeal?'

'You go ahead. I'll follow.'

As soon as Dolbreuse had gone, Victor hurried to leave. Once outside he caught sight of a man elegantly dressed in the English style.

'Antonin Clusel!'

'Legris! Victor Legris! My good fellow, it's been an age!'

'Almost two years. How is *Le Passe-partout* going?'

'Wonderfully well. We've moved to number 40 Rue de la Grange-Batelière, beside Passage Verdeau. I'll await your visit! Excuse me, must dash. I don't want to miss our Eudoxie's number. She's sensational, Fifi Bas-Rhin – who would have thought it, eh?'

On Boulevard de Clichy the crowd thickened. Carried forward by the throng, Victor turned off the boulevard. The bitter taste in his mouth indicated that his system was objecting to the mixture of alcoholic drinks he had swallowed in that accursed Moulin. His mind was filled with the image of Tasha sitting beside the bespectacled painter, squeezing his wrist and laughing, laughing . . . What would he say to her when he arrived back at Rue Fontaine? Would he be able to feign indifference? All this for a trifle, for an incoherent note from one Gaston Molina, whom he was not even sure was Élisa Fourchon's suitor. Or perhaps the note had been sent to Gaston by someone else?

'It serves you right, poor imbecile! The only thing you've discovered is that Tasha associates with libertines.'

CHAPTER 6

THE steam from the coffee pot was like a finger raised to impose silence. Bundled up in a shawl, Tasha nibbled bread and butter between yawns. Victor tried to cure the effects of his sleepless night with coffee. He regretted having feigned sleep when she had come home, shortly after him. Had he unburdened himself to her, he would not now have so much trouble meeting her eye.

As he prepared his preamble, including a subtle allusion to the quadrille at Le Moulin-Rouge and to Eudoxie Allard's second career ('It's an amazing progression, isn't it? Did you know about it?') Tasha baffled him by exclaiming:

'*Ia nié mogou!*'

He jumped.

'Pardon?'

'I can't! I'll never be able to! Never, never, never!'

'Be able to what?'

'To paint as well as him!'

'Him? Who?'

'An artist I saw yesterday. I've already mentioned him to you, Henri de Toulouse-Lautrec.'

So she admitted it! He put his cup down, his hand trembling.

'Your meeting was with him?'

'Yes, at Le Moulin-Rouge. The *Gil Blas* has commissioned me to do a series of caricatures: "Personalities from Parisian nightlife".'

'But I thought . . . You said . . .'

'Don't leave your mouth hanging open; you look like a carp!'

'I thought you'd stopped working for that paper. Your book illustrations pay you enough to live off! And, Tasha, I pay the rent, you sold a picture . . .'

'My passion is more expensive than photography. Frames, paints . . . It's so sweet of you to take on this studio. But as for that wretched canvas bought by Boussod & Valadon, that wasn't enough to cover my expenses! Besides I like keeping up my contacts in the press. It's stimulating, don't you agree?'

Victor did not know how to respond. It had been difficult to convince her to accept his financial support. Their communal life – parallel would perhaps be a better description – rested on a fragile equilibrium. Tasha had declined his offers of marriage, claiming that marriage changed an independent woman into a minor with a guardian. And she intended to pursue her career in her own way. What arguments could he use to persuade her?

'Be careful of that little runt. Apparently he's keen on redheads.'

It was her turn to be stunned.

'Where did you hear that?'

'I have my sources,' he retorted drily.

She hid her face in her shawl, her shoulders shaking. Was she crying? But when she sat up, he saw she was laughing.

'Oh, Victor, you're so funny! "I have my sources." Anyone would think you were Inspector Lecacheur!'

She was hiccupping with laughter. Outraged to be compared to that plodding policeman, he leapt from his chair and attempted to grab her shawl. She deftly slipped out of his reach.

'Stop it, sorry! I just couldn't help it, I . . .'

She let out another hoot, then succeeded in controlling herself.

'It's true, Henri likes girls with red hair, and he has made advances to me; in spite of his deformity he is not without charm. But even if he were Adonis himself he would stand no chance with me. You are my only love. Did your sources tell you that?'

Why bother to pretend he was interested in the last works of Armand Charpentier and Abel Hermant? Victor just could not focus on them. Joseph swept several orders up from the counter. He tried to concentrate, but it was impossible; his mind kept wandering back to Rue Fontaine. He was surprised to feel such fulfilment; it was as if his very existence had been given new meaning by those words, 'You are my only love.' A long embrace had followed Tasha's announcement. Reassured, he had relaxed and had almost revealed that he had also been at Le Moulin-Rouge. It was as well he had held back; everything would have been ruined had he told her. There was no point in betraying his fascination with the new investigation; she hated it when he involved himself in mysteries. And when she had wondered aloud about the new tenant of the hairdresser, he had whistled softly.

He was to meet her at seven o'clock at the studio and accompany her to Le Chat-Noir, where she wanted to sketch a young writer.

'Boss, I've finished the window, only prim little stories. "*It was so beautiful, but so sad, the Fire Brigade Captain wept into his helmet*," mimicked Jojo. I'll close up the storeroom.'

Furnished with his apple and his notebook, he settled down to skim through the dailies.

'You'll make yourself ill if you don't eat more than that,' remarked Victor, suddenly solicitous.

'Don't fret, I fill up in the evening, and not just on any old thing; my mother makes sure of that. But don't let me keep you from your Crayfish à la Bordelaise . . . if Monsieur Mori leaves you some . . . What do you think of *Blood and Betrayal*? It's the title of my novel.

'Very catchy. So you're abandoning . . . *Love and Blood*?'

'Yes, too sentimental. I'm teeming with ideas for the book; I'm going to use lots of unconnected news items and fashion them into a mystery that'll keep everyone guessing.'

'That seems a rather random approach,' murmured Victor.

'Exactly, a plot woven out of episodes. I just have to put the finishing touches to the key to the mystery. My point of departure is inspired by the murder at Killer's Crossing. I'm calling her Red Cinderella. I'll graft on to it some of the cases I've been keeping warm all these years. It's amazing the number of bizarre things that happen in Paris; you just have to keep your eyes peeled. Look, today for example I've unearthed this gem:

CORPSE FOUND IN WINE CASK

Yesterday morning before opening time an employee at
the wine market . . .

'Victor! Your lunch is getting cold!' shouted Kenji, his
mouth full.

'Coming.'

Joseph wearily closed his notebook.

'I'm wasting my breath. Grub, that's all people think about!'

He bit violently into his apple.

The concierge at L'Eldorado wore a lugubrious expression, but
a generous tip perked him up.

'She lives beside the Théâtre des Variétés, number 1 Passage
des Panoramas. You can walk there – it's very near.'

'I know. Which floor?'

'Second, I think.'

Victor was beginning to be quite familiar with the road
between Boulevard de Strasbourg and Boulevard Montmartre.
He noticed, not without apprehension, that Noémi Gerfleur
lived near Killer's Crossing. He slipped into the alley, where
bookshops beloved of bibliophiles sat side by side with
perfumeries and confectionery shops. He lingered in front of a
fan-maker, wondering whether an imitation eighteenth-century
fan might tempt Tasha and if going to see Noémi Gerfleur was
really necessary. The most important thing was that Élisa
was with her mother, safe and sound. But how could he be
certain without asking?

As he started up the stairs, a man in an alpaca overcoat, his hat crammed down on his forehead, murmured an apology and pushed past him, striding up the steps to the upper floors two by two.

Victor rang the bell. Eyes cast down, nose streaming, apron filthy, the maid who answered was rather unprepossessing.

'I would like to speak to Madame Gerfleur.'

'She's not here.'

'Will she be back soon?'

'Not likely. When she goes to her milliner it takes her all day; with all the frills and baubles she orders for her ridiculous hats, they wouldn't look out of place at a carnival.'

'I'm sorry, a carnival?'

The maid wet her finger and stooped to collect a stray crumb from the carpet.

'Oh yes,' she said, straightening up. 'Fruit, flowers, feathers – the works.'

'Perhaps her daughter will be able to see me?'

'Her daughter?'

'Yes. Mademoiselle Gerfleur. Or Fourchon, Élisa.'

She stared at him a moment, then relaxed and sniffed.

'What are you talking about? She doesn't have a daughter.'

'Are you certain about that?'

'She doesn't tell me everything, so, no, I'm not certain. What I know is that officially Madame Gerfleur is single. Leave me your card and I'll pass it on to her.'

She smiled conspiratorially and the door closed softly.

'I'll come back later,' said Victor.

The man in alpaca who had passed Victor on the stairs leant

over the third-floor banister and watched him go back down. Deep in his pocket, his right hand caressed the handle of a knife. It comforted him to keep this memento with him, and he had not been parted from it for years. Would he use it again? Even if he did not, how soothing to feel its bulk weighing down his coat, like a loyal soldier ready to second him! A trusted companion in the absence of a real friend. So Noémi was not there. That upset his plan, but no matter, he would just have to rearrange their charming rendezvous. After so many years, he could certainly wait another few hours. He was amused at the maid's reply: 'She doesn't have a daughter!' That was not quite correct; there should be a qualification to the denial: 'She doesn't have a daughter any more!'

Victor hailed a cab on Boulevard Montmartre, in a state of uncertainty.

When he reached Rue Fontaine, he spied the deformed painter on the other side of the road. Had he just left Tasha? She was painting, naked beneath her paint-stained smock.

'I must be hallucinating. I thought I just saw Lautrec.'

'You've just missed him; he was here two minutes ago. He's our neighbour, he moved into number 21 in April. I'm just going to change quickly.'

Was she mocking him? Did she not realise that he was upset at her having received the painter here, and in that get-up?

He could not resist the impulse to unveil the canvas she was working on. What he saw only increased his anxiety: a dishevelled cancan dancer whirling her petticoats to reveal black stockings. It imitated Lautrec's style without having any of the life of his paintings; it was static, soulless. Why had she chosen such a subject? She was coming back! He just had time to put the cover back over.

'Do you like this?'

She was wearing her best hat, and had put on a Russian blouse with sleeves gathered in at the wrists, and a black skirt. She was wearing the lapis lazuli necklace he had given her for her birthday and embroidered gloves belonging to her mother. She was un-corseted and her curves were shown to best advantage.

'You look ravishing.'

Calm again, he kissed her neck lightly as he helped her into her coat.

They were only five minutes from Rue Victor-Massé and the former studio of the Belgian painter Alfred Stevens, which had since 1885 had housed Le Chat-Noir cabaret. Victor admired the façade. A massive terracotta cat backed by a glowing sun concealed the second floor window. Two enormous lanterns illuminated a wooden sign on which he could make out the first and last words of text marked in yellow letters:

Ladies and Gentlemen! [. . .] Enter the modern world!

They went up a short flight of stairs and bumped into a man in Swiss national costume with halberd and silver-topped cane, who led them along a corridor to a hallway ending in further steps.

'Thank you, Bel-Ami,' said Tasha.

Once they were alone they took a turn around the ground floor, the François-Villon room, and the guard room, which was a superbly decorated tavern. A stained-glass window by Willette representing the worship of Mammon reflected the flaming fire in the hearth of the grandiose fireplace. A real life black cat was asleep, perched at the top of a potted palm.

They climbed a large oak staircase. Tasha indicated a closed door.

'That's where the editorial meetings take place.'

'Do you often attend them?'

'I have sold some drawings to the journal; their print run can be as many as twenty thousand copies. But I never got on with Willette and now I don't care, since he's fallen out with the club's owners.'

They went on up to the heart of the cabaret. About a dozen spectators were already seated. An athletic-looking man, with red hair and beard, wearing a collarless waisted frock coat welcomed them in a booming voice:

'Good evening! Welcome aboard the pleasure train. Make yourselves at home!'

Victor paid. A waiter in academic garb led them to their seats.

'Who is that yelling buffoon?'

'Rodolphe Salis. Unkindly know as "The Red Donkey". A genial smooth-talker – you either love him or loathe him.'

'Which is it with you?'

'I don't want to make you jealous, so I'll just say I admire him. He created this cabaret, and he makes sure the cabaret artists get their due.'

Victor had imagined finding billiard tables and card or domino players, not this bourgeois interior dominated by a piano, near which a blonde woman stood, smiling – Madame Salis. The small amount of space left by the pictures, drawings and engravings on the walls was filled with earthenware trinkets and copper bric-a-brac, creating a medieval ambiance. Above an enormous composition by Willette entitled *Parce Domine* were depictions of many Pierrots and Colombines escaped from the cabarets of Montmartre.

The room was filling up with men in tailcoats, gently mocked by Salis who called out in a raucous voice:

'Goodness me, we've got a conventional bunch in tonight! Welcome, admiral. Excuse me, I mistook you for one of those dreadful politicians.'

He scoffed at the parliamentarians with the air of a naughty child. Although that was nothing, according to Tasha, compared with the coarse insults beloved of Bruant at Le Mirliton cabaret.

'Mesdames, Messieurs,' he declared, 'this evening we have the great pleasure of welcoming our esteemed friend Louis Dolbreuse, in honour of whom the nymphs of the hill have adorned themselves with crowns! He is going to regale you with his poems!'

Even though he knew that Dolbreuse performed at Le Chat-Noir, Victor had not expected to see him again so soon. The lothario, in his sombrero, took his place at the piano.

'Although it does not operate here as strictly as it does at Le Mirliton, censorship is the enemy of the artist. Our colleagues in the theatre and in the *café-concerts* experience it every day. That is why I have dedicated my poem "Anastasia" to them.'

He began to declaim:

> *How does the press tell the truth?*
> *With silent tongue.*
> *Why does the press tell the truth*
> *With silent tongue?*
> *Because the truth is not always worth telling*
> *Even when there's a public scandal?*

'Is that him — your Personality of the Parisian Nightlife?' whispered Victor.

'No, I don't know him. Shh, listen to the poem.'

> *And what does the journalist eager for truth opine?*
> *He follows the dictum: he who is silent will dine.*
> *Hungry bellies hear no evil!*

Louis Dolbreuse raised his sombrero in response to the laughter and applause, then went over to a spectator in an Inverness cape and muttered something to him. Victor prayed that Dolbreuse would not notice him; he wanted to draw a veil over what he had been doing the night before.

'Montmartre, granite breast at which the idealistic youth come to suckle! Montmartre, the centre of the universe! Never will you have heard a work like the one we are about to admire!' bellowed Salis.

A pianist sat down at the keyboard.

'And here is our maestro, Charles de Sivry, and the famous author and narrator Maurice Donnay!'

'That's who I have to caricature,' said Tasha when a young man with horsy features and a pointed moustache joined the composer.

'You won't see the illustrious Henri Rivière,[20] creator of the figures and plays of light that are about to enchant you; he operates behind the scenes. Prepare to dream; to be carried off to far off places with a Gallic poem that is mystical, socialist and absurd, depicted in twenty tableaux and dedicated to our master of all, Paul Verlaine!'

The lights went down and the piano began a bright little tune. The curtain opened to reveal a pale, circular screen. Steel scenery mounted on frames appeared against this background, which was gradually filled with a sky shining with stars. A coppery light revealed Paris and the terrace of the Institut, with the statue of Voltaire in the middle. An astonished silence gave way to gasps and whispering. The statue of Voltaire had just jumped from its pedestal to go and greet a poet called Terminus. Ruined and discouraged, Terminus threw himself into the Seine, dragging Voltaire into the depths of the river. Their shadows, bathed in the clear light of the moon, overhung the buildings, the rocks and the trees, as they were buffeted by the wind. In a toneless, funereal voice Maurice Donnay read a poem by Chopinhauer: *Adophe ou Le jeune homme triste*,

> *He was foul and weak of chest*
> *Having sucked the watery breast*
> *Of a nurse who was so sad*
> *He became a whining lad*

As the poem progressed through Adolphe's stages of dis-illusionment, a man came and sat down next to Victor. Turning slightly, Victor recognised Louis Dolbreuse.

'So, dear friend, you're doing a tour of the nightspots of the capital? Yesterday Le Moulin-Rouge, today Le Chat-Noir, a nicely spiced itinerary! Or perhaps you're still looking for Gaston Molina?'

'I'm here for pleasure,' murmured Victor, disconcerted.

Tasha did not react, but her puzzled expression and slight frown did not bode well.

In the middle of the applause the lights came back on. Salis announced:

'There will now be a half-hour interval! I hope Your Lordships will use it to imbibe some libations at ridiculously inflated prices!'

'Can I buy you a drink on the ground floor?' proposed Dolbreuse. 'Don't worry, it's just a beer served in a Madeira glass.'

'I would . . . but I'm not here on my own.'

'Oh! Mademoiselle or Madame is with you? The more the merrier . . . Have we met?'

'I would have remembered,' replied Tasha. 'Excuse me, I have to go and talk to Maurice Donnay.'

'Exquisite,' pronounced Dolbreuse, leading Victor away. 'A journalist?'

The guard room was packed. They succeeded in finding a seat under one of the iconic Steinlen posters dedicated to the feline race: *Apotheosis of Cats*.

'Drink, my friends, drink, it's your contribution to our artistic endeavours!' brayed Salis.

The man with the Inverness cape murmured something in Dolbreuse's ear and then melted into the crowd, a glass of bitter in his hand.

'That's Navarre, an acquaintance who would be of interest to your lady friend. He's going to edit a literary review. For three months now he has been a regular at our soirées. He has good contacts at *L'Écho de Paris* and he's asked me to write some articles. Shall I introduce you to him?'

'No need,' muttered Victor, anxious to know whether Tasha had picked up the reference to Le Moulin-Rouge.

Without waiting for Dolbreuse, he went back to take his seat and found Tasha just finishing a sketch of Maurice Donnay, an engineer fresh out of the École Centrale, but more attracted by poetry than industry.

Victor hoped he had shaken off Dolbreuse, but when the show ended at about midnight, as he followed Tasha into a sort of screened off area attached to the inside wall behind the stage, he glimpsed him at the back of the hall.

The cramped space contained ladders up to three platforms, one above the other, the first for musical instruments, the next for the stagehands who operated the discs of coloured glass and the highest reserved for the puppeteers. There were an impressive number of strings.

'It's complicated, but we never make even the smallest mistake,' explained Henri Rivière, who reigned over his team like a captain over his sailors. 'Everything must be done with extreme precision. You have to manoeuvre the three layers of zinc silhouettes at the same time and angle the mirrors so that they recreate a rising sun or a storm.'

Victor listened distractedly to the painter's explanations; he was observing Tasha. Had she heard what Dolbreuse had said?

'How do you make the stars shine?' she asked.

'By flapping a shutter in front of this box pierced with pin holes.'

'And the flashes of lightning?'

'Easy: you light paper dipped in saltpetre and then release it into the air.'

Victor's attention was caught by that word: saltpetre. He suddenly remembered the note found the previous night in Molina's cupboard: *sale pétriaire*. At the time the two words had seemed meaningless. But now he realised what they meant: the Hospice de la Salpêtrière, built on the site of Louis XIII's gunpowder arsenal.

They left Henri Rivière. Dolbreuse was hanging around, determined to offer them one for the road. They refused. Victor did not like the way Dolbreuse was looking at Tasha.

'And did you solve Gaston Molina's cryptic message?'

'No, I'm stumped, it makes no sense,' mumbled Victor.

'Come on, make an effort!' said Dolbreuse.

Victor managed not to lose his temper, but he could not hide his exasperation. Dolbreuse took the hint and bowed, smiling.

'Here come some friends less frightened at the prospect of a nightcap!' he declared, greeting several visitors who had just arrived in the guard room.

'Jean Richepin, Jules Jouy, Xanrof,[21] Maurice Vaucaire, the flower of modern song,' explained Tasha. 'And that one there, already drunk, do you recognise him?'

'Verlaine,' responded Victor immediately, relieved to see that she did not seem to be in a vindictive mood.

But they had scarcely gone ten yards towards home when she turned on him.

'Why didn't you tell me you were at Le Moulin-Rouge yesterday evening? Were you spying on me? Who is Gaston Molina? You accuse me of duplicity, but it's you who's leading a double life!'

He weathered a hail of stinging reproaches without flinching, as he stood rigidly, trying to come up with a plausible explanation. He was amazed to hear himself say:

'I was simply trying to save a friend from embarrassment.'

'A friend? Which one? Joseph? Kenji? You don't have any others.'

'All right, I admit it; it was Jojo. I was worried he was going to do something stupid. He is in a furious rage with Boni de Pont-Joubert for marrying Valentine de Salignac, and he knew that Pont-Joubert was going to be at Le Moulin-Rouge last night. I followed him and succeeded in convincing him to go home and sleep off his rage.'

The words seemed to come to him of their own accord.

'Did you see me with Lautrec?'

'No, you know that I can't stand that kind of place. I left very quickly.'

'And Gaston Molina?'

'A relation of Boni. He sent Joseph a threatening note, ordering him not to see Valentine on any account; that's why Joseph was so angry. But I couldn't find Molina or Pont-Joubert.'

Victor was sweating in spite of the cold. He felt like a

schoolboy digging himself deeper into trouble after a reprimand from his tutor. He had rarely reeled off so many lies. And, worst of all, Tasha would probably grill Joseph about it, and then he'd have to spill the beans in exchange for Joseph's complicity, thus involving him in this new investigation.

'Tasha, are you angry with me?'

'I am neither resentful nor jealous; you on the other hand . . .'

He silenced her with a kiss.

Boulevard de Strasbourg was buffeted by gusts of wind. Noémi Gerfleur had to hold tightly to her feathered turban as she hurried to the cabriolet waiting to take her home after her performance. Before getting in she studied the area around L'Eldorado. She held herself defiantly as she scrutinised the passers-by. Was the sender of the roses watching her from under a porch? She was obsessed with the idea that he would show himself sooner or later. Well, let him dare! If it were his intention to stir up old history, she would know how to receive him. She rapped on the frame of the hood and the coachman registered her signal. She sank back against the banquette and hummed a song from her childhood:

> *To man and bird alike on earth*
> *God says softly, make your nest!*

Her childhood had been difficult. Her mother and sister had died when she was five years old and her father, a miner, had been killed in June 1869 during the strikes of La Ricmarie. After that she had lived in Lyon with her aunt Suzanne Fourchon, a cook for a household of weavers, and had been started off in the art of spinning. She still remembered the boorish boy who used to take her to the *café-concerts*. The owner of the Taverne des Jacobins had noticed her pretty voice. She had rapidly acquired notoriety, and people travelled from far and wide to hear the vivacious Léontine Fourchon. When Élisa came along, she did not try to discover who the father was, and refused to be parted from the child:

> *To man and bird alike on earth*
> *God says softly, make your nest!*

She had split her existence in two, devoting her days to the little girl and performing in the evening. Later, she sent Élisa to boarding school, to the Veuillot sisters where piano, English and good manners were taught. At twenty-two years old she had been bursting with ambition. She knew she was seductive, she attracted men, she wanted to embrace life in the fullest possible way, broaden her horizons and become a lady . . .

The cabriolet was struggling on through the crush, but the noise of the traffic and the brouhaha of the spectators leaving the Théâtre Gymnase, where they had savoured *Numa Roumestan*,[22] failed to distract Noémi from her thoughts. Eight years, it had taken her eight years of effort, to draw up the plan that would buy her freedom. She had conceived a scenario without flaws, chosen the ideal dupe and promptly set about carrying out her plan. The results had exceeded her wildest expectations. And now the imbecile had raised his head again, putting her entire way of life at risk! She felt spied on, and as if actual blows had rained down on her. What a mistake to have given in to homesickness! She had been safe in London. What was he after? Did he hope to collect his share?

'You can whistle for it my friend! You have no proof – if you think you'll make me talk, you're out of luck!'

A downpour had emptied the terrace of the Grand Café de Suède, and the Salle des Variétés was closing its doors. At the crossroads, inquisitive onlookers drawn to the spot where the body of an unknown woman had been found defaced by acid were flowing along the pavements, like a flock of stupid sheep. She despised them just as she despised the men bleating outside her dressing room. They should all be taken off to the abattoir – they were animals, lovers of fresh meat!

The cabriolet dropped her off near Passage des Panoramas. The rain was icy. She reached number 1, turning round as she went to check that no one was following her. The passage was deserted. She forced herself to climb the dark stairs. Mariette opened the door, yawning. As always, Noémi would have liked to order her to cover her mouth, but she desisted, too weary to try to instil manners in the girl who was so badly raised that nothing could cure her slovenly ways. She contented herself with asking for tea with milk and some buttered toast, and hastened to take refuge in her room.

The wallpaper depicted an infinity of downy mimosa petals, and amongst this excess of yellow, the rosewood furniture took on a sickly pallor. She let her cape fall to the ground and parted the saffron drapes at the window overlooking Boulevard Montmartre. There, opposite, beside the Musée Grévin, that man waiting about near a poster advertising a re-enactment of the Gouffé affair,[23] was that him? No! A plump young miss on tottering high heels threw herself into his arms and led him off towards one of the restaurants lighting up the pavements.

She settled down at her dressing table, and leant towards the mirror.

Look at you! The creases at the corners of your mouth, little wrinkles everywhere, bags under your eyes . . . At thirty-five!

How many times had she longed to hurl her fan, mantilla and wig into the dustbin, pack her trunks and give it all up! But she lacked the courage. Becoming Noémi Gerfleur had cost her too much time, too much effort. Even if she had been a fool to think she could capture happiness with money and success, she was too old to give up what was certain for a chimerical hope. She would have to be satisfied with fading glory and passing lovers. And as for love? A delusion, a cheap little ditty:

> *A nest is like a tender berth*
> *A haven that the spring doth bless*

And yet she had determinedly sought this unreachable tender berth. But at the end of it all she found herself alone, without a shoulder to lean on, without a friend to confide in, except for Élisa. Thank God she had been careful to keep her apart from the mire, in the hope that one day she might find a good husband who would provide for the declining years of his mother-in-law.

Mariette came in bearing a tray. The tea was chalky, the toast burnt. Noémi sighed. Did she really deserve such injustice?

'Put that there for me and run my bath. Don't forget the lavender salts and stop sniffing. Don't you have a handkerchief?'

Mariette produced a large linen square and blew her nose noisily.

'Dreadful,' murmured Noémi. 'Wait . . .'

Mariette stared at her with her frog eyes.

'Do you have a suitor?'

'Oh yes, Madame, Martial. He's training to be a baker. He gives me brioche every Sunday. When we marry, our children will always have bread.'

Noémi studied her maid's irregular features and lank hair and told herself that life truly was unfair.

Mariette had not been gone five minutes when she returned, much excited.

'Madame, you have a gentleman caller!'

'Not this evening!' cried Noémi, tying the belt of her negligee. 'What does he look like? Young or old?'

'I don't know, Madame, the hall is dark. He says he's an old friend; here's his card.'

Noémi glanced at it then sank on to a chair.

'Are you all right, Madame?'

'Yes, yes . . . take the gentleman into the drawing room.'

'What about your bath, Madame?'

'You go up to bed; I'll see to it. Go on, hop it!'

She was trembling with emotion, could not even tidy her hair. Dragging on a peignoir took enormous effort. Her heart was racing. She staggered as far as the drawing room. Standing in front of the fire, a man was contemplating the flames. She could only see the back of him. At the sound of the door, he spun round.

'You . . . it's you,' she breathed.

'Good evening, Madame de Saint-Meslin. I'm overjoyed that we meet again. We'll be able to recreate the past. Did you appreciate the ruby roses? I see from your expression that you did.'

He spoke calmly, in a monotone. She supported herself against the door frame. He smiled and indicated an armchair.

'You must sit down. I have news of your daughter, Élisa. I'm very much afraid that it's bad news . . .'

CHAPTER 7

His long roam through the lonely streets brought him an immense feeling of peace. He was able now to view the evening's events with the detachment of an onlooker.

When he had rung the door bell at Noémi's house he felt his resolve wavering, but as soon as she joined him in the drawing room he had regained his composure. She had immediately recognised him. As for her . . . How could a face and figure change so much in five years? He was in the presence of a stranger. He remembered the young woman with whom he'd been madly in love when her name was still Léontine Fourchon; her silky blonde hair, her guileless face, her voluptuous body. That image rekindled the pain he had experienced when he discovered he'd been used. The candlelit room appeared to grow darker; he had to rid himself of this thorn in his side.

He invited her to sit down, and delighted in describing Élisa's last moments to her, relishing the spectacle of her increasing despair as he furnished each fresh detail. She remained silent; not even weeping, her sorrow too great for words. Then suddenly she stood up, clutched her chest and fell to the floor. Faced with this stranger's prostrate body he felt numb. He had longed to savour the sweetness of revenge, but all he experienced was a deep sense of weariness. He knelt down beside her unconscious body and tied the thin band round her neck, to finish her off. When he rose his legs were trembling. He paused for a moment, his mind blank. Then, gradually, he felt his will to live return, like the distant echo of a half-forgotten melody. With the spontaneity of an actor at ease in his role, he pulled the petals from the roses, deposited the shoe and the notes and left.

As he wandered through the empty streets it occurred to him that life was in constant flux. Just as Paris was a bustling metropolis from dawn to dusk and at night a ghost town, he was no longer the naïve man who six years earlier had been taken in by sweet lies.

'I promise you,' she had kept telling him, 'everything will go according to plan. Trust me. We'll live the good life. No more money worries. We'll go away – just the two of us!'

Day in day out, week after week, she did not let up until he had agreed. He would play a very small part. She had a brilliant imagination and a formidable talent for acting. A talent so great, she had taken him in too. He knew her farewell letter by heart:

Don't try to come after me. I wouldn't hurt a fly as you know, but if you talk I'll swear it was you who dreamt up the whole scheme and forced me to go along with it by threatening my daughter. To the devil with you and your soppy senti-mentality, just hold your tongue or else . . .

He knew what it was to be heartbroken. The hardest part had not been her running off with the money, but that she had played with his feelings, that she did not love him, she had never loved him. The poison of humiliation, despair, anger and hatred had taken him over, dulling his mind. One night in a drunken rage he had attacked a police officer. During his detention he had elaborated his plan for revenge. And yet this dish best eaten cold had lost all flavour now.

He wandered until he came to a halt, surprised to find himself at the end of his street. The air in his unheated bedroom was chilly and damp. He sat beside the only window, watching the mist swirl among the branches of the chestnut trees. He liked to sit up until dawn giving free rein to his thoughts, one or two of which would linger in his mind. The next stage of his plan would require complete self-control. The die was cast. He decided not to sleep.

The wild life Victor was leading did not agree with him. He was tired and his sole wish was to laze in bed.

'On my own or with Tasha?' He put the question to himself as he crossed the boulevard. What were all those people doing beside the entrance to Passage des Panoramas?

A little baker's boy, his dish of pies balanced on his head, was trying to push his way through to the front of the crowd.

'Has there been an accident?' enquired Victor.

'A murder,' whispered the boy.

Victor made a beeline for the nearest officer, a police sergeant, and pretended to be a reporter.

'A woman's been strangled. The maid found her this morning. Some of your colleagues are already there. How do you lot manage to sniff these things out? Like a pack of dogs trailing a meat cart you are!' said the officer, twirling the ends of his moustache.

'Where did the murder take place?'

'At number 1. Move along now, please.'

'What times we live in!' cried a stooped old woman. 'When you think that only last week another one was bumped off just round the corner!'

A man joined in:

'In any event, burglary clearly wasn't the motive. It appears the lock was intact which means she knew her killer – she must have if she allowed him in.'

'And you were there, I suppose?' remarked the police sergeant.

'You ought to read the newspapers. The statistics are all in there. I'm an accountant and I can assure you figures don't lie. In sixty percent of cases, the killers are known to their victims.'

'That's true!' exclaimed the old woman. 'Those hussies attract a type of man that brings nothing but trouble; if I were you . . .'

'Mariette alerted my mistress; she was white as a sheet,' interrupted a chambermaid. 'She said a fellow called after midnight, but she never saw his face. La Gerfleur was covered in rose petals, and she had a red shoe stuffed down her front.'

His legs feeling like jelly, Victor moved away from the crowd and found the nearest cab rank. He was only half aware of murmuring an address to the cabman. The name Iris kept running through his mind.

*

Victor had never seen Kenji in such a state; a single well-thought-out sentence had been sufficient to cause him to drop the pile of index cards he had been filling in at his desk.

'Iris is in great danger at Mademoiselle Bontemps'.'

'W-what did you say?' Kenji stammered, turning the shade of scarlet he went when he had drunk too much sake.

'Her best friend, Élisa Fourchon, has been . . .'

'Who told you that Iris was in France?'

Victor had to think on his feet again. Luckily, Joseph was out delivering some novels to Mathilde de Flavignol and the shop was empty.

'Joseph overheard the address you gave the cabman the day that shoe was brought here. You were upset and he thought you were having a relapse, so he told me about it. I was worried and decided to go to Saint-Mandé.'

'So it was you who brought back my cane . . . Did you speak to Iris?' Kenji asked in a stern voice.

'I did indeed meet your goddaughter. She told me she had lent a pair of red shoes to Élisa Fourchon. And I am afraid that this young woman might have met with a fatal accident, particularly since I discovered that her mother, the singer Noémi Gerfleur, has been murdered.'

'How did you know about this?'

'I read it in the newspaper.'

Kenji stood up. Victor could not help noticing how white his hair was growing, and the shadows under his eyes. He suppressed a surge of affection.

'We must go at once to fetch your goddaughter. She can stay in my apartment and I'll stay with Tasha. It's high time I fended for myself, and there's no reason why it should affect our partnership.'

Kenji paced back and forth, tapping together the two index cards he was still holding, and then stopped in front of Victor.

'You are forcing me to disclose something I would have preferred to keep secret. I suppose in a way it's a relief. Iris is my daughter.'

'I suspected as much. Does she know this?'

'No . . . Yes, but I only told her recently. Her mother died when she was four years old; she was a married woman. Iris has no memory of her. I wanted to spare her from a scandal.'

'Why did you keep her hidden from me?'

'The frog that resides in the well knows nothing of the big wide ocean and is better off in ignorance.'

'Spare me the oriental wisdom and give me a simple explanation, will you please, Kenji?'

'You were a withdrawn, nervous and possessive young man at the time. Your mother had put you in my charge and I felt a responsibility towards you; why should I burden you with my worries?'

'But then I grew up. You really are a terribly complicated fellow. Did you not envisage the consequences of your little secret? I was convinced Iris was your mistress.'

Kenji moistened his lips.

'A child her age . . . You're mad! Have you been spying on me?'

'Of course not! You are simply very bad at hiding things. Remember the saying: truth will out.'

'Please do not inflict your crude sayings on me and promise me you will tell no one about this, not even Tasha.'

'I promise.'

Kenji slipped on his frock coat and bowler, picked up his cane and went out of the shop, still holding the two index cards. Victor addressed himself to Molière's bust in a jaunty voice:

'Indeed, Tasha, the young girl is his mistress and I must make way for her. I have little choice in the matter . . .'

'A sixteen-year-old girl!' Tasha exclaimed indignantly. 'Men! Young or old, you're all obsessed with the same thing: proving your virility!'

'Not all of us. You should be grateful that you've found the exception to the rule.'

Victor took her in his arms and she resisted a little, as a matter of form.

'I expect you're just like him,' she murmured, 'one official relationship and ten unofficial ones.'

'Referring to our relationship as official is a little optimistic, my darling. So far we only snatch occasional glimpses of one another. Aren't you worried we'll end up forgetting each other's faces?'

'If you want us to see more of each other, then stop running off to Rue des Saints-Pères every five minutes.'

'Are you saying you want us to live together?'

She gestured at the untidy studio.

'I feel comfortable with my mess, but you're an orderly person. Do you really see yourself living here? We would end up quarrelling over nothing. I loathe cooking, and housework bores me to tears. Painting is my only joy!'

'And how do you feel about me?'

'I adore you! But you're possessive and I need to go out and meet other painters, to compare my work with theirs.'

'The easiest solution would be for me to live across the courtyard. We'd each have our own space – me to develop my photographs and you to paint in peace. Then we could meet more regularly. Would Saturday afternoons between five and seven be convenient?'

'What on earth are you talking about?'

'I've rented the hairdressing salon and the adjacent apartment.'

'You've . . .'

'Close your mouth, darling, you look like a carp.'

The man in the grey alpaca coat took a swig, dried his mouth on his sleeve and put the flask back in his pocket. The appearance of the sun had made him thirsty. He walked alongside the rusty railings, into the Botanical Gardens, past the chrysanthemum beds and up the gravel path towards the maze. From the top of the hillock he took in the view of the dome of the Panthéon, then sat down on a bench circling the cedar of Lebanon. Buffon[24] had planted the tree over a hundred and fifty years earlier; it had seen the Monarchy swept away by the French Revolution, the First Empire and the Restoration of the Monarchy, and the Second Republic succeeded by the Second Empire that had finally ushered in the Third Republic. Millions of people had killed each other in the name of ideas that had since run their course, but this tree was still standing.

'I am still standing too, and I'm free as a bird, which is how I intend to remain.'

In spite of the murders he had committed his thirst for life was insatiable, and he would do anything in his power to escape retribution. He watched a crow cleverly taking pieces of rubbish one by one from a bin and pecking at them tenaciously. He smiled at the thought that the litter would be attributed to some negligent passer-by. 'People break the rules and others get the blame. That's life!' He looked at his fob watch: three thirty. It was time for him to make sure the old man he had been stalking all week was keeping to his routine.

He spotted him in the deer enclosure, stroking one of the does after changing her straw. He had become accustomed to the man's wrinkled face and walrus moustache. The old fellow had spent so long caring for animals that he had become like them, docile, timid and withdrawn; and each afternoon without fail he made the same rounds. The old man walked past the bison and antelope and down a path leading to the aviary. There he stopped for a moment to look at the Sunday painters attempting to reproduce the beaks and talons of the vultures and the priest-like silhouette of the marabou storks.

The old fellow exchanged a few words with a skinny little woman who was struggling to make a lump of clay look like a bearded vulture. He shook his head doubtfully and carried on, past the crocodile pit and the bear enclosure, before finishing his rounds at the lion house, where the wild beasts languished behind double bars in twenty cages.

Satisfied, the man in the grey alpaca coat sat down on an iron bench near a nursemaid who was reading an illustrated fashion newspaper and rocking a perambulator with the tip of her boot. He brushed off his coat sleeves with a brisk gesture, and reviewed his plan. At first he had considered getting locked in after the place closed, but that was foolish – he might be seen climbing over the railings. Then he'd had another idea. The Botanical Gardens, like all other public places, were cleaned each night by municipal workers.

'All I have to do is mingle with them. Two days is more than enough time to find a straw hat and smock and pass myself off as a road sweeper.'

The occupant of the perambulator, feeling it was being rocked too vigorously, began to wail. The man jumped up, his nerves on edge, and snapped at the nursemaid:

'Just give it some bromide!'

The clouds drifted like huge, dark sails over the rooftops. A poor, skinny wretch with unkempt hair, his clothes in disarray and gasping for breath, was running as fast as he could behind a cab that was making its way up Rue des Saints-Pères. The concierge, Madame Ballu, leapt out of the way on to the porch, but was still splashed as the cab drew up alongside the gutter.

'Hooligans!' she muttered, picking up her broom.

She stood hands on hips at the entrance to *her* courtyard and watched Monsieur Mori jump from the carriage and help down a young lady she had never clapped eyes on before. Pignot's son staggered after them carrying a pile of hat boxes followed by the skinny fellow who had just heaved a huge trunk on to his shoulders.

'Well now! I hope that porter won't be going up my nice shiny stairs! I nearly broke my back polishing them!' the concierge cried out crossly.

'Please, Madame Ballu, he has my permission,' Kenji Mori said, doffing his hat.

'Permission, says he! Permission! What do I care about his permission? And what's he doing bringing this hussy here? Who's in charge of this building anyway?' muttered the concierge, following closely behind them. 'Oh, and don't bother wiping your feet, will you!' she barked at Joseph, who was bounding up the stairs.

'They're here, Monsieur Legris,' he said, bursting into the bookshop. 'Between you and me, the young lady is a little young for . . . for . . . Well, you know what I mean. Will she be staying long?'

'I have no idea, Joseph, and I fancy you're being rather nosy.'

'That's a bit rich; accusing me of being nosy when you're the one doing all the ferreting about!'

'If the cap fits . . . They're expecting me upstairs, Joseph. I'll see you later.'

Father and daughter were standing side by side in the kitchen making tea. In contrast to Kenji, who looked almost embarrassed, Iris had a joyous expression on her face.

'Monsieur Legris! How kind of you to give up your apartment to me. Finally I shall see how my godfather lives!'

She laughed. 'Tongues will wag, but let them. Who cares? I'm so happy!'

'I just need to pack a few clothes into a suitcase and then you can settle in.'

Victor looked around his apartment and picked up a few of Tasha's things. He dropped a pair of gloves, some pieces of charcoal and a few crumpled sketches on to the counterpane then carefully folded his shirts, waistcoat and trousers. He remembered the little picture, a nude of Tasha, leaning on the dresser in the dining room and was afraid it might shock Iris. He was looking for somewhere to hide it when Iris walked in.

'I've been exploring my godfather's rooms; an interesting mixture of styles. Please don't worry on my account. I have already seen the picture of the woman bathing so you can leave it where it was. She's your sweetheart, isn't she?'

'I'm not sure that . . . your godfather . . .'

'This is your home, and I'm not a child any more,' she replied, following him into the bedroom. 'She's very beautiful. What's her name?'

'Tasha,' Victor murmured.

'The tea is ready,' Kenji said, interrupting their conversation, which he had overheard.

'And who is she?' asked Iris, standing in front of a photograph of Daphné Legris. 'She has a sweet, thoughtful face.'

'My mother,' Victor replied, pointing to an oval frame above his bed.

Kenji silently left the room and hurried through his apartments to the bathroom, where he seized the photo of Daphné and the young Victor and hid it in the trunk at the base of his futon.

Joseph cupped his chin in his hand and contemplated the stack of frames leaning against the wall of the studio. Mademoiselle Tasha was really coming along. Maybe one day, when his reputation as an author was established, he would ask her to illustrate his books.

What's keeping the Boss? He left his suitcase in the alcove and said he'd be back in one minute. One minute! An eternity, more like!

He moved the potted palm he had given Tasha last spring away from the stove. It seemed to have grown so much that if it got any more warmth it might burst out of its pot!

'There he is, and about time,' he grumbled as he heard the key in the lock.

Victor came in without saying a word, slumped into a chair and opened a copy of *Le Passe-partout*.

'What's new, Boss?'

The main headline read:

MORE FAT ON THE FIRE
NOÉMI GERFLEUR FOUND MURDERED
AT HER HOME

The article, signed by The Virus, described the career of the singer who, after humble beginnings in Lyon, had triumphed in London and Brighton. Returning to Paris at the time of the Universal Exhibition she had become a roaring success at L'Eldorado. The world of entertainment had been brutally deprived of her talent, for in the early hours of the morning her strangled corpse had been found strewn with red roses in her drawing room. On her chest lay a red shoe containing the label *Made in England, Dickins & Jones, Regent Street, W1.* The odd thing was the shoe did not fit her foot.

'Well I never! That's the same make of shoe as the one that strange fellow left!' exclaimed Joseph, who was reading over Victor's shoulder.

Irritated, Victor went to close the newspaper, but checked himself and looked up at his assistant with a kindly expression.

'Tell me, Joseph, when did we last collaborate on a case?'

'Have you started another investigation, Boss?'

'Yes and no . . . Funnily enough it was I who advised Monsieur Mori to bring his . . . to bring Mademoiselle Iris to Rue des Saints-Pères. I was concerned for her safety.'

'Why, Boss?'

'One of her classmates, Élisa, went missing from their residence. Mademoiselle Iris had lent her a pair of red shoes, they were a little big for her and . . .'

Joseph clutched his head in both hands.

'I've got it! It's her! Élisa is the girl at the crossroads! And would I be right in saying that her murder is related to that of Noémi Gerfleur?'

'We cannot be sure yet. I'm following a trail that has led me to Le Moulin-Rouge. Élisa's lover worked there. The annoying thing is that Tasha saw me, and you know how she hates this hobby of mine. I was obliged to put her off the scent by implicating you and . . .'

'Me and who?'

'Boni de Pont-Joubert.'

'Not that dandy! And what was I supposed to be doing at Le Moulin-Rouge?'

'Challenging him to a duel.'

'A duel! Hang on a minute! Let's not get carried away! I value my life, you know! So you want me to back up your story, is that it? And what do I get out of it?'

'You can assist me.'

'Word of honour?'

'Word of honour.'

As soon as Joseph had left, Victor examined the card he had pocketed in Noémi Gerfleur's dressing room: *In memory of Lyon* . . .

Lyon. Where La Gerfleur had begun her career. He looked again at the scrap of paper he had found in Gaston Molina's locker.

Charmansat at uncle. Aubertot, rite cour manon, sale pétriaire. Rue L., gf 1211 . . .

Apart from the reference to 'Salpêtrière' he could make no sense of it for the moment.

'*Cour manon*,' he murmured, his face pressed up against the window.

On the other side of the courtyard, the windows of the hairdressing salon stared back at him blankly.

'Tomorrow I must get in touch with a decorator . . . by Christmas time I should have a home of my own.'

CHAPTER 8

A SUDDEN breeze scattered the pile of index cards Kenji had just filed as a brunette waltzed into the shop flaunting feathers, flowers and jewellery in the most audacious fashion.

'Monsieur Mori . . . Do you remember me?'

Kenji was at a loss to recall where he had seen those dark eyes and that sensuous mouth. He stammered:

'Mademoiselle . . . Mademoiselle . . . Allard? You . . . you look more beautiful than ever!'

'Call me Eudoxie. Thank you for the compliment. Do you mean it?'

'Yes . . . yes, in . . . indeed. I . . . Please have a seat . . .'

She found his embarrassment amusing, and when he pulled up a chair she moved closer, brushing against him. He tried to rearrange his index cards, but they fell through his fingers.

'I came here to see Monsieur Legris. Is he out?'

'He's down in his dark room developing photographs. I'll call him for you.'

Eudoxie grabbed a catalogue and buried her face in it as Victor came up the stairs. He walked unsuspectingly over to the studious customer, who lowered her mask with a giggle. He was trapped.

'What are you staring at, darling? Your associate was far more gallant – he at least offered me a chair.'

'In that case make the most of it. You've caught me at a bad moment; I have nothing to offer you.'

'Don't be so sure. At least allow me to try to change your mind,' she said loudly enough to be heard by Kenji, who had retreated behind his desk.

She gave a mocking smile, and brushed Victor's cheek with her glove.

'Darling, I'm challenging you and all you can do is frown! You were in a much nicer mood the other night. I only wanted to tell you about Gaston Molina! Ah, that's better! I prefer your face when it's relaxed. What do you think, Monsieur Mori, should I accept your offer of a chair and tell my tale to horrid Victor?'

'I-I do not know to what you are referring,' Kenji stuttered.

'Well, well, how wrong I was. I could have sworn you two were as thick as thieves! Hasn't Victor told you about the awkward situation one of your customer's daughters is in? What's all that noise? Are you moving house?'

Kenji looked up abruptly. Iris was banging about upstairs, rearranging the furniture to her liking. Victor had a sudden fit of coughing.

'Have you caught a cold? It must have been when you were at Le Moulin-Rouge; we certainly get chilled lifting our legs to do the quadrille. Grille d'Égout insists that the immoral atmosphere corrupts men's minds. Maybe that's what brought Gaston to an early grave.'

'Is he dead?' cried Victor.

'As dead as a doornail. Don't worry it wasn't consumption or the pox that carried him off. Some joker stuck a knife in his belly, no doubt for services rendered. Josette went to the morgue to identify her lover, shed a few crocodile tears and then began screaming at him. And well she might! He relieved her of her life savings and left her in the lurch. Be thankful that your customer's daughter is out of harm's way. Has she returned to the bosom of her family, by the way?'

Eudoxie picked up a piece of blotting paper from the table and began fanning herself nonchalantly. Victor made an evasive gesture.

'I am grateful to you for this piece of information and I shall relay it to my customer,' he muttered.

'Poppycock! You can't fool Fifi Bas-Rhin! No one can. You can cut off my hand if there's not more to this than a girl's honour. Come on, tell me everything. It's to do with one of your investigations, isn't it?'

'I'll cut off your tongue, not your hand, if you don't pipe down,' Victor hissed out of the corner of his mouth, casting a meaningful look towards Kenji, who was hunched over his index cards.

'Oh, I see. This is our secret. In that case fair's fair. I'll keep silent in exchange for a few afternoons with you.'

She had lowered her voice to a whisper. He replied in equally hushed tones:

'I was under the impression that you were involved with Monsieur Dolbreuse.'

'Does that pose a problem for you, darling? Louis is a nice boy but utterly conceited. His entire conversation revolves around what he's done, what he's doing, what he's going to do and how talented he is. It's terribly dull!'

'I ought to warn you that I am already . . .'

'Hush! Never say never. Here's my address. Who knows, I might be able to assist you in rushing to the aid of some new maiden in distress.'

EUDOXIE ALLARD
16, Rue d'Alger, Paris 1er

He stooped to kiss her hand after reading the card and then hurried back downstairs.

'Men are a veritable mystery to me, Monsieur Mori. They beg for your help and when you give it they send you packing! No doubt your bookshop is full of novels about the folly of women. How would you describe that of men?'

'A man most loves a woman who loves him not.'

'Do you really think so? I'd be interested to put your theory to the test, but unfortunately I'm in a hurry. Please accept this complimentary ticket. It'll give you a chance to become acquainted with Le Moulin-Rouge, if you don't already know it, and you will be able to enlighten me as to the intimate practices of the Orientals. Be sure to wrap up warm; I don't want to be responsible for anyone else catching cold!'

She had barely closed the door behind her when Victor shot out of the front of the main building.

'Where did you spring from? Like a jack-in-a-box!'

'Forgive my rather cool reception, Euxodie.'

'Is that a euphemism?'

'I didn't want to talk in front of my associate. I assume the police are already investigating Molina's murder?'

'Yes, that delightful Inspector Lecacheur has honoured Le Moulin-Rouge with a visit. Thank God he didn't recognise me, or I'd be suspect number one. He still bears a grudge against *Le Passe-partout*.'

'Do you know whether my name was mentioned?'

'You aren't celebrated enough for the cabarets to be proclaiming your attendance from the roof tops! Don't worry; Lucienne and Josette were unable to describe the dark, handsome gentleman who was hot on Gaston's trail. However, if the police continue their questioning, they might ask to interrogate Alcide, Louis or me and . . .'

'It is vital my name is kept out of this!' he growled, squeezing her arm.

'You horrid man, you're hurting me! When you request such things of a lady you should use tact and diplomacy.'

She pulled away in a pretend sulk.

'I thought I'd explained . . .' Victor began, and then plunged his hand into his pocket and extracted his cigarette case just as Joseph, whistling nonchalantly, returned from a delivery.

'You have very strange manners. Do redheads find them especially attractive? Come now, Victor, let us part on friendly terms. I shall do my best to ensure that you remain anonymous. After all, my ungrateful darling, who else at Le Moulin-Rouge cares about you enough to remain silent under threat of torture!'

Victor went back into the bookshop to find Joseph battling with a ball of string he was using to tie up a parcel of books. The muffled voices of Kenji and Iris were audible upstairs.

'Another delivery?'

'Alas! The complete works of Zénaïde Fleuriot[25] for a certain Salomé de Flavignol, Madame Mathilde's cousin who lives at Passy! Damn, damn and triple damn, what a pain!' groaned Jojo, trying without success to tie a knot.

Victor helped by pressing his finger down on the string.

'Much obliged, Boss. By the way, do you know who Diogenes was?'

'He was a humble Greek philosopher who chose to live in a barrel. Why do you ask?'

'Well, that's what Monsieur Gouvier calls the fellow they found in a barrel at the wine market. Though actually the police already know him; he had a record. Shall I go on?'

'Yes.'

'This will help me with my book. His name was Gaston Molina, a petty criminal, only if I were to include him in my novel I would change his name. He could fall madly in love with . . .'

'Brilliant idea!' cried Victor, rushing out of the door.

'That'll teach me a lesson. He couldn't care less! He'll change his tune when I'm famous!' muttered Joseph, savagely finishing tying up the most dreadful parcel of books that had ever come his way.

Victor strode down Rue des Saints-Pères, *Le Passe-partout* under one arm, reflecting on the article he had just read by Isidore Gouvier. It described how a man had been found stabbed to death and stored in a barrel of wine at the wine market. His body had been there for several days. Gaston Molina had been born in Saint-Symphorien-d'Ozon in 1865. His father had been a silk worker and his mother a washerwoman, and he was known to the police. Caught thieving red-handed, he had been sentenced to six months, which he'd served in a Lyon prison in early 1891. He would have done a longer stretch had the authorities been able to establish his involvement in a series of robberies in the Saint-Étienne area three years earlier. The only witness to his guilt was a peddler who was too fond of his drink to stand up in court.

Victor tried to make sense of the facts. Molina had been the lover of Noémi Gerfleur's daughter, Élisa. But why had the three of them been murdered? He reread the card he had picked up in Noémi's dressing room at L'Eldorado, sensing that it contained the key:

> *To the Jewel Queen, Baroness of Saint-Meslin, a gift of ruby red roses in fond memory of Lyon – from an old friend.*

He was about to cross the road to the bookshop when he saw Jojo closing the door and putting up a sign that read: *Back at half-past two*. He had forgotten that he was supposed to be having lunch with Tasha!

He bought two portions of sauerkraut and a bottle of white wine at the Brasserie d'Alsace on Boulevard de Clichy. Then, his coat collar turned up against the icy wind, he hurried in the direction of the studio, whistling the tune to *L'Alsace et Lorraine*, but paused at her door. She had company. Standing next to her beside the stove, looking as though he owned the place, was a man wearing a sombrero and striking a handsome pose. It was Louis Dolbreuse, the charmer from Le Chat-Noir he had met at Le Moulin-Rouge. He was after Tasha! Victor's suspicions became instant certainties: she was deceiving him with this dandy.

'Have you brought lunch? Excellent timing; I'm famished!' Dolbreuse cried.

'It was meant for two,' muttered Victor.

'Oh! I wouldn't wish to intrude. I shall sit in the alcove.'

'In that case we'll need another portion.'

'Let me see. There's more than enough for three! Look, I don't mind admitting I'm penniless, so I'd be only too delighted to share your lunch. Do you know what I've been living on for the last week? Spinach kindly donated by my landlady, and horribly bitter because I cannot afford the luxury of cream.'

'You're exaggerating, of course!' Tasha laughed. 'Take a plate from the dresser, pile it with food and go and sit on the bed. And try not to make a mess!'

Victor waited until Dolbreuse was out of earshot.

'What's he doing here?' he muttered angrily.

'Salis gave him my address. He came round yesterday to look at my work. He likes my style. He's a good person to know. He's well-connected in the entertainment world and thinks I should try my hand at set design. I invited him here today to sketch his portrait.'

Victor was so furious he couldn't swallow. For a moment he thought he would choke on his sauerkraut. When he finally managed to breathe again he remarked drily:

'He won't be able to pay you for his portrait; he's penniless.'

'I don't mind. I need models.'

'I can't believe it! You're attracted to him!'

'Calm down, Victor, please! You're always imagining . . .'

'Monsieur Legris!' Dolbreuse shouted from the far end of the room. 'Have you seen the newspaper? That chap you were looking for, Gaston Molina, he's kicked the bucket. They found his body in a vat of wine. Funny coincidence, isn't it?'

'Gaston Molina . . . Isn't that the name you mentioned at Le Chat-Noir?' Tasha asked, glaring at him. 'And now he's dead? Victor, what are you cooking up?'

That was the last straw. Consumed by jealousy and anxious at the prospect of being peppered with questions, Victor put down his plate, picked up his hat and muttered something about having to go and buy a book. Tasha looked at him, frowning.

'Aren't you going to finish your sauerkraut?' Dolbreuse called.

The door slammed.

Victor walked into a café where he took a glass of rum and lemon to lift his spirits. He must stop thinking about Tasha with other men, or he would lose his mind. He forced himself to unroll a newspaper on a pole. It was a special edition of *Le Passe-partout*.

The article on the first page, signed by The Virus, was devoted to the Gerfleur affair and gave details of the crime scene. A red shoe containing two cryptic messages had been discovered close to the wretched woman's body and would doubtless provide the police with a lead. Victor was so intrigued by this new piece of information that his disastrous luncheon went right out of his mind. He resolved to head straight for Rue de la Grange-Batelière.

The hue and cry was at its peak. On the corner of Rue Montmartre and Rue du Croissant, Victor glanced at a bust of Émile de Girardin and dawdled in front of one of the cheap bookshops, plastered with posters. At the entrance to the print-works, the pavement was encumbered with bundles of the evening editions wrapped in thick yellow paper advertising in big letters the name of the newspaper. High-wheeled carts trundled over the cobblestones, returning to dump their unsold copies. *Le Passe-partout's* offices were a few doors along Rue Grange-Batelière from the auction house.

Victor made his way through the turmoil of the typesetting room, which was on the same floor as the editorial offices.

'We're running late,' the typesetter groaned.

Discarded pages of newspaper were scattered all over the floor. Telegraphists hurried to and fro delivering dispatches. *Le Passe-partout* employed a staff of twenty including five journalists.

When Victor asked a buck-toothed secretary whether he might see the journalist who signed himself The Virus, she showed him in to the editor's office.

Dressed in one of the tailored English suits that had earned him the nickname Beau Brummel, patent leather ankle boots and a cravat that was a work of art in its own right, Antonin Clusel was engaged in dictating his leader article to a shapely blonde.

'My dear chap, what a surprise!' he exclaimed, advancing towards Victor. 'You may go, Eulalie.'

'So, you're The Virus!'

'I'm filling a variety of roles at the moment, out of necessity. If you want something done, it's better to do it yourself! Not that Gouvier and the others don't do an excellent job, but I've noticed that our readers particularly like The Virus's mordant style, especially when Lecacheur and his henchmen are on the receiving end of it. Care for a cigar?'

'No thank you, I am on my way to the auction house. I just dropped by to see your new offices. When you say they are "on the receiving end" do you mean you know something they don't about Noémi Gerfleur's murder?'

Clusel broke into a broad grin. He poured out two small glasses of cognac and handed one to Victor.

'You don't beat about the bush, do you? I'd call it your weakness. Settle back in my chair; you'll find it wonderfully comfortable,' he said, pushing back the two telephones and various papers scattered over his desk so he could perch there. 'It's a scandal all right! La Gerfleur is still well remembered from the years she spent on the London stage between '86 and '89. And when she returned to Paris she triumphed each night at L'Eldorado. What a waste.'

'Why have you not divulged the contents of the two messages left in the shoe?'

'I can see what you're up to, old chap, but you're shouting into the wind. I'm not giving anything away. "Silence is golden" is my motto. Facts should be revealed gradually, as in the serialised novels the people love so much. It's the secret of success. Three magic words send the average reader to the kiosk every day to buy our paper: *"to be continued"*.'

'Are the notes authentic?'

Clusel lit a Havana cigar. He was clearly enjoying himself.

'Who can say? The good inspector becomes very cagey when he feels he's getting nowhere, which is often! All I know is that these texts are of interest to the police, as well as to me and my fellow journalists, and they will soon captivate my readers. Incidentally, you're a secretive fellow. You let me do all the talking, but you don't give much away . . . Any news of Fifi Bas-Rhin? Don't look so disapproving! Have you seen her dance? You haven't! I recommend you go down there this instant, and don't miss the *chahut*. Our darling Eudoxie is sublime! I wouldn't be surprised if she ended up marrying a grand duke!'

Victor could see he'd get nothing more out of Antonin Clusel, so he took his leave, plunging back into the commotion of the editorial office.

'My article has to go in!'

'No, I said. It'll take up nearly the whole of page two.'

'Leave out the piece on equipping the army.'

'Are you being deliberately dense? We don't need your drivel, for goodness' sake. What we need is ideas. New ideas. Brilliant ideas!'

Victor immediately recognised the slow delivery and timbre of the voice. He made his way over to the plump figure gesticulating at the far end of the room.

'Good day, Monsieur Gouvier.'

'Ah, Monsieur Legris! You've come at a bad time. We're

running late – yet another ace reporter who goes berserk if we move a single comma. I'm fed up with it. It's good to see you again. What brings you here?'

'I need the benefit of your wisdom.'

'Are you still doing research for your detective novel? I thought you'd have finished that by now.'

'I'm at the editing stage; I belong to the Flaubert school. Actually, I'm interested in the Noémi Gerfleur case.'

'And you thought you might worm something out of me? All I can tell you is that Lecacheur is following a lead.'

'Is he really?'

'It's no use turning on the charm with me, Monsieur Legris; I'm not giving anything away. You might get caught up in more trouble.'

'Come on, Gouvier, you know I have a passion for solving mysteries.'

'"To be continued . . ." Tomorrow, *Le Passe-partout* will reveal all.'

'And what am I supposed to do between now and then? I'm not Sherlock Holmes, you know.'

'Who?'

'He's the hero of a novel.'

'Oh! You and your detective stories! No, I mean it. I'm not giving anything away.'

'Come on, Isidore, as a special favour to me, your old friend. What has your friend at headquarters been telling you?'

'Oh, all right then, I give in, but only if you promise to keep mum until after tomorrow's edition is out. And not a word to Beau Brummel either!' he added, pointing towards Clusel's office. 'It seems the singer was strangled with a piece of gauze, and that's the trail Aristide Lecacheur is following.'

'But what does it mean?'

'Don't play the innocent with me, I wasn't born yesterday. It's obvious what it means. Gauze suggests the murderer might be a doctor or a chemist.'

'But why leave behind such an obvious clue?'

'Not all criminals are infallible.'

'Is that all?'

'You are the most obstinate man I have ever met. No, that isn't all. A shoe manufactured in England was found near La Gerfleur's body, but it didn't fit her foot. However, because the poor woman spent time in London, Lecacheur has wasted no time in dispatching two of his henchmen over to investigate her past in Albion. And . . .'

'And what?'

'There were two love letters.'

Isidore fished a couple of crumpled leaflets out of his pocket. 'I jotted them down. This is the first:

> *My love reigns at the hospital,*
> *Most infamous of all creatures*

And this is the second:

> *The dear one was naked and knowing my desire*
> *Wore chinking gems as her sole attire*

It's signed *A. Prévost*. I'll wager that oaf of an inspector is going to question every Anatole, Alphonse, Auguste and Anselm

Prévost he can find in every hospital between here and Navarre! A complete waste of time, of course, as A. Prévost is almost certainly a pseudonym. Do you know what I think, Monsieur Legris? The murderer is testing us by leaving clues in the form of riddles. He's playing with us! We're dealing with a criminal who is well-versed in the art of poetry – unless of course he copied them from somewhere. You're the scholar. Do you recognise them?'

'No,' Victor sighed, careful not to reveal that he knew the name A. Prévost.

He felt exhilarated. Once again, he was a step ahead of both the police and the press. For the wily Gouvier appeared not to know that Noémi Gerfleur had a daughter.

Jojo was nodding off, his notebook open on the counter. Victor's arrival nearly caused him to fall off his stool.

'Oh! It's only you,' he mumbled.

'You look worn out.'

'It's not surprising, two deliveries in one day, and to top it all one of the battleaxes, Raphaëlle de Gouveline, kept me talking for hours because of an accident at Bullier.'

'What sort of an accident?'

'A crash. Madame de Flavignol and Helga Becker collided when they were each astride their infernal machines. The outcome: a twisted ankle for the Fräulein and two sprained ones for the battleaxe. They asked whether you might take them some detective stories to keep them amused during their convalescence.'

'I'll see to it. Where's Kenji?'

'Upstairs. He doesn't come down any more. A certain person requires his complete attention.'

Joseph's demeanour was so funereal that Victor felt quite sorry for him.

'Do you think Helga Becker might appreciate *Tales of the River Rhine* by Erckmann-Chatrian? And would *Voyage Round My Bedroom* by Xavier de Maistre, or *No Tomorrow* by Vivant Denon suit Madame de Flavignol? I hesitate in case she makes a connection between the titles and her future career as a cyclist. Speaking of which,' Victor said nonchalantly, 'it turns out there is a connection between Noémi Gerfleur and the murdered girl at the crossroads.'

Joseph's eyes lit up.

'Are you feeding me a line in the hope of buying my silence regarding your little excursion to Le Moulin-Rouge?'

'Absolutely not! I am telling you the truth because I know you will end up wearing me down anyway.'

'And so you should – only the day before yesterday you gave me your word that I could assist you.'

'You must keep absolutely quiet about it. Iris's safety is at stake.'

Joseph leapt off his perch with renewed vigour and stood a couple of inches from Victor. All but clicking his heels together, he murmured: 'You can count on me Boss – "the hunting lion never growls" – it's an African proverb. It's quite something isn't it! I'm all ears.'

*

A resounding roar dispersed a flock of sparrows perched on top of a cage. It was followed by two, then three, then four formidable snarls. Basile Popêche, his hands behind his back, contemplated with an air of contentment the cage containing his post-prandial charges, who were aiding their digestion with a deafening recital.

'They don't seem very friendly,' squeaked the skinny woman, who had given up trying to sculpt the bearded vulture and moved on to Tiberius the lion.

'Don't worry, my dear, lions are least dangerous after they've eaten their fill. It's only that, instead of downing a glass of something like you or I, they voice their contentment.'

'Yes, but I can't hear myself think. And I can't see a thing in this light. I'm going home. Goodnight!'

The painters and sketchers packed away their materials and walked towards the exit, along with the few visitors to the Botanical Gardens who had braved the damp weather. The street lamps came on. Basile Popêche felt strangely euphoric as he took possession of his territory. During this interval between closing time and his departure, he was free to imagine that he was at the helm, under God's command, of a great arc floating at the heart of the city. He strolled alongside the railings, greeting the lions as he passed: massive Tiberius, beautiful Cleopatra, lithe Mercedes and her two cubs – Castor and Pollux, old Nemea and finally young Scipion.

'Oh! Why is he walking round in circles like that, growling? If I didn't know better, I'd say he was hungry. Am I going barmy? I'm sure I gave him his piece of meat.'

He leant against the bars. The lion was certainly behaving

strangely. He was twitching his tail along the ground like an angry cat and scratching himself furiously with one of his hind legs.

'Something's aggravating him. Strange, I don't see any sign of meat.'

He entered the building and walked down the passageway that ran alongside the cages. When he reached the one marked 'Scipion' he paused for a moment. He only needed to step inside quickly to see what was wrong, and then go for help if needed. He pulled out his keys, opened the door as slowly as he could and went in. Scipion, who was at the far end of the cage pacing up and down angrily, stopped to lick his fur in rapid circles. Basile Popêche noticed something glinting in the middle of his right haunch. Curious, he moved closer.

'What is that? It looks like . . . no, it can't be . . . it's a dart! The work of some pesky kid.'

A sudden clanking made him swing round. The cage door had closed, and he had left his keys on the outside. Trying not to panic, he turned the handle slowly. It would not move. A growl warned him that the lion had sensed his presence. Basile turned round very slowly to face the animal. Above all he must not show his fear.

It'll be all right, it'll be all right, he reassured himself. That's it, that's it, easy does it, my friend, easy does it . . .

Scipion lay on the ground licking his fur more and more frantically until a noise stopped him short. He remained motionless, turning his ears to try to pinpoint the rustling sound outside the cage. Someone was walking over from the garden. Basile Popêche flattened himself against the cage door. He had heard the muffled footsteps too. If he cried out, it might alarm the lion, who was staring in the direction of the path. Risking everything, Basile slid along the inside of the cage.

'Help,' he whispered, 'I'm locked in. Get me out of here!'

He felt his whole body freeze as he recognised with horror the face emerging from the darkness. In the light of a street lamp a road sweeper was staring at him with a look of profound pity. The man extended his arm in a rapid movement. A second dart pierced Scipion's flesh. Crazed with pain, the ravenous lion tensed its muscles and crouched, ready to pounce. Basile Popêche curled up in a ball and began to scream.

A pile of books toppled over. Joseph cursed as he searched through the scattered volumes. He picked up an armful and set them down on the old packing case that served as his desk. He curled up in his rickety armchair and began leafing through an anthology. A bulky shadow clad in a night cap and holding a candle glided into the study.

'Do you know what time it is, my pet?' Euphrosine Pignot bawled.

'Maman! You scared the wits out of me! I thought you were asleep!'

'Off to bed with you, quick; it's freezing in here. You'll catch your death, then you won't be able to go to work tomorrow. I'm confiscating all these books or you'll wear your eyes out!'

'You forget that I work in a bookshop . . .'

'And what of it? Nobody says you have to read every book you sell.'

'How am I supposed to recommend them to my customers if I don't read them?'

'Your customers can do what I do and go by the titles. For example *The Loves of Olivier* is very enticing while *Roger the Rogue*[26] sounds awful!'

'Maman, you don't know what you're talking about.'

'Don't be rude, my pet, and go to bed. I've given you a foot warmer.'

Joseph reluctantly did as he was told. While he was undressing he repeated to himself out loud the beginning of the message Victor had relayed to him.

'The dear one was naked . . . the dear one was naked . . .'

Euphrosine, leaning back against her bolster, was listening. She sat bolt upright and groaned: 'And what's more he's reading smutty novels! Oh, the cross I have to bear!'

CHAPTER 9

BERLAUD was bored. He sat between Mélie Pecfin and Nini Moricaude, watching the six goats pawing the ground, impatient to get home and not understanding the reason for the prolonged stop. He stood up, stretched and growled at an insolent pigeon, then decided to abandon his post just long enough to go and mark his territory on an area of Place Valhubert.

'Holy Mother of God, what is Basile up to?' said Grégoire Mercier crossly, shaking the bowl he had brought to fill with Pulchérie's milk. 'Hoy! Berlaud, stop messing around, you mutt! That coxcomb is past it. He cuts and runs at the slightest provocation instead of staying at his post; he forgets everything when he feels the need to raise his leg. Monsieur! Monsieur!' he shouted, running towards the gate of the Botanical Gardens through which he could see a park keeper. 'I've come to see Monsieur Popêche. Have you seen him by any chance?'

'Popêche? The wild animal keeper? A lion mauled him yesterday evening. He had terrible injuries and they've taken him to the emergency section of the Hôpital Pitié. Do you want to come in a minute?'

'No, no . . . Poor Basile, that's terrible! Do you think he'll pull through?'

'I couldn't tell you,' said the keeper over his shoulder as he left the dismayed goatherd.

'My God, what am I going to do? I'm his only relation . . .'

Grégoire Mercier thrust the bowl into his satchel and whistled at length for Berlaud, who lolloped excitedly over, his tongue hanging out.

'Calm down now, you great oaf! You want to play games like little Pervenche, but at your age you should be like Mémère; at least she behaves with dignity! Go and stand beside her. There, that's good – birds of a feather stick together. Now let's go, no dawdling!'

They hurried up Rue Buffon – never had a herd of goats passed so rapidly along that street – turned off at Rue Geoffroy-Saint-Hilaire and walked along the side of the Pitié as far as Rue Lacépède, where the monumental gates of the hospital loomed.

'Berlaud, you're going to have to behave like a leader. I'm entrusting our flock to you. Protect them as if they were your own puppies and when I come back, if you've been a good guardian, I promise you a feast you'll never forget!'

Overcome with anxiety, Grégoire Mercier paced up and down a few times before entering the building. Inside, he spotted a young doctor and asked where he might find Basile Popêche in one of the six hundred beds of the hospital. After wandering from wing to wing, holding his nose against the stench of carbolic acid, the goatherd finally succeeded in finding a man swathed in bandages stranded at the back of a room whose windows looked out on the Botanical Gardens. A doctor had just checked on the wounded man and was about to leave.

'Don't tire him; his life is hanging by a thread,' he whispered.

Grégoire Mercier removed his hat and, kneading it with his fingers, timidly approached the mummy, whose breathing was barely perceptible.

'Basile? Is that you?'

'Who's it by? Who's it by, for heaven's sake? I've read it somewhere, damn it, but every time I think I've remembered the poet, it slips out of my mind! "The dear one was naked and knowing my desire . . ." '

Victor paced about the bookshop, now empty of the few customers who had ventured in since opening time. He was so absorbed that he forgot Joseph was there. Those two mysterious verses had cost him a sleepless night. The previous evening he had thought that they had given him a trump card, but this would disappear as soon as *Le Passe-partout* hit the news kiosks. He was enraged at not having been able to use his knowledge to his advantage, and exasperation pushed him to soliloquy.

' "The dear one was naked . . ." '

Joseph, who was engaged in collating the ten volumes of Casanova's *Memoirs*, blew his nose noisily and regarded Victor as he marched about.

'I looked through at least fifty books, Boss! I was up till dawn. I had to wait until Maman was asleep to get up and ransack the study from top to bottom; the only thing I gained was a cold!'

'Joseph, I can't concentrate if you talk!'

' "The dear one was naked and knowing my desire, wore chinking gems as her sole attire . . ." '

' "Her rich apparel gave her a vanquishing air," ' intoned a solemn voice from the floor above.

'Kenji! Do you know who wrote that?'

'Is this a new game? What does one win?' asked Kenji, coming downstairs, impassive.

He sat down at his desk and spread out his index cards and his catalogues, under Joseph's admiring eye.

'The Boss is a mine of information!'

'Who's the author?' Victor demanded.

'Baudelaire, from *The Flowers of Evil*. I'm amazed you didn't know that. The poem is called "The Jewels", but it doesn't appear in every edition, because it's one of the poems banned in 1857 by the courts, and published clandestinely with other unpublished works, in 1866 in a pamphlet called Scraps.

'And this one, Boss, "My love reigns at the Hospital, most infamous of all creatures . . ." ' recited Joseph. 'Do you know where that is from?'

'Alas, I am not omniscient, sorry,' said Kenji.

He went to greet an old dealer, who was bent over a wallet, from which he extricated various works bound in hide. Joseph dragged Victor over to the bust of Molière.

'M'sieu Legris, do you know what it means, "My love reigns at the Hospital"?'

'No, I don't.'

'M'sieu Legris, why would a murderer, who's trying to escape detection, leave two lines from Baudelaire and an incomprehensible text, apparently signed with a pseudonym, at the scene of the crime?'

'I don't know. But it means he's a cultivated man . . .'

'Or woman.'

'. . . And he chose those lines with a very specific aim in mind; he did not pick them at random. So first he chooses a poem entitled "The Jewels". Next . . . *Wore chinking gems as her sole attire* . . . Wait a minute.'

He took the card he'd found at L'Eldorado and read:

'*To the Jewel Queen, Baroness of Saint-Meslin, a gift of ruby red roses in fond memory of Lyon – from an old friend. A. Prévost.*'

'What strikes you Joseph?'

'The Jewel Queen; the ruby roses! This must surely be all about jewels! We're getting warm, Monsieur Victor, we're getting warm!'

'And there's another thing. Noémi Gerfleur's death has in common with the death at the wine market, think.'

'My brain's turned to mush; I'm at a loss.'

'Read the note again: "*in fond memory of . . .*"'

'Lyon! Noémi Gerfleur began her career in a *café-concert* in Lyon! Oh that's it, I get it! M'sieu Gouvier's article . . .'

Joseph flipped feverishly through his notebook.

'Well, I'll be darned! That bloke who was topped in the wine market, that Gaston Molina, he did a spell in prison in Lyon!'

'Bravo! Lyon is the golden thread that links the two murders.'

'Three murders, Boss,' corrected Joseph excitedly. 'You're forgetting Élisa, Noémi Gerfleur's daughter; you told me Gaston Molina was her lover . . . So, there's no doubt – the body at Killer's Crossing; it's definitely her. Her body was left near her mother's building. So we now know it's something to do with jewels . . . and the city of Lyon. But when? We need more facts – should we go to Lyon? But we've no leads . . .'

'Let's not get carried away; it's probably much simpler than we imagine. Let's see, Noémi Gerfleur was born in 1856. So the jewels incident could have taken place between . . . let's say 1875, the year the *café-concerts* began, and 1886, the date she crossed the Channel.'

'Great Scott! Eleven years, that's a long time! You'd have to wade your way through tons of newspapers to unearth a story about corruption and jewels taking place in Lyon. Perhaps it's a sordid family drama, a stolen inheritance, and no one has said a word. Do you have any other clues?'

'No. Although . . . I thought no more about it, it seemed to make no sense, but who knows . . . '

Victor extracted the note, picked up in Gaston Molina's cloakroom, from his wallet and held it out to Joseph.

'So my friend, what do you make of this gibberish?'

Charmansat at uncle. Aubertot, rite cour manon, sale pétriaire. Rue L., gf 1211 . . .

'I did my best to decipher the jargon. Apart from the fact that whoever wrote it can't spell, I worked out that Charmansat and Aubertot must be people, that "sale pétriaire" means the

Salepêtrière and that Rue L. gf 1211 is an address. Can you think how this might have a bearing on our case? Could Charmansat be someone Molina was supposed to meet at his uncle's house?'

Joseph looked at him mockingly.

'Oh! M'sieu Legris. That says a lot about you! You've obviously never been hard up! When I was a lad, Maman regularly pawned our linen "with uncle"; it's what you call the pawnshop. Maybe Molina had a rendezvous with Charmansat at Rue des Francs-Bourgeois . . . Or maybe Charmansat was a clerk at the "casino", that's another name for "uncle". We'll have to find out; that would be a lead worth pursuing. So that's that one! As for M'sieu Aubertot, I suspect he's a chap living at the Hospice de la Salepêtrière, on the right, in a courtyard where someone called Manon – his mistress perhaps? – also lives.'

Victor did not reply.

'Boss?'

'I'm thinking. What if we're barking up the wrong tree? What if the sibylline message I stumbled on by accident has nothing to do with the murders?'

'What about "sale pétriaire" then? "My love reigns at the Hospital, most infamous of all creatures." I know that the Salepêtrière is a home for old women, but under Louis XIV it was called "the hospital". And today they treat mental health problems there . . . Perhaps Inspector Lecacheur is on to something. But you're a step ahead; you know things he doesn't.'

'Time will tell . . . In view of the way this note is written, it's possible that Molina, or whoever wrote it, meant a building named Aubertot situated in the left wing of the Salepêtrière, where a certain Manon was supposed to have an appointment, probably for treatment.'

'Steady on, Boss, you're getting muddled up. You have to think logically and calmly about this. I'll wager that Aubertot is a patient or a member of the medical staff. That's the second one. Now let's move on to that street, Rue L . . . That's a nuisance, because streets starting with L are ten a penny in Paris. It must be incredibly long to have a street number 1211. And gf, do you think . . . ?'

He was unable to finish his sentence. Iris had suddenly appeared like a glorious apparition on the spiral staircase. The four men turned to look at her slim figure moulded into a fuchsia dress in vicuña wool, decorated with lace. She wore a soft, wide-brimmed hat in the same colour. Smiling at Victor and Joseph, she joined Kenji, giving him his frock coat and bowler hat. Kenji saw the old dealer out and announced: 'We're leaving now, we have some purchases to make, have lunch without us.'

As soon as they were out of sight the door chime pealed. To Joseph's despair, a corpulent man entered the shop, removing his top hat to reveal a bald pate: the Duc de Frioul.

'Dear friend, you can guess why I'm here; I'm persuaded that you have acquired a property that might interest me – an in-quarto in yellow morocco leather, the work of the wonderful Michel! I owe my nephew a wedding gift. Let's not beat about the bush. How much?'

While Victor was showing the Montaigne, Joseph went into the back office. There, amongst the travel books, he nursed his grievance against the Duc's nephew, Boni de Pont-Joubert, who had stolen his Valentine away.

I would rather go to uncle than see Frioul; he revolts me. At least at uncle's, when you abandon an object you love, you harbour hope of seeing it again . . . if only the Boss would let me go to the pawnshop, I would show them all what I'm capable of.

Enraged, he seized a feather duster and went to dust the books behind the two men sitting at the table, engaged in a lively discussion of the price of the Montaigne.

'That man is hardly better than his nephew,' he said to himself. 'Listen to him whining *you understand, it's a gift, blah blah blah*; we're not carpet merchants! So I'm too humble to marry Valentine, am I? Well, at least when I buy something I don't I argue about the price!'

He shook his duster under the nose of the Duc, who sneezed and gave him a murderous look. Victor frowned, indicating that Joseph should leave them in peace.

The arrival of the postman created a diversion. Victor signed a receipt for a parcel, which he placed on the counter. The Duc de Frioul wrote a cheque and left with a sullen 'Good day'. When he'd gone, Victor rubbed his hands together with pleasure.

'Kenji will be delighted. You'll have to deliver the Montaigne this afternoon to Auteuil, to Monsieur Boni de Pont-Joubert.'

Joseph froze, ashen-faced.

'I won't go – you know very well why – you can't force me.'

'All right, all right, don't worry. I'll take care of it,' Victor replied, hastily concealing a smile as he untied the parcel.

'You're provoking me – it's not funny!' complained Joseph.

'Stop grousing and come and look at this book that I ordered specially from London: *The Sign of Four*. The author is a Scottish doctor, an admirer of murder mysteries. He's invented a detective who solves crimes using his powers of deduction. Three or four years ago I read his first novel published in an English magazine and I think his detective, Sherlock Holmes, is even better than Monsieur Lecoq.[27] I thought you would like to have a first edition of the second Sherlock Holmes novel.'

Thrilled, Joseph was at a loss to express his gratitude.

'I'll have to make a big effort to learn English so that I can read it.'

'I'll translate it for you,' promised Victor. 'The first chapter is called "The science of deduction".'

'Oh, that's right up our street, M'sieu Legris, my mouth is watering. By the way, talking of deductions, why don't I go and ferret about at the pawnshop and try to find out for you about Charmansat?'

'But that will take up the whole afternoon and I'll be stuck here.'

'Please, Boss, just this once . . .'

'Very well, off you go, Sherlock Pignot, but don't forget to give me a detailed account of your activities!'

Joseph made the cab stop outside the Archives Nationales, and jumped to the pavement, almost colliding with an old woman laden with baskets. He did not react to her barrage of insults. His mind was occupied by the thought that perhaps the author of the note had not been referring to the principal pawnshop as 'uncle', but to one of its branches. He resolved to stick to his original plan, however; he could always go to Rue du Regard, then Rue Servan afterwards if he was mistaken.

He crossed Rue des Francs-Bourgeois and reluctantly ventured into the waiting room. Inside, he was transported back to childhood.

Euphrosine Pignot, one hand clutching a bundle of linen, the other holding tight to a slightly hunchbacked little boy with straw-blond hair, surveyed the room. The sudden death of her husband a year earlier had left her destitute. Not daring to approach the counters, she remained planted in the middle of the comings and goings, a black-clad statue, unable to make up its mind. She, who had never had to solicit help from anyone, considered it the highest indignity to have to pledge her inheritance. In the end little Joseph had raised his head and piped up suddenly:

'Are we going to thell the sheeth today or tomorrow? I don't care; they itch anyway!'

They had left five francs richer. It had been the first of many trips to the pawnshop.

The memory collided with reality: a woman obviously in mourning was struggling under the weight of an enormous clock that began to belt out a Mozart melody. Joseph became aware of a strange ritual dance that was being played out around him. Bearing an eclectic mix of utensils, from wicker hampers to petrol lamps or copper jam pans, people were waiting fretfully, anxious to obtain some centimes to pay their rent or fill their bellies. Beloved everyday items, work tools, useless trifles that evoked happy memories, all these treasures would be used to pay for more ordinary necessities: underlinen, bedding, overcoats, skirts. People were forced to give up their pitiful belongings in exchange for precious little. There was a section for bundles and rags. In another corner, mattresses were taken in to be sent to the steam room for cleaning and disinfection. Further away was the section for jewellery and trinkets of some value.

Joseph went and stood at the back of the queue. In front of him he recognised the old woman who had cursed him. In her baskets she was carrying plates and glasses wrapped in straw. Someone tapped him on the shoulder. A student in threadbare clothes held up a chipped vase and asked him timidly: 'Do you think there's any chance I'll get something for this?'

A lanky fellow with a bilious complexion intervened: 'You're dreaming, son, dreaming. You have to be a bit cunning. I know what I'm talking about; I was a pedlar on the boulevards – they called me The Emperor, d'you know why? I had the gift of the gab; I could sell things in double quick time. I knew to keep my eyes open and to make myself scarce at the sight of a *flic*.'

'But you've fallen on hard times?' Joseph asked.

'My lucky star deserted me; it was sick of the sight of me. In this world, once you have white hair and no flimsies, you have no choice but to throw in the towel or become an accomplished crook. That vase of yours, it's worth a hill of beans.'

'But it's Sèvres,' insisted the student.

'Well, it might be, but look at the state it's in. It's not the Sisters of Mercy here; if they pay money it's because they can smell a mile off that they'll be able to sell it on for more! Have you any idea how many auctioneers there are lurking in the back?'

Joseph and the student shook their heads.

'Eight! If we poor buggers don't come and take out of hock what we've pawned, those eight blighters will sell them at auction for the very great good of public assistance. When it comes to valuing our possessions at the lowest possible price, then they stir themselves. You'd be lucky to get a hundred sous for the *Mona Lisa*. So you and your chamber pot . . .'

'But I tell you it's genuine Sèvres!'

'You can tell me all you like. You'll see, and don't blame me! It doesn't stop them weighing the silver and gold and offering four fifths of their weight. As for the rest, if they offer you a third, you're doing well. You'll soon see how it works! When I get in here I say goodbye to hope. I've come to pawn my ticker and that'll be the last I ever see of it!'

'But surely there's a way to stop them selling what you leave here?' said Joseph.

'Oh, there is! With a renewal, a slip of paper that entitles you to pay loan interest every year until you hit better times. All in all, some people end up paying ten or fifteen times the value of their item. The dice are loaded; the administration knows how to turn a profit.'

Discouraged, the student was about to leave when Joseph whispered to him: 'Don't listen to him; you might as well give it a go. It's daylight robbery but it does help you out. As my Boss says: "Better to empty your house, than languish with an empty stomach."'

His spirits lifted, the student took his place in the queue again.

At a neighbouring counter it was the turn of the musical clock. It was duly weighed and passed through the grille to the valuer under the anxious eye of its owner, where it was briskly given a valuation of ten francs. The widow exclaimed indignantly, arguing that her parents-in-law had paid a fortune for that clock, that the chime played twelve different operatic extracts, one each hour, and that she desperately needed money to pay the baker and the butcher who were threatening to cut her off. Unmoved, the woman behind the counter was already leaning towards the next woman in line, a giggling girl who had brought a man's suit belonging to her cousin.

'He became all roly-poly in the army, and now it's like doll's clothes on him – how much can you give me?'

But the widow changed her mind. She pushed the girl out of the way and gave up her precious clock, receiving in return a receipt and two five franc pieces.

'Thieves,' she murmured.

'Why would I try to swindle you?' retorted the valuer. 'I'm just doing my job. I'm only an employee.'

'Do you think it's acceptable to fleece people?' returned the widow.

'Now do you see how it works?' said the old pedlar.

Joseph finally reached the counter where a surly-looking cashier chewed the inside of his cheeks as he sharpened a pencil. Without looking up he drawled: 'So, what do you have?'

'Hello, Monsieur. If I were to say "Charmansat" to you, what would you say?'

'I would say what on earth are you talking about? What is it, a "charmansat"?'

'It's not an object; it's a bloke, my mother's brother. Someone told me he works here.'

'Your uncle Charmansat?'

'Yes, very funny, my uncle at uncle. I'm Gaston Molina. Is he here?'

The employee stared at him, chewing his cheeks harder, then announced gruffly: 'Wait a minute. I'll have to find out.'

The minute stretched out interminably and the people behind Joseph in the queue were starting to protest when the employee returned saying: 'He's busy in the shop.'

'Look, it's urgent, a question of life or death. I just have to tell him something. Do me a favour and just go and tip him the wink . . .'

The flash of a coin caught the employee's eye and he swiped it and disappeared again.

'Hey there, my boy, you're not the only one here, and I've got better things to do than stand in this queue!' roared the old street pedlar.

Giving the student a conspiratorial look, Joseph pushed through the crowd and went to lose himself on a bench among the pledge agents. He took a copy of *Le Passe-partout* from his pocket so he'd be able to keep an eye on the counters from behind the newspaper. The surly employee soon returned, in the company of a short, pot-bellied man in a grey smock with a bald head but an abundant beard.

'So that's what a Charmansat looks like,' murmured Joseph, buried behind his newspaper. 'Like a villain.'

The employee scratched his ear, shrugged his shoulders and abandoned Charmansat, who hung around uncertainly. His myopic goggle eyes blinked as he scanned the lines of people waiting, then he swung round and disappeared back into the bowels of the pawnshop.

Joseph retraced his steps and asked one of the men in charge where the staff exit was. Lying in wait on the opposite pavement, he kept watch until Charmansat appeared surrounded by colleagues and set off with a jerky gait towards the omnibus station.

'It's too late today to follow the fellow, but next time I'll know which burrow to flush him out of.'

It was almost seven thirty by the time he got back to the bookshop. Kenji did not rebuke him, but told him crossly that Victor had hopped it the minute he had returned and that he also had to be out that evening.

'I was beginning to feel abandoned. I'll be home by midnight. Would you be able to dine with Mademoiselle Iris and keep her company?'

Joseph, bristling with impatience, put down the broom he had just picked up.

'Your wish is my command, Boss. I'll warn Maman that I am required to work late.'

'Thank you. I'm going to change. Please close up the shop.'

Joseph closed the shutters and was sweeping the floor when he saw Iris at the foot of the stairs. He turned scarlet.

'Take off your apron and come and eat. I've prepared a little dinner for us.'

She carefully filled his plate with pâté and crudités and poured him a glass of Bordeaux. The sudden intimacy made him pensive; for a brief moment he imagined that he and this charming young girl were married, dining together in their own kitchen. But the memory of Kenji brought him back to reality, and he could not suppress a peevish gesture.

'Is something wrong?' she asked.

'Oh no, it's just that . . . I know it's none of my business, but I can't help asking . . . You're so young and he's so . . .'

'What are you trying to say?'

'The Boss and you. Excuse me but I find it shocking!'

She covered her mouth in an attempt to stifle her laughter.

'Why is it shocking? Love is blind to age.'

'You're right. I'm just a little old-fashioned.'

'Old? You?'

'If you're in love with the Boss, then of course that changes everything. Besides, he deserves it, he knows everything about everything.'

'And he's very handsome, don't you agree?'

Joseph hesitated. He had never before considered Kenji's physical attributes. Now that he thought about it, he had to admit that, in spite of his wrinkles and his greying hair, Monsieur Mori did possess a certain charm. He nodded vigorously as he tucked into his grated carrots.

'So you approve of our union.'

She was more beautiful than ever. Resignedly, he managed to smile and said: 'Absolutely. But it is a shame.'

'For whom?'

'I don't know, for other men. Not for Monsieur Victor of course; he has Mademoiselle Tasha.'

'For . . . for you?'

'You're joking, a hunchback like me!'

'What hunch are you referring to?'

She was looking at him in such a friendly way that he blushed again, ecstatic to be with this beautiful girl. Valentine's halo slipped a little.

'Listen, I'm going to tell you a secret, and you mustn't tell anyone or I'll be very angry. I'm Monsieur Mori's daugh– goddaughter.'

He was not sure he had heard correctly.

'So there's nothing between you?'

'Nothing but enormous affection.'

'Good! That's very good! I mean, very good carrots, don't you agree? I would love to have some more. I suppose you're going to be staying here quite a while? You lived for years in England; perhaps you can help me . . .'

'With what?'

'Monsieur Victor gave me an English novel, and as English is a closed book to me . . .'

'Lessons? What an excellent idea! I'm bored to death, and Kenji doesn't allow me to go for walks. When would you like to start?'

'Straight away.'

'Perfect. Repeat after me: "*My father is not at home.*"'

185

'That's difficult!'

'You haven't even tried. Put your tongue against your teeth: "*My father*" . . . Come on, "*ther*".'

'I can't; I have rabbit teeth!'

Wherever Kenji looked were rumps emphasised by the tightness of corsets, and breasts on display. It mattered not that this abundance was contrived. Bosoms and bustles, wigs and fake diamonds; all were designed to satisfy one master: the desire of men. Le Moulin-Rouge really was the temple of Eros, where gossip columnists and novelists came to feed their fancy. Woman, in all her manifestations, enticed man: whether humble errand girls or high-class prostitutes, bourgeoise women come to mingle with the masses, or street girls with shrill voices.

Completely at ease in this universe, which was the world of his fantasies, Kenji felt both seduced and contemptuous as he watched one of the courtesans. She was given flowers by a besotted provincial lad, then promptly left him in the lurch and went off to sell them to a flower seller.

'It's interesting to watch, is it not?' said a rather affected voice in Kenji's ear.

'It illustrates a proverb that comes to mind: "Life makes bad vaudeville. You miss the beginning and you don't know how it ends."'

'Well said! Would you by any chance be a philosopher?'

'Only a bookseller,' replied Kenji, taking his card out and glancing briefly at his interlocutor. He saw a bourgeois man, silver at the temples, an Inverness cape thrown over his evening dress.

'Delighted to meet you. Jules Navarre. I work for *L'Écho de Paris*. Would you be interested in furnishing me with other aphorisms of that sort, for my coming literary review?'

'Unfortunately, they're only for my private use.'

'I'm sorry to hear it. Will you at least have a drink?'

'I'm meeting one of the dancers.'

Navarre burst out laughing.

'Well, that's frank! Would it be indiscreet to ask which one? I have first-hand knowledge of all the dancers! Would it be the gorgeous Chiquita, perhaps?'

'Eudoxie Allard.'

'Alias Fifi Bas-Rhin! She haunts the dreams of the most virtuous men. She has an imperious eye, a disdainful lip and a haughty air, but everything else is so winning! She is much less vulgar than most of them, but she flirts, or rather she likes to make conquests. You see that lothario with the sombrero sitting opposite the dwarf in pince-nez, Henri de Toulouse-Lautrec, a painter whose star is on the rise? That's Louis Dolbreuse, one of her would-be lovers. He's a poet, who recites at Le Chat-Noir.'

Kenji had spotted the table indicated by Navarre, but he looked away immediately, disagreeably surprised to recognise Tasha amongst the drinkers. What was she up to? Was Victor with her? Was that why he'd left the bookshop in such a hurry?

He turned back, concealing his anxiety.

'I have no designs on Mademoiselle Allard; she's a customer, that's all.'

'Excuse me.'

'Juju! It's been a long time! La Môme Fromage and I were worried you'd kicked the bucket!'

'I've been busy, my angel. Can I offer you cherries in brandy?'

A voluptuous creature, who Kenji found rather unattractive, was blocking their way.

'I wouldn't say no, but the *chahut* is about to start. See you soon . . .'

As she took the arm of a sinister-looking, skinny, middle-aged man, Kenji saw Tasha coming towards their table. He just had time to sit down hastily and unfold a handkerchief in front of his face.

Tasha passed by without looking at Kenji, but she had seen him. She was astonished to find him here. Victor had told her how he was devoting himself heart and soul to his young conquest installed in Rue des Saints-Pères. She resolved to get to the bottom of it.

'I'm delighted you've changed your mind, I'm dying of thirst. Waiter, a bottle of champagne!' Navarre sat down next to Kenji. 'Do you know her?'

'Who?'

'The girl who just accosted us. That's Nini Patte-en-l'air, used to be a shopkeeper, married, a mother. She gave it all up to dance the cancan! The same goes for the lamp post with her, Valentin le Désossé.'

'Curious nickname . . .'

'A journalist used it after he heard him singing '*La Chanson de Valentin*' and it stuck. His real name is Étienne Renaudin; his brother exercises the noble profession of notary. Valentin was already well known at the balls of the Second Republic. When the urge to dance has you in its grip, you become a slave to it, just as others are slave to ether or morphine. But that's not the worst thing. The most fearsome infection is invisible and is passed on in the privacy of the bedroom. I love the delicacy of the expression "sickness of the century". When the evening starts to become boring I entertain myself by trying to guess how many of these puppets will have caught it by morning . . .'

Kenji congratulated himself on always using protection and on having strongly advised Victor to use prophylactics, tiresome though they were. He was listening with half an ear as Navarre discussed the women dancers when the orchestra, conducted by Mabille, struck up the opening bars of '*La Vie Parisienne*'.

Midnight approached and it was time for the cancan. The crowd pressed into the middle of the hall. The brass section heralded a whirlwind of dancers escorted by their partners who bounded on to the dance floor, making it tremble with a flurry of petticoats and black stockings. The four leading dancers – La Goulue, Nini Patte-en-l'air, Grille d'Égout and Rayon d'Or – launched into a succession of complicated steps – shouldering arms, guitar, military salute, crossing over, legs behind the head. Fifi Bas-Rhin lifted the creamy avalanche of her petticoats to reveal elegant calves in frenetic contortions. She threw herself up and landed in the grand split, spreading out her five yards of black satin skirts.

'Do you see the pink line between the garter and the flounces of the drawers?' shouted Navarre. 'It's that glimpse of naked flesh that keeps the indomitable men coming night after night!'

At the height of all the excitement Kenji had wandered up to the front row. The *chahut* finished with an improvisation from each dancer, who searched the circle of spectators for the man whose top hat she would send flying through the air with a well-aimed kick. Before he realised what was about to happen, Kenji found himself uncovered by Eudoxie, who sent his opera hat clattering into the middle of the crowd, under the watchful eye of Navarre. Blushing, Kenji retrieved his headgear, more exhausted than if he himself had been dancing for hours. The cancan had only lasted eight minutes.

Navarre led Kenji to a table, where Eudoxie wasted no time in joining them, still out of breath.

'The grand split is a little too acrobatic; I'll end up breaking my bones!' she cried, flopping on to a chair.

'Bravo, my dear! The precision of your leap is incomparable. Your friend here seems overwhelmed.'

'Oh, Monsieur Mori, it's so kind of you to come, but you mustn't be so shy! What a beautiful purple cravat!'

'The more the merrier . . .' murmured Louis Dolbreuse, sitting down in his turn. 'Good evening, comrades. Have you seen who's here? Wales himself,' he said, indicating the future Edward VII with a movement of the head. The prince was disporting himself nearby in joyous company.

'Pah, I don't give a toss about the royals when we have a visit from a celebrated bookseller from the left bank!' exclaimed Eudoxie.

She put her hand on Kenji's.

'Monsieur is a bookseller?' asked Dolbreuse.

'You met Monsieur Mori's associate, Victor Legris, the other evening.'

'Ah, the one with the painter girlfriend? Delightful enough to eat! Can you believe she has undertaken to paint my portrait? I think she may have taken a fancy to me.'

'Victor and Tasha are engaged,' Kenji announced drily, quite prepared to lie in a good cause.

'That's wonderful! I haven't the least faith in feminine fidelity,' retorted Dolbreuse, never taking his eyes from Eudoxie. 'Yvette Guilbert explains it admirably, go and hear her sing *"Le Fiacre"*, it's edifying: *"Léon! You're hurting me, take off your glasses"*,' he cooed.

Navarre, chuckling, went one better: 'I heard her at the Concert Parisien, sensational! She more than deserves her nickname – Sarah Bernhardt of the Gypsies! You have to have heard her reciting *The Virgins*, replacing all the censored words with a cough!'

'Yes, it's even better than the production of *Le Père Goriot*. Antoine has put it on at his Théâtre-Libre,' said Dolbreuse. 'That's the kind of razor-sharp book you sell in your bookshop, I suppose, Monsieur Mori.'

'Oh, we have books for all tastes, including collections of pictures for those who don't like to read, Monsieur Dolbreuse.'

'Ouch!' cried Eudoxie. 'That's put you in your place, Louis! Monsieur Mori, you're not leaving so soon?'

She tried to hold Kenji back, as he seemed to be about to get up.

'It would be a shame to leave; you'll miss the best part. When Le Moulin closes its doors, the dancers offer their most daring displays to the regulars,' said Navarre.

'True, in comparison, the naturalist quadrille is a trifle,' added Dolbreuse. 'Come on, no hard feelings. Let's shake hands Monsieur Bookseller! And give me your card, so that I know where I can find something to read in case Morpheus and love both desert me!'

Kenji looked at each of them in turn carefully for an ironic expression, then, convinced that he really was wanted, especially by Eudoxie, he slowly sat down again.

CHAPTER 10

Buried under a heap of newspapers that rose and fell to the rhythm of snoring, a human form lay slumped on a wonky armchair. Toes sticking out of holey socks beat a steady rhythm, and one hand dangled to the ground, where a slipper and a candle watched over a mountain of tattered papers.

Joseph had scoured his newspapers one by one, in vain, going directly to the page of miscellaneous news, convinced that if a case involving jewellery theft had caused a stir in Lyon between 1875 and 1886, it would have been mentioned in the Parisian dailies. It was after one in the morning when he had given up his fevered search. Exhausted, he had fallen asleep.

His sleep was troubled by a dream, a nightmare about an enormous library in which he searched interminably for a precious manuscript.

The church bell of the Église Saint-Germain-des-Près sounded three o'clock. Joseph started awake in his armchair, ready to go back to work, but then realised with anguish that he had stopped collecting periodicals in 1885, the year he started at the Elzévir bookshop.

Unable to face switching off the petrol lamp, he remained immobile, transported back six years. He pictured his mother's radiant face as she gave him the news.

'My pet, you're going to take up your Papa's mantel; I've organised everything. We'll live like kings! Just think, your salary added to mine . . . and the bookshop is only round the corner. If your father were alive, he would be so happy!'

Joseph remembered the words of Marcel, his childhood friend.

'Goodbye, dear freedom, farewell to adventure! But take heart, you'll have a fixed income and your future will be assured. Books, that's right up your street; you're a real bookworm.'

Determined to become a model assistant, he'd not had time to see Marcel more than two or three times since that day. When they did meet they would remember fondly how they used to wait at dawn by Rue du Croissant for the first editions of the papers to come out of the printworks. Between the ages of nine and fifteen, they had worn out the soles of their shoes racing madly across Paris to sell their local rags before the other hawkers. Their numerous friends among the typographers, the apprentices and the kiosk owners had enabled Joseph to accumulate nearly five thousand papers, now shelved along the walls of his study.

A head topped with a nightcap appeared at the door.

'Jesus, Mary and Joseph, what on earth's going on!' exclaimed a hoarse voice. 'Look at him sleeping among his newspapers. Perhaps his glands are bothering him? My pet, are you asleep?'

'I'm not asleep now that you've woken me up,' complained Joseph.

'Well, so much the better, because it's time to drink your coffee. I'll go and heat you a big bowl.'

Joseph stood up, cursing, overcome with cold and fatigue. He brushed his trousers with the flat of his hand, and slipped on his jacket.

'It's too stupid! What if the jewel affair was written about during the months in which I neglected my newspaper collection! But I haven't entirely wasted my time, because I swear that if that article exists, I'm going to root it out! Isn't that right, Papa? You should never give up, and if you want something enough you can achieve it.'

He looked up at the photograph pinned up above the old packing case that served as his desk. A jovial-looking bookseller in a smock and beret smiled out at him.

'Coffee!' yelled Euphrosine.

'Com-ing!'

He went to drink his coffee standing up by the red-hot stove in their tiny kitchen. His mother handed him some bread and dripping, looking disapprovingly at his crumpled clothes.

'Next time you decide to turn your room upside down instead of kipping, warn me and I'll spend the night at Madame Ballu's. The racket was as bad as when the German cannons were bombarding Paris!'

'I didn't think I had disturbed you; you were snoring.'

'I'll thank you to show a little respect! He accuses his mother of snoring! Oh the cross I have to bear!'

She left the apartment, muttering to herself, and loaded up her costermonger's cart with fruit and vegetables. Joseph rinsed the bowls and made his bed, feeling all the while that he had forgotten something important. Every time his mother reproved him, he felt so guilty that he was impelled to busy himself as if his life depended on it.

When the little apartment was as clean as a new pin, he set out with a heavy heart for Rue des Saints-Pères. His brain was fizzing with ridiculous or tragic news items and his mouth was stiff with the effort of not yawning.

He opened the wooden shutters and seized a feather duster, whistling as he passed it over the shelves.

'How do you do it? I've tried but I just can't whistle,' declared Iris from the door of the back room.

'You startled me!' cried Joseph, letting go of his feather duster.

'I didn't know how to amuse myself so I came down to have a look around. I'm just amazed that people can earn their living selling books. Why is anyone interested in such trifles? All these thousands of words aren't going to change anything.'

'Have you never felt the desire to escape, to lose yourself in a good mystery or an adventure story?'

'I would rather learn to whistle.'

'That's not as hard as pronouncing English, all you have to do is make an 'o' with your mouth . . .'

'Good morning, darling. Would you like breakfast now?' asked Kenji in English, from halfway down the stairs.

'Yes, coming!' replied Iris, giving the disappointed Joseph a smile.

'Charming, the Boss speaks in English because he doesn't want me to understand; he'll get a shock when Mademoiselle Iris has taught me the ins and outs of the language,' he muttered to himself, continuing his dusting in a desultory fashion.

'Good morning, young man. I hope you have received the three copies of *Giselle* promised me by Monsieur Mori?'

Joseph jumped, and adopted an affable expression with which to greet the Comtesse de Salignac, who wore a brocaded wool coat and an air of hostility.

'The battleaxe doesn't believe in saying please, of course!' he said under his breath, as he went to consult the order book.

'What did you say, young man?'

'Only that you have mistaken the date. The books are not due until tomorrow.'

'That's most provoking. Well, I shall make a sacrifice as is my wont, and make do with a present for my friend Adalberte de Brix. The poor thing is convalescing very slowly from her hemiplegia. The stay at Lamalou-les-Bains recommended by Dr Charcot only allowed her to regain part of her mobility. Half of her face is still paralysed.'

'She must talk like a duck.'

'Don't be impertinent, you little lout! Spare me your comments and find me *The Vicar*, *The Son-in-law* and *Precocious*, three novels by George Bois, published by Dentu. I also want *A False Start* by Max de Simiers, a story in which Mathilde de Flavignol assures me the first surprises of the heart are painted with spring-like lightness,' she concluded to Kenji, who was advancing towards her.

Kenji calmly sent Joseph to the stockroom.

'And where does he want me to dig out this spring-like book, from amongst the gardening manuals?'

After a longish pause, which he had deliberately extended,

Joseph reappeared with *The Vicar* and *A False Start*. The Comtesse had left the shop.

'That was worth the effort,' he told Kenji. 'Isn't Monsieur Victor coming?'

'He's at Rue Drouot. There are some deliveries to make: the two books you're clutching for Madame de Salignac, this one for Rue du Louvre, and that other one, the Montaigne, for Monsieur Boni de Pont-Joubert, Rue Michel-Ange. Monsieur Legris wasn't able to do it himself.'

'You amaze me . . .'

'Don't start complaining. You can take a cab – does that make it more acceptable? Make up the parcels and try not to waste yards and yards of string.'

'It's slave labour; you're sending me to the four corners of Paris,' protested Jojo.

'I only count three deliveries,' retorted Kenji. 'Do you want me to add a fourth?'

As soon as he had gone through the main gates bearing the inscription: Hospice for Elderly Women, Victor felt as though he were a prisoner in an enclosed town. The Salpêtrière resembled a monastery that jealously guarded the secrets of its past. Over an adjoining gated entrance the *tricolore* fluttered. Victor entered Cour Saint-Louis, where the wind had denuded the puny trees of their leaves. Opening off this courtyard was a refectory that was like a veritable market. There were grocers, a café, a tobacconist and fruit stalls in a large area where elderly women milled about; some, formerly refectory staff, were smoking pipes. There was also a laundry, always very busy because on visiting day the old ladies liked to have fresh white bonnets and ironed, frilled bodices. The immense hospice also included a section for the mentally ill.

Victor crossed a garden bare of flowers at this time of year and followed an alley of flagstones that led to a vast, imposing religious edifice crowned by a dome. On both sides of the Chapelle Saint-Louis rose the façades of buildings, to the left the Mazarin Wing, to the right the Lassay Wing. Victor hesitated. Last year he had come to the Salpêtrière to view Albert Londe's pictures. At the request of Professor Charcot, Londe had produced snapshots of the patients, demonstrating the various aspects of hysteria. But where was his office? Victor was hoping that the author of *Photography in the Arts, Science and Industry* would tell him what or who bore the name 'Aubertot'. He met a house doctor in a white coat, an overcoat thrown over his shoulders, who gave him a complicated explanation of where he could find Londe.

Stretching out before him was a vista dotted with bare trees and hemmed in by grey walls and tiled roofs. He trampled across patchy grass that spilled on to a path where hunched women tapped along, the noise of their canes breaking the silence. A young member of staff was guiding this flock, who seemed to mark the frontier between this world and the world beyond.

At the entrance to the Cour Saint-Claire, he noticed on his left the sinister prison where, in September 1792, a group of angry revolutionaries had raped and murdered thirty-seven unfortunate women detained under the common law, accused of royalism. The courtyard in which he now found himself had been renamed the Cour des Massacres in their honour. This gave on to a second courtyard with a large well in the centre.

Elderly residents sat immobile and silent on benches, warming themselves in the pale sunshine. What were they thinking about, these women whose lives had been nothing but hard graft? Were they back in the distant days of their childhood? Victor stopped to observe them. He felt such a wave of empathy that he entered a reverie. He saw himself old, gout-ridden, abandoned in an asylum and anguished by the realisation that life is short, that whatever one does time passes ineluctably by, and had already passed for him. Oppressed by the thought that everything is transitory, he continued on his way. Only a hundred and twenty years earlier, delinquents, beggars, prostitutes, madwomen and vagabonds had all been callously crowded together in the Salpêtrière. These cloistered women had been convicted of causing public disorder; they mouldered in cells, frequently branded with a hot iron. If there was no room for new arrivals, the girls were deported to Martinique, Guadeloupe or Louisiana.

He went behind the prison and passed the old quarters of the archers who, in former times, had been housed in identical dwellings. Lost, he found his way into a cemetery, where a watchman pointed him in the right direction. He retraced his steps and finally made it to the Pariset Wing, where Charcot ran his clinic and Londe his photographic laboratory.

Victor spotted a house doctor examining a set of negatives and approached him. They exchanged opinions about the use of photography in medicine.

'Do you know where I can find Albert Londe?'

'He's not here today. Are you a doctor?'

'I'm a specialist. And Aubertot . . . do you know him?'

'Dr Aubertot?'

'That's right.'

'He runs a course in the lecture hall on Wednesdays, on other days, not Saturday or Sunday, he's at his clinic in Rue Monge. I'm not sure what number . . . 68? 168? . . . There's a brass plate.'

'I'll find it, thank you.'

'If it would interest you, I can show you part of the hospital.'

'Very kind.'

Following the doctor, Victor realised that Joseph's intuition had been sound; Aubertot was on the medical staff. Pleased to have solved one part of the puzzle even if he did not understand its significance in the Molina–Fourchon affair, he paid little attention to his guide's explanations.

'Those women wandering about took part in a hypnosis session this morning – hypnosis is Charcot's favoured treatment. Here's the ward for lunatics who're calm, mostly cases of senile dementia, with reversion to childhood. The management provides them with more than the bare necessities; their lives are made agreeable. Singing teachers come several times a month to give them lessons to break up the monotony, and they have parties and dances.'

The doctor crossed a room where forty beds were lined up on either side of a central aisle with a wood stove that took up a great deal of space. Now and then, without interrupting his discourse, he would lean over one of the beds, separated not by curtains but by narrow gaps. Some women were knitting, others were chattering, intrigued by the man in the frock coat who threw them embarrassed glances. Too often for his liking, Victor was forced to stop behind the doctor and look down at some dying wretch, eyes unseeing, reduced to little more than a digestive passage.

'I hope the smell doesn't bother you? We do air the room regularly but it's hard to get rid of . . . Now we've come to the ward for the more excitable cases – the megalomaniacs, people suffering from hallucinations, idiots of all ages.'

Victor was about to make an excuse, but the doctor was already charging through the ward and plunging into the next one.

'Here we have the agitated patients, who struggle and can be violent, in which case the doctors have to resort to restraints: straitjackets – thick linen jackets with very long sleeves that they knot round the patients' back, to restrain their arms. Would you like to see? Just this morning we were obliged to put one on a patient.'

Victor was appalled and succeeded in escaping on the pretext of an urgent meeting.

'That will teach me to pretend to be a doctor. If there's one profession I'm really not cut out for, it's medicine,' he said to himself as he fled along the corridors.

Lost again, he passed through a series of arches and ended up on Rue des Cuisines. Through the half-open gates he could see the enormous red copper cauldrons and saucepans evoking a giants' banquet. He hurried over to a gate opening on to the Pinel Wing and realised with horror that he was back where he had started: in front of him were the lodgings of the lunatics. He set off again in the other direction and reached the courtyard where he had seen the old ladies sitting limply on benches. Exhausted, he went to sit down. A wrinkled old woman turned towards him.

'Pretty, isn't it, our Manon well? I remember the well of Three Windmills farm. I had my first kiss there, sitting on the little wall of the well.'

'Madame Bastine, come and have your tisane – it's getting cold!' shouted one of the nurses.

'Coming, coming,' sighed the old lady.

Victor fished the crumpled note out of his pocket.

'*Aubertot, rite cour manon . . .*' he muttered. 'I'm here in the Cour Manon! Why on earth is it called that? . . . Think for heaven's sake, you're nearly there . . . Manon . . . Manon . . . *Manon Lescaut!* Yes! It must relate to the novel by Abbé Prévost . . . Of course! This is where Manon rests before her deportation to America . . . Abbé Prévost . . . *A. Prévost.*

He stood up, trembling with excitement.

'*Manon Lescaut*, Abbé Prévost. Why?'

He walked aimlessly, trying to order his thoughts. He did not much like the characters in Abbé Prévost's novel and did not understand the indulgence of readers and men of letters towards the Chevalier des Grieux, who became a swindler and murderer through the love of a woman who sold her body to old men. Manon and the Chevalier did not hesitate to cheat, to fleece people, to lie, while still respecting God, the King, the aristocracy and especially large fortunes. Was Noémi Gerfleur's personality similar to Manon's? Had her murderer been meting out 'justice'? Through jealousy? Greed? Or for vengeance?

'Flush out the motive, you will have part of the solution . . . So they say . . . So they say . . .'

His throat tightened. The text was clear:

My love reigns at the Hospital, most infamous of all creatures . . .

'It's a quotation from *Manon Lescaut*! I'm sure of it! The Hospital! Cour Manon, Doctor Aubertot. That makes no sense . . . Is Dr Aubertot a murderer? . . . Acid. The bandage round La Gerfleur's neck. No, that's ridiculous! . . . What is this "rite"? The location of the lecture hall where Aubertot teaches?'

He wrote in his notebook: *68 or 168 Rue Monge.*

'I'll have to wait until Monday to go and see him . . . Until then I absolutely must compare what I've discovered with whatever Joseph gleaned at the pawnshop. How provoking that I had to sign the lease on the hairdresser's yesterday, otherwise I would be much further ahead! And this morning I had to dash straight to that Rabelais sale at Rue Drouot because Kenji insisted I should attend.'

According to his watch it was one o'clock; he had promised Tasha he would introduce her to Thadée Natanson, one of the bookshop's customers, who had just relaunched *La Revue Blanche*, an avant-garde literary and artistic journal, with his brother Alfred, and moved its offices to Rue des Martyrs.

'I'm going to be late! Hurry, hurry, I'm sick of hurrying! Everything is conspiring against me!'

The coachman was extremely relieved to be free of the

passenger who had made him roar around the capital like one of those useless stinking petrol automobiles, the plaything of the engineers Panhard and Levassor.

Joseph meanwhile was delighted to have knocked off his three deliveries in double-quick time, having promised the cabby a generous tip if he went as fast as possible, and went to take up his position near the pawnshop. He had decided to wait for the staff to leave, and to follow Charmansat home.

'I must strike while the iron is hot. The Boss will be pleased – at least I hope so – you never know with him . . .'

He found himself a suitable doorway.

' "In the midst of darkness, the most lowly watchman glows like a beacon",' he quoted from Émile Gaboriau, his favourite author. Jojo resolved to be the beacon that would shine light on the murders of Killer's Crossing, even if he had to take root on that pavement.

Had anyone been able to see inside Prosper Charmansat's mind, they would have encountered a void. The model employee did not burden himself with thoughts as he fulfilled his daily tasks. The interior of the pawnshop cocooned him in a haven of peace. In the belly of that closed universe, out of sight of the world, nothing could reach him, not the wickedness of man, not fear, not loneliness. He was master of a modest domain, where the silent witnesses of so many lives were heaped up waiting to be packaged, and he dreamed of hiding in here for ever. He wrapped, labelled and accounted, drugged by the routine as if it were a narcotic.

He handled the imposing clock that had brought its owner ten francs and wondered how he was going to wrap it. Each of the objects left required meticulous attention. The valuable items – jewellery, shawls, watches, lace – were packed away in boxes, while the precious stones and pieces of gold were carefully kept in envelopes. Prosper Charmansat had the privilege of sealing the flaps with wax. In pushing the seal into the warm wax he experienced the joy of a breeder branding his livestock. He delegated the stamping of the parcels to a lame boy; another boy he gave the task of folding the valuation dockets in four and attaching them to the strings. The harvest was then consigned to baskets and sent to join the other pawned items in the tunnels beneath the shops, numerous storerooms lined with wooden and latticed metal pigeonholes, a labyrinth three miles long, where mounds of carpets, dishes, clothes and umbrellas had accumulated. It resembled not so much Ali Baba's cave as a beehive, and as he walked past the cells filled with antique busts, eiderdowns, pillows and thousands of lorgnettes, Prosper Charmansat imagined himself master of the store room of an enormous cargo ship with no home port.

He fitted the packaged clock between a parasol and a psalter, stood back to let a porter carrying boxes pass, and headed reluctantly to the cloakroom. He took off the uniform provided by the management – with no pockets, to prevent theft – and put on his own clothes.

There was already a crowd of employees at the omnibus station. Prosper Charmansat hauled himself up to the top deck, not noticing a blond, slightly hunchbacked young man who followed him.

At Place Maubert, Joseph jumped off the platform and tried not to lose his prey, who crossed Marché des Carmes and Rue des Écoles to reach Rue de l'École-Polytechnique. At number 22, he turned off into Impasse des Bœufs. Joseph paused, and saw Charmansat stop in front of a woman sitting shelling nuts. They exchanged greetings and Charmansat raised his hat then disappeared into a narrow opening at the foot of the alley. Joseph hurried after him. A little boy appeared, carrying a cup of milk.

'Can you tell me which floor Monsieur Charmansat lives on?'

'Second floor on the left. But be careful, Mère Galipot's always drunk!'

Undeterred, Joseph climbed the steps and almost collided with a dishevelled shrew, who gripped his shoulder.

'I've got you, boy, where have you hidden the dough?'

'Dough? You can find it at Les Halles,' retorted Joseph, pulling away sharply.

He knocked at the floor on the left. No answer. The crone clung to him, regarding him balefully and breathing her killer breath in his face.

'At Les Halles, eh? Which pavilion?'

'With the bread and the cake!' Joseph cried, and headed back down to the ground floor.

He reached the bottom just in time to see the little boy with the cup of milk push open a gate at the end of the alley. Intrigued, Joseph followed hard on his heels. To his great surprise, he found himself on the mezzanine of a neighbouring building. He ran downstairs, coming out in another narrow passage with little dark yards off it, leading to Rue de la Montagne-Saint-Geneviève. In the distance, the squat figure of Charmansat loped in the direction of the Panthéon.

'For heaven's sake, he didn't waste any time,' he muttered, struggling not to let him out of his sight.

Charmansat suddenly disappeared. Joseph thought he had lost him, but, noticing that the door of the Église Saint-Étienne-du-Mont was slightly open, he told himself it would do no harm to check inside.

He saw Charmansat make the sign of the cross and genuflect, then head for the finely sculpted balustrade separating the choir from the nave and the side chapels. He stood near the pulpit and opened a missal. Joseph hid behind a pillar, hoping that a crisis of faith would not keep him there for long. But then a slim, well-built chap, elegantly turned out and wearing a top hat, approached and tapped Charmansat on the shoulder. Arm in arm, the two men whispered together as they strolled over to the tomb of Sainte Geneviève, where they conferred at length. Joseph passed slowly behind them and bent over the monument, pretending to admire the decorative detail. The slim man moved away, his face remaining bathed in shadow.

Finally, Charmansat turned away as his companion slipped a coin into the contribution box and lit a candle. Which man should he follow? Joseph opted for the slim chap, whom he knew nothing about, reasoning that he now knew Charmansat's address.

The man in the top hat walked rapidly and with much greater ease than Charmansat. After skirting round the Lycée

Henri-IV and bearing off up Rue Rollin, he entered the Roman arenas at Rue de Navarre. It was the first time that Joseph had seen the ancient remains and his attention was distracted by the few remaining steps of the crumbling tiers and the partly excavated arena; all the rest was being buried under new constructions, notably the stables and offices of the Omnibus Company.

'When you consider that they dug up a skeleton six foot six tall, you realise that the gladiators were strapping fellows, most likely as a result of hitting each other over the head all the time!'

He spoke aloud, startling a Sister of Charity, who crossed herself and fled. Joseph suddenly remembered the man in the top hat, but, search as he might, he could see no trace of him.

Joseph frowned. His investigations might well prove more prolonged and arduous than he had anticipated. Annoyed with himself, he went back towards Impasse des Bœufs, where he found the woman still clamped to her seat shelling nuts like an automaton. When he went up to her and coughed politely she looked up; she had a moustache and reminded him of a scraggy goat.

'Excuse me, Madame, could you tell me the name of the bearded, slightly tubby man who lives in this building? I ask because he looks rather like the photo of my Uncle Alfred in our sitting room, taken ten years ago. He went off to Venezuela and no one knows what became of him . . .'

'Oh, yes, Monsieur Charmansat,' replied the woman who was so toothless that every other syllable was garbled. 'Prosper, that means happy in Latin, but that doesn't fit because he's had so many troubles, that man. He never smiles, but then you don't choose your Christian name. It's a shame, I would have been happy to have escaped my name, Angelique, since there's nothing angelic about me. But he's nice all the same, Monsieur Charmansat, very pleasant, a compatriot of mine; he's from Lyon. I'm also from the Rhône region, from Crémieu. I bet you've never set foot in Crémieu.'

To stop the flow of words, Joseph agreed that this was so, and repeated with exaggerated interest: 'Lyon?'

'Yes, a town, whereas Crémieu . . . I'm not surprised you have avoided it; it's a right hole. Monsieur Charmansat moved in here six years ago, I came in '88. It was my grandson who wanted to come up to Paris to find work on the building site of the Exposition. He's a slater and he brought me to run his household. He's not married, my grandson, on account of his wooden leg, after the accident. So he's your uncle, Monsieur Charmansat?'

'No, no, I must be mistaken, they do look alike but apparently we all have a double. My uncle's from Arras, but Lyon, I've heard about it – people say it's the home of good cuisine, known for its quenelles . . .'

Although he detested fish balls, he smacked his lips, hoping the woman would divulge some important detail about Charmansat's past.

An hour later, stuffed with tales of the Rhône region, he arrived back on Rue Visconti, having learned nothing about Charmansat, who had not returned home.

Euphrosine had shut herself in the kitchen and was preparing gnocchi with parmesan. Joseph took advantage of this to record what he had learned that day in his notebook.

'Lyon, Lyon, that's the nub of the affair; I must at all costs manage to find out what happened in '86 . . . Monsieur Gouvier would be able to help me in three shakes of a lamb's tail . . . Yes, but that would arouse his suspicions and I might find myself with Inspector Lecacheur on my back. Not to mention Monsieur Legris. I'll have to find out on my own; I'm going to impress the Boss with my skill.'

He did not like to admit to himself that he was hoping also to impress Iris. Disconsolately, he contemplated the heaps of newspapers stacked against the wall. Inspiration struck.

'Marcel! Marcel Bichonnier! The fun we used to have selling newspapers! And the games of hide and seek in his father's factory! If he's still working at Rue du Croissant, he won't refuse me help. I'll go and find him tomorrow at the crack of dawn. For now, I'll have to concentrate on the best approach to take. I need to start with Rue L. gf 1211 mentioned in Molina's note.'

He went into the study and pushed back the stacks of paper, Prussian sapper helmets and cartridge shells covering his packing case-desk, exhuming two apple cores and a two centime piece as he did so.

'I'm totally baffled,' he murmured, leaning over his notes. 'I must take stock. Let's think . . . It's this gf in that interminable Rue L. that's thrown me. Number one thousand two hundred and eleven – it's not possible! And gf . . . gf . . . what's that mean? It means I've been an ignoramus, that's what it means – gf, ground floor of course! So, ground floor, 1211 Rue L. If only

I could narrow it down to one quarter. Think. The slipper was dug up by the goatherd's dog at the Botanical Gardens . . . Are there wolves at the Botanical Gardens? Yes, triple ignoramus, there are wolves and lions as well. I'll have to look in my Paris street map; I think I'm on the right track!'

He was sure he was close to a revelation, something was about to become clear, but what? It was impossible to guess. He searched feverishly through the debris on his trunk.

'It's reasonable to assume that Molina lived in that area and that he lured the girl there, because she said you could hear wolves howling from his apartment. There's no way out of it, I'm going to have look at all the streets that begin with "L" in the area. And there are more than one thousand two hundred numbers! That's not a street; it's a bad joke . . . In the name of belts and garters, where's my street map!'

He searched through a teetering pile of issues of *Magasin Pitoresque*, which collapsed on the floor with a crash. This was not what he had intended at all. He stared in stupefaction at the fruits of his efforts, and then got down on all fours to read the title of a full-page heading:

ÉGLISE SAINT-SEVERIN IN PARIS

'A church! That's it! THAT'S IT! The chap with the top hat at Saint-Étienne-du-Mont, talking in a cloak-and-dagger manner to Charmansat, who then escaped my clutches at the Roman arenas . . . right next to the Botanical Gardens. I've got it! They're all in this together! Molina, Charmansat, the man in the top hat: all from the same neighbourhood! Where have I buried my map? I'm sure I left it here somewhere. I use it all the time . . .'

'My pet, you can come now!'

'Eating, eating, always eating,' he grumbled, abandoning the search.

'What's wrong with you; you look like you're coming down with something,' remarked his mother, serving him.

'It's just that I've lost my Paris street map.'

'Oh, don't worry, he'll bring it back.'

'He? Who are you talking about? Don't tell me that you . . .'

'Lent your map? Yes, I lent it to Madame Ballu's cousin, you know, Alphonse, the one who's just come back from Senegal. His officer was dying to show his fiancée all the best parts of Paris but the poor fellow hadn't a clue what to suggest – terrible for a talented soldier – so Madame called on me to help. Don't make that face; she wasn't about to buy one at that price!'

'Maman, I've told you a thousand times not to touch my things!' exploded Joseph.

'I don't deserve the scaffold, none the less! Go on, eat, otherwise it'll get cold. They're not too sticky, are they, the gnocchis? I wanted to make black pudding with mashed potato, but then as I had some semolina . . .'

'Good, I don't like black pudding,' said Joseph with approval, soothed by the appetising smell of the parmesan.

He was about to take a bite when there was a knock at the door.

'What now?' groaned Euphrosine. 'Don't move, I'll go.'

The next thing Joseph knew, Victor was sitting down beside him. Ignoring his protestations, Euphrosine served him a plate of gnocchis. He had already dined with Tasha and the Natanson brothers, but he forced himself to swallow what was on his plate, drank three glasses of water to help it down, politely refused a baked apple and led Joseph off to the study.

'Was your harvest fruitful?'

'Do you know Impasse des Bœufs?'

'Come on, out with it!'

'That's where he lives, the Charmansat "at uncle". Here's what I found out; afterwards you can tell me everything you know . . . One minute, the walls have ears.'

Just as he was about to closed the communicating door, Euphrosine said loudly, 'I labour to prepare them a dish fit for a king! Would it kill them to show their appreciation? Oh, the cross I have to bear!'

CHAPTER 11

JOSEPH peered through the window as he heard the clatter of wheels crossing the cobblestones in the courtyard outside. The light of a lantern cast the shadow of a bent figure pushing a pair of barrow handles. It was Euphrosine, bundled up in layers of knitted shawls, setting off to Les Halles to buy her produce. He could get up now.

Teeth chattering, he groped for his clothes and was soon leaving the house too, an apple stuffed in each pocket. He felt bad about letting his mother go alone. She was beginning to have difficulty hauling her costermonger's cart, and he could have helped her that morning. But he made up his mind to ignore his conscience and stick to his plan.

His blood was tingling after an hour of walking through the deserted streets. The city was beginning to stir as he reached Rue Montmartre, where he saw sleepy clerks and shop girls disappearing through the already open doors of the fabric and lingerie stores.

Rue du Croissant was dim and narrow, and invaded by a crowd, mostly of men, lounging on the pavement or leaning on bistro counters. Beer glasses of varying sizes jostled with one another and the cigarette smoke and murmur of conversation evoked a station buffet.

Revisiting the atmosphere that had permeated his youth stirred Joseph to the depths. He remembered as if it were yesterday being one of those street vendors bundled up in a threadbare frock coat and cap or bowler and listening with half an ear to the rotary presses inside the printing shops, and with the other half to the bragging accounts of a comrade's amorous exploits. He too had waited for the dailies that provided an irregular income. After paying his two francs for a hundred copies, he would hurry to the kiosks on the outskirts of the city to resell his merchandise at five centimes a piece. He remembered the routes he took through the maze of streets so well he could have walked them blindfolded.

All of a sudden the vendors, as though alerted by a sixth sense, gathered at one of the entrances. Those reselling to the kiosk owners moved off in silence, their heads sinking into their shoulders under the weight of the bundles they had to deliver. The news vendors scattered, brandishing papers in the air and crying out the headlines:

'*La Patrie*! Court in session!'

'*Le Passe-partout*! Special Sunday edition on Noémi Gerfleur murder!'

'*Le Petit Parisien*! Gruesome death of zoo keeper!'

Clerk and labourer alike devoured this fodder on their way to work, which was as vital to their nourishment as Euphrosine Pignot's wares. Bicycles insistently tooting their horns cleared the way for the horse-drawn carts that distributed the manna at the railway stations in bundles tied up with string.

As the hubbub died down, Joseph spotted a familiar figure loading the previous day's unsold newspapers on to a cart.

'Marsouin!' he shouted.

'Pignouf!' replied the other man.

This had been their rallying cry in the days when they had walked the city's streets together. Marcel Bichonnier, a tall, hefty young man with a slight squint, greeted his old companion with open arms. Joseph, afraid he would be smothered, kept him at arm's length.

'I was hoping I might find you here. Are you working for your father?'

'The old man has gone to join his ancestors, and I've taken over the running of the factory. Now it's "Bichonnier, suppliers of confetti and paper decorations". And I've branched out. We do streamers and penny whistles now, and we're about to launch a new range of lanterns and paper windmills. And how about you?'

'Oh! I'm still at the bookshop and I'm working on a project, a novel, that'll set all Paris atremble. But it is early days yet; let's not count our chickens . . . Actually, that's why I came to see you. I need some information. You wouldn't happen to have any newspapers from 1886?'

'Do you suppose I remember the exact years? Why not the dates too while you're at it! We keep piles of old papers in the warehouses as well as some loose pages in case we need to stretch the pulp. But they're not all in order. You'll be a lucky devil if you find what you're looking for. You never know, though. Climb aboard, if you don't mind being shaken about a bit. My mare goes like the clappers so hold on tight! Gee up, Finette! Are you sitting comfortably, Pignouf? You're about to meet my lady wife.'

'You're married!' exclaimed Joseph, not without a hint of envy.

'Have been for two years. And I've got a son and heir: little Émile. If you think you're going to wriggle out of having a slap up meal, you're mistaken. My Caroline does an excellent leg of roast lamb on a Sunday!'

As they rode up Rue du Sentier, Joseph imagined himself sitting opposite a faceless assassin who stood over a sizzling joint of meat, sharpening his knife.

Victor, his hands warmed by the fresh croissants, was resisting the temptation to put one in his bag for later, when he looked over at a kiosk and saw the headline on an illustrated supplement of *Le Petit Parisien*:

ZOO KEEPER MAULED BY LION

He bought the paper and devoured the article:

On Thursday evening, after closing time, one of the keepers at the Botanical Gardens, Basile Popêche, 56, was mauled and fatally injured by a lion in his charge. Basile's colleagues found him lying in a pool of blood. He was taken to the Hôpital de le Pitié, where he died from his wounds this morning. How did the man come to be locked in the cage . . .

That name, Basile Popêche, he knew it from somewhere. He

raced back to the studio, where Tasha, dressed in a plain black taffeta blouse and skirt, was setting out cups on the table.

'Tea or coffee?' she asked.

'Mm,' he mumbled, frantically leafing through the notebook he had found at the bottom of a bag stuffed with his belongings.

There it was! In his handwriting, dated *Friday 13 November*:

Basile Popêche, lion house at Botanical Gardens, Grégoire Mercier's cousin.

'Well, I'll be damned!' he cried.

'What is it?'

'Er . . . nothing, I've just remembered I have to be at the bookshop.'

'On a Sunday?'

'Yes. It completely slipped my mind. The Comtesse de Salignac is supposed to come by the shop and pick up a book today. She didn't say what time, but I don't want to upset her by not being there.'

What was he concealing from her? Was it something to do with that girl he was putting up? The siren from England who had seduced Kenji? Had she put her claws into Victor too? Tasha was not naturally jealous, but she felt wounded; how could he run off like that using such a flimsy excuse? They had planned to open a celebratory bottle of Champagne in the hairdressing salon, and now he was leaving!

'You haven't answered my question, so you'll have to make

do with tea. I didn't know the Comtesse had such a hold over you,' she said coldly as she filled the kettle.

'I'm sorry, darling, tea would be lovely.'

She relaxed. She had no desire to become like him, suspicious and jealous if she excluded him from her plans for half an hour. In any case, she did not think there was another woman. No, his sudden departure had something to do with what was written in his notebook. Dolbreuse's hints at Le Chat-Noir and later at her studio had aroused her suspicions, and now she was convinced: Victor was working on another case. But what was it? Could it be connected to the spate of grisly murders that were splattered all over the headlines at the moment? Or was it something completely innocuous? Of course, he wouldn't put her in the picture until it was all over, regardless of whether she was worrying sick and tearing her hair out at the thought of him being in danger! She was on the point of questioning him, but he was eating his croissant with such gusto and looking at her so sweetly and innocently that she realised she would need to use all her guile if she were to get anything out of him.

'What a shame. It's so rare that we're both free at the same time . . .'

'It'll only take up part of the morning!'

'That's not what you said. You said that the battleaxe . . .'

'Oh no! Not you as well as Jojo! Kenji is there, so if she doesn't show up this morning I'll ask him to deal with her this afternoon.'

'Admit it. You're scared she'll have a fit if her darling bookseller isn't there.'

'To hell with the battle . . . I mean with Madame de Salignac! I prefer your company a hundred times.'

'And I prefer yours a thousand times, so I win!'

As soon as Joseph set eyes on Caroline Bichonnier, a brunette with a turned up nose, he felt as if he had known her all his life. She welcomed him as a friend, told him how often she had listened to Marcel's tales of their youthful antics, then obliged him to go into ecstasies over a bundle of bedclothes with the bald head of a chubby sleeping baby protruding from it.

According to Madame Bichonnier, their location on Rue de Chaligny between Hôpital Sainte-Antoine and the Reuilly fire station was heaven-sent: if there were a fire, they'd have doctors on one side and the fire brigade on the other.

Notwithstanding how kindly disposed Joseph felt towards Marcel's wife, he declined a tour of the house, which abutted the factory and its adjoining warehouses. But he could not wriggle out of being shown the property's luxury feature – a modern sanitation system, and the vats filled with a colourless magma, the smell of which made him nauseous.

'Plug your nose if you find it too overpowering. It's the chlorine; it makes me feel sick too! We use it to bleach the pulp, then we mix in the colours – green, yellow, red – and make cheap and cheerful decorations for parties. I go on at Marcel about branching out, making masks and hats for Mardi Gras and carnival. But he's like a bear with a sore head at the moment; he's got all the Christmas orders to do. I'd appreciate it if you could work on him for me.'

Joseph promised he would champion the masks, and in return received a double helping of lamb and spinach and a large slice of mocha cake, which he had difficulty finishing.

At last he and Marcel took their leave of Caroline, who said she had to see to the baby, and went to have coffee with three of the factory workers, whose job was to sort the newspapers for shredding.

'Père Théophile, you wouldn't happen to know where my friend here might find newspapers from 1886?' Marcel enquired of a burly fellow who, despite his greying hair, still looked as strong as an ox.

'Well, if there are any, they'll be in the second warehouse, but he'll have to dig deep. Your father stored the rejects there – the newspapers he picked up for a song because they were badly paginated or damaged. There should be some left over, but I can't guarantee it,' he added, turning to Joseph. 'He passed away in '87, so if I were you I'd take a ladder and start on the tops of the piles. With any luck you'll find what you're looking for first off. Otherwise you might find it a strain on your back.'

Jojo refrained from answering that his back was already aching from the weight of his full belly.

His heart sank when he saw the towering wall of paper that made his collection look like an anthill. But when he considered what was at stake, and how a successful outcome to the case would not only provide inspiration for his novel but cause Iris to fall into his arms, he stepped on to the bottom rung of the rickety old ladder.

He was in his shirtsleeves and, despite the cold, sweating copiously after three hours of unstinting effort. He attacked another stack of papers, which he had painstakingly excavated from the wall. Amongst them were odd copies of *L'Illustration*, *Le Petit Journal*, *Le Monde Illusté*, *Le Gaulois*, *Le Siècle*, *Le Figaro* and twenty other publications. Faced with this sea of words, that was powerless to change people's destinies, he began to think that Iris might be right. By what twist of fate had Monsieur Bichonnier senior failed to buy a single newspaper from November 1886, when all the other months in that year were present and correct? Then he spotted a colour illustration of a woman in a dark coat, her face hidden under a veiled hat, clutching a set of jewels in her gloved hand. She was standing beside the counter in a jeweller's shop – the name of which was printed backwards on the window – looking at a chubby man who was showing her a case containing a diamond necklace. Underneath the picture was the caption:

STILL NO CLUE AS TO THE WHEREABOUTS OF THE BARONESS OF SAINT-MESLIN

And further down:

What has become of Prosper Charmansat? Where are the jewels?

His heart pounding, Joseph checked the date on the colour supplement of *Le Petit Journal:* 20 November 1886. He opened it.

The story behind the picture. For four days now the whereabouts of . . .

He read through the brief article carefully, overjoyed at

having found the key to the mystery. Turning to the back page for the continuation, he discovered to his horror that it wasn't there. Cursing his luck, he glanced up the wall of paper. It would take him at least a year to find it, like looking for a needle in a haystack! It was a task worthy of Hercules!

'It's too bad! This will have to do. We should be happy – at least now we know the name of the murderer and his motive for the killings!'

'Come back here, you ninnies!'

Grégoire Mercier was charging down the street after his panic-stricken goats. Berlaud, who had been keeping a close watch over them, had nevertheless failed to notice a brigand attempting to snatch Pervenche. While the goatherd was busy threatening the thief with his steel-tipped cane, his animals had taken flight.

He finally caught up with them at the entrance to Rue des Reculettes, where the excited neighbours gathered round and fired him with questions. Berlaud took advantage of the diversion and slunk into the building, though not without his master noticing.

'If that old bandit's eyesight goes the same way as his sense of smell, my business will go to the dogs!' he complained to Mère Guédon. 'I'll end up a beggar in a hospital bed, surrounded by drudges and idlers!'

'Don't be such a pessimist. There's a gentleman over there who wants to talk to you,' she said, pointing at Victor who was leaning up against a fence.

Grégoire Mercier whistled for his dog, who re-emerged, head bowed.

'Good day to you, Monsieur Leblanc.'

'It's Legris, actually.'

'Oh! What a to-do! I should have stayed on the farm in the Beauce, growing oats and wheat. Only the big city lights lured me away, didn't they? When you're young you dream of having money in your pocket, so you pack your bag and learn another trade and the years go by and those bright lights end up burning your wings . . . My dog is fast becoming a worthless old scavenger and in a few years I'll be put out to pasture . . . When I'm finished you city-folk won't feed me or my animals!'

'Forgive me for bothering you,' Victor interrupted him, keen to call a halt to the goatherd's grievances. 'I wanted to ask about your cousin . . .'

Grégoire Mercier's face froze in dismay, and he forgot his own troubles.

'You know about it then,' he whispered. 'It's terrible, poor Basile . . .'

'Did you see him again before he . . .'

'In a manner of speaking. Imagine! Being torn limb from limb, like in the days of the Commune! He managed to tell me with his dying breath that it was no accident.'

'What did he say?'

'He was doing the rounds at closing time when he noticed that the youngest lion, Scipion, hadn't eaten his meat and was spinning round faster than a weathervane. He went straight into the cage and what did he find? A dart in the animal's rump! And when he turned to leave, the cage door slammed shut! Then he saw the road sweeper and knew he'd clapped eyes on him before. It was around midnight on the twelfth of the month. The man was wearing a grey coat and he was trailing the tenant from the flat below. Basile was leaning out of his window taking the air and the fellow looked up and saw him. And you wouldn't believe this, but it was Basile who later fished the tenant out of a wine barrel.'

'Gaston Molina,' Victor breathed.

'But before he could say "knife", the man dressed as a road sweeper, who was the man in grey, threw a second dart at the lion, which roared in pain and pounced on poor Basile . . .'

Grégoire lifted his hands to his face.

'I am terribly sorry,' Victor said softly. 'Have you said anything to the police?'

'Don't you consider I have enough troubles? Holy Virgin! They're too fond of killing humble folk. No. Basile has left this wretched earth and no policeman can bring him back!'

'I shall say nothing to them either, I promise. Oh! There was one other thing. Where did your cousin live?'

'Number 4, Rue Linné. Come along, Berlaud, back to the stables. We've earned our crust, now let's go and enjoy it!'

Victor was kicking himself for not having guessed the meaning of Rue L. gf 1211. It was as obvious as a rebus when you've sneaked a look at the answer. Rue Linné, ground floor flat 12 November. Child's play!

He hesitated over what to do next. Should he knock on all

the doors of the drab building only a stone's throw from where he was now? That was the surest way to arouse people's suspicions. He decided on a method he had used before.

The concierge shuffled to the door and his bull-dog face peered out at Victor.

'I'm from the police,' said Victor sharply, prepared to invent an excuse if the man asked for proof of his identity.

'Oh! If it's about Monsieur Popêche, the tenant on the first floor, your colleagues have already been here pestering me. He had no family, except for a distant cousin who is from the same region, near Chartres. The problem is I've never clapped eyes on him and I don't know his name or where he lives. I can't tell you any more. It's sad, but there you are – if you work with wild animals, you take risks.'

'I didn't come here about him.'

'Oh! Is it on account of old Sédillot then? He promised me he wouldn't do it again,' sighed the concierge. 'But what can you expect? It can't be much fun living like a hermit in that room. He's bored out of his brains and he finds it amusing.'

'May I come in?'

'Be my guest. Only you'll have to excuse the mess. Antoinette was the perfect housewife, but since she left me I've let the place go and it's a pigsty.'

He ushered Victor into a narrow, airless room stuffed with reproduction Empire furniture that was piled high with dirty plates and clothes. He tipped up a seat, brushed off the crumbs and offered it to Victor while plonking himself down on a stool in front of a bottle of red and a greasy glass.

'You're not going to arrest him, are you?'

'No, I just wanted to find out what the actual charge was; a routine enquiry.'

'All right then. He's a malicious old man who sees no harm in spitting at passers-by all day long. He's got bats in the belfry since he was run over by a milk cart, and he hasn't a soul in the world. I take him his vittles, and it leaves me out of pocket. Luckily he owns his flat, but apart from that he's skint.'

'Don't worry. I'll try to smooth things over with the neighbours on the ground floor.'

'And who might they be?'

Victor immediately regretted having spoken too soon. How would he extricate himself?

'Somebody in this block claims to have taken a direct hit on the back of the head.'

'And you say they live on the ground floor? Well, it can't have been Mademoiselle Bugne because she's visiting her sick mother in Dijon. And the others didn't arrive home until late in the evening, when Sédillot would have been in bed.'

'If they made it up, they'll be in trouble. Are they tenants?'

'Yes. There were three rooms to let and a man calling himself Duval came and paid two months in advance, thank you very much! That was mid-September. "It's for my daughter and son-in-law," he said. "They're from Montargis and want to have a place to stay when they come to Paris."'

'What did this Duval look like? Square beard, bald, stout, blue eyes?'

'I couldn't tell you, my friend. It was Antoinette who dealt with him. All she told me was that the man paid up. The next day she cleared off, leaving a laundry ticket and three jars of her sister's homemade plum jam. They're in the kitchen right where she left them. Life's wicked. You fall in love with someone, live with them and see yourselves growing old together and then one fine morning you wake up alone in a cold bed.'

He filled his glass to the brim and took a swig.

'I comfort myself with the juice of the grape. It helps me pass the time until Antoinette returns. Because she will come back, I know she will. A little voice keeps telling me. I hear it all the time in here, echoing,' he said, tapping his head.

'Could you describe Monsieur Duval's daughter and son-in-law to me,' Victor persisted, 'so that I may identify them correctly as the plaintiffs?'

'I'm afraid I can't help you. On the two occasions I opened the door for them I had such a blinding headache I was nearly out for the count, and the next day they were gone. They never open their shutters. But they've paid their rent, haven't they? The landlord's happy and he owns two-thirds of these apartments. I am not here to spy on people. That's your job, which takes us back to old Sédillot. The best thing would be to put bars on his windows so he can't lean out. If you want to talk to him, I'll have to warn him first or you might get a gob!'

'No, no, leave it. I'll try to play the thing down to my superiors.'

The concierge accompanied him out to the street, and as Victor was walking away the man cried out: 'You're not bad for a *flic*! Do you like plums? I'd be only too glad to give you my jam.'

*

The studio was like a little island of contentment. The pleasant fug made Victor drowsy as he lounged in his underwear in the alcove, watching Tasha languorously brushing her hair. She often put her hair up after their love-making, and then he would have the pleasure of untying it again. Their leisurely afternoon had washed away all thoughts of Popêche's death and Charmansat's presence at Rue Linné. What had most troubled him about the concierge's story, making him hurry back to Tasha with an urgent need to whisper words of love in her ear, was the image of Antoinette flying away one fine morning leaving three pots of jam. Their passion aroused, they gave up the idea of a walk followed by a meal at a grand restaurant. Victor apologised for his childish behaviour of the past few days, and solemnly promised to be jealous no more. Behind her pretence of amusement and scepticism, Tasha was deeply moved, and Victor went up in her esteem. They had tea and bread and butter, playing at tea parties, like a couple of children. Tasha felt relaxed enough to show Victor the canvas she had been working on. Not wishing to discourage her, Victor feigned admiration. Perhaps later on he might allow himself to make a couple of suggestions. And yet, he didn't feel within his rights to give advice, since he hated it when anyone criticised his photographs.

There was a scratching noise at the door. He sat up.

'Are you expecting someone?' he asked Tasha, who had turned round to face him, her brush suspended in the air.

She shook her head. He groaned, pulled on a dressing gown and went to open the door a crack.

'What on earth are you doing here? Is something wrong?'

'No, Boss. I mean, yes, Boss. I know who did it!'

Victor was about to push Joseph back outside when Tasha, who had followed him over, cried out: 'Don't stay out there. You'll catch your death!'

The two men stood in awkward silence beside the stove as she fluttered around them, preparing a snack for Joseph.

'Here you are,' she said, setting down a platter of bread, cheese and wine on a chair for him, 'that'll fortify you.'

Suppressing her desire to listen in to their conversation, Tasha engrossed herself in a novel, leaving Jojo and Victor at liberty to speak in hushed tones.

'Honestly! You might have chosen a better time and place!' hissed Victor.

'When you hear what I have to tell you, you'll agree it was urgent, Boss. Now we know there's no time to lose.'

'Now we know. Now we know. You keep saying that!'

'And it's true. I spent the whole day breaking my back trying to find a newspaper from 1886. Don't concern yourself about the state of my health, though; I'm only starving, freezing and cross-eyed from reading, regardless of which I've brought you printed evidence of . . .'

'All right, have a bite to eat and pass me the newspaper – discreetly.'

Offended, Joseph opened the newspaper as noisily as he could and Victor, worried Tasha might see him, grabbed it from him and turned away.

Lyon, 20 November 1886
For four days now the whereabouts of Monsieur Prosper

Charmansat, a jeweller from Place Bellecour, has been unknown. His assistant reported his disappearance last Thursday. Monsieur Charmansat left the shop that morning in the company of a customer, Baroness Saint-Meslin, with the intention of showing her husband some precious jewels. There has been no sign of him since. So far the police have mounted an unsuccessful search for Baroness Saint-Meslin.

'Isn't Saint-Meslin the name on the card you picked up in La Gerfleur's dressing room?' whispered Joseph, who was reading over his shoulder.

According to the assistant the lady owns a house named Les Asphodèles somewhere in the Lyon area. The jewels in Monsieur Charmansat's possession are worth half a million francs. The police heading the investigation claim that no one in Lyon has ever heard of this mysterious Bar—

The article ended there. Frustrated, yet pleased with this new information, Victor stared at the palm tree, imagining he saw floating in its fronds a frieze of protagonists. This Baroness robbed a jeweller named Prosper Charmansat in Lyon in 1886. Five years later, the vengeful jeweller, now an employee at the pawnshop in Paris, comes across the woman who fleeced him at the L'Eldorado in the person of Noémi Fourchon, alias Noémi Gerfleur, the singer. After murdering her daughter, Élisa, he kills her, no doubt with the aid of Gaston Molina, a crook known to the police in Lyon. Fearing betrayal at the hands of this swindler, Charmansat bumps him off and conceals his body in a barrel at the wine market before proceeding to silence another witness, Basile Popêche, who was a tenant at the same address, 4 Rue Linné.

He gave an account of his reasoning to Joseph who hung on every word.

'Well, Boss, it looks like you've unveiled the truth. Bravo!' he said, his mouth stuffed with food.

'There's just one snag. What part does this Doctor Aubertot, mentioned in the note from Le Moulin-Rouge, play in all this?'

'Possibly none; I mean, that scrap of paper might have no bearing on the case at all.'

'We cannot just ignore a piece of evidence. I shall pay him a visit tomorrow morning. Here, take a cab and go home to bed. I'll drop in at the bookshop before lunch tomorrow to let you know of any progress. We can discuss where to go from there. If Monsieur Mori asks where I am, tell him I've gone to do an evaluation.'

'Yes, Boss!' said Joseph, pocketing the banknote. 'Goodnight, Madame Tasha!'

'Goodnight, Jojo!'

Victor turned to her, yawning.

'That boy wears me out, coming here to pester me about buying bookshelves!'

'You seemed rather absorbed – just like a couple of conspirators cooking up some dastardly plot. It had all the elements: whispering, averted eyes, notes changing hands in secret. Are you sure you aren't hiding anything from me?'

'No, my darling, I assure you I'm not.'

'Because if I discover that you've been involved and the police question me I shall have to put on an act and that's not my forte.'

'The police? Why would the police want to stick their nose in my business? I'm not dealing in stolen goods, I promise.'

'Be careful you don't perjure yourself, my love,' she whispered, pressing her body against his.

They tried to outstare one another, Victor wearing an expression of pure innocence that broke down under her insistent gaze. He lowered his eyes and, embarrassed by her victory, she stood up to put out the light.

CHAPTER 12

VICTOR asked the cabman to drop him off at Rue Linné, where he battled against the wind and rain that had transformed the morning into dusk. He wanted to have another peek at the building where Père Popêche, Gaston Molina and Élisa had all stayed. As he walked past the semi-detached house – the side wall of which was adorned with a painted advertisement for *Le Balnéum, Turco-Roman Baths* – he reflected on the proximity of the places where, as on a chessboard, the pawns of his investigation were laid out:

Rue Linné, Botanical Gardens, Hôpital de la Piété: Basile Pôpeche.
Wine market: Molina's corpse.
Impasse de Bœufs: Prosper Charmansat.
Hospice de la Salpêtrière and Rue Monge: Doctor Aubertot.

All seven squares were situated in the eastern part of the fifth arrondissement.

Without knowing how he got there, he found himself in Rue Geoffroy-Saint-Hilaire. The gusty wind had been replaced by icy rain. He felt disheartened. He was well acquainted with the cycle that seemed to mark out human existence: the euphoria when an idea first occurs, followed by anxiety and misgivings. He carried on walking, his mind blank. He had the impression of being in a provincial town where, other than a handful of visitors bringing an orange or some brioche to the patients inside the bleak walls of the Hôpital Pitié, passers-by were a rare sight. The shops waited for their regular customers to rouse them from their lethargy. Indeed, the whole neighbourhood, largely inhabited by men of independent means, teachers and museum curators, had a sleepy feel, as though it had been placed under a spell, which the distant trumpeting of an elephant or the repetitive cry of a peacock could not break.

Servants carrying shopping, safe from the rain under their broad umbrellas, hurried past nannies walking arm in arm with soldiers. Pedestrians waited impatiently for the Glacière omnibus to go past before venturing across the slippery road. It occurred to Victor that the student hurrying towards him with a shabby briefcase under his arm must tread this same piece of pavement every morning at nine fifteen. He rejoiced at not being a slave to an invisible clock that ruled every minute of his life and, suddenly depressed by the thought, he looked up and found himself in Rue Monge.

The brass plaque advertising the clinic of Doctor Aubertot, psychiatrist at the Hospice de la Salpêtrière, was at number 68. Not without some trepidation, Victor stepped into the hydraulic lift. It was an invention which, unlike Kenji, he did not really care for, though he could see that it was useful. He was let in to the fourth floor apartment by a valet who appeared to be mute. He mumbled his name, and followed the man across a plush carpet that led from an entrance hall hung with dark red fabric, to a Louis XV drawing room that had been turned into a waiting area. A baby grand, an Empire clock and several pieces of medieval furniture broke the harmony of the décor.

Where does this craze for the pseudo-Gothic style come from? Victor wondered, deciding not to sit down on one of the oak choir stalls that ran along two of the walls. He opted instead for a bishop's chair with a latticework back which, despite its embroidered cushion, proved extremely uncomfortable.

Is this meant to give patients a foretaste of the torments to come or make them glad to leave such an unwelcoming place?

Indeed, the trembling old man, the bilious looking fellow with twitchy eyes and the woman bent double with curvature of the spine all sat staring with anticipation at the closed door of the consulting room.

Victor, his back aching and his legs stiff, stood up to avoid getting cramp. A window hung with chiffon curtain revealed a gap between two buildings, through which was a view of the Botanical Gardens, where the imposing cedar, more than one hundred years old, towered like an emperor over the other leafless trees in the maze. Smoke rising from the chimneys of Sainte-Pélagie prison and the Hôpital Pitié fused with the leaden clouds that hung like a menacing blanket above the quietly pulsating city. On the pavement opposite, a baker's boy carrying a basket covered in a white cloth was buffeted by the wind as he darted out of the pâtisserie and headed for the door of a dilapidated building. Victor amused himself by imagining the boy racing up the stairs to an attic room, where a bachelor and former squadron leader stood, watch in hand, awaiting the boy's arrival at ten o'clock sharp. The image saddened him, and he resumed pacing up and down the room, where someone suffering from ataxia had just been wheeled in by a nurse. He picked up a couple of magazines that were lying on an escritoire, but his own thoughts were already too clamorous for him to concentrate. He glanced at the painting above the fireplace: a professor of medicine examining a patient in an amphitheatre packed with medical students. Just as he was reading the caption at the bottom of the frame, a man's voice called out:

'Monsieur Pignot?'

Intrigued by what he had read, he walked into the consulting room. Its bareness was in stark contrast to the cluttered waiting area: a desk strewn with books, three chairs and a few engravings, all with a medical theme. Doctor Aubertot smiled politely and asked him to take a seat. His stern manner and serious expression lent him the air of an office clerk. In fact his face, which was still youthful despite the greying hair, was familiar to Victor, though he could not for the life of him recall where he had seen him before. The doctor took a sheet of paper and dipped his nib in an inkpot.

'First name, surname, date of birth and profession, please.'

'Pignot, Joseph, 14 January 1860, shopkeeper,' Victor stated.

'What are your symptoms?'

'Well, I . . . er, they are difficult to describe, a sort of generalised pain, and . . .'

'Do you suffer from headaches?'

'Sometimes, yes, but . . .'

'Do you feel any pressure around your skull? Do you have pains in your stomach?'

'Yes, especially after a meal.'

The doctor glanced up at him.

'And your sexual function?'

'No problems in that department.'

'Please remove your clothes.'

'Look, I'm afraid I haven't been entirely honest with you,' Victor hastened to explain. 'I'm a journalist and I'm writing a series of articles about people's fascination for certain types of murder. One motive that particularly interests me is vengeance. I would very much like to have a psychiatrist's point of view. However, I imagine you must be terribly busy.'

'And you waste even more of my time with such convoluted preambles! I dabble in journalism myself, and one of the first things I learnt was to be concise!'

He softened and, putting down his pen, went and stood with his back to the window.

'What is it you would like to know? Crime is not my speciality. The patients who come to my clinic seek words of reassurance rather than drugs. What they tell me rarely gives me an insight into the darkest recesses of their psyches. Indeed, they are usually the primary victims of their inner demons.'

'Are any of your patients obsessed with revenge?'

'A string of them, yes, but they rarely act on it.'

'What do you think motivates someone to seek revenge even though it might take years?'

'The conviction that without the intervention of another, their life would have taken a more favourable course, would have flourished instead of being destroyed. The more they suffer, the more they want to punish the person they feel is responsible for their suffering.'

'Is there any other driving force behind this need to punish?'

'A corollary of suffering is hatred – a violent emotion that drives people to destructive acts.'

'What does someone who takes revenge feel? Revenge cannot right the original wrong.'

'No. What is done is done. However, whether or not they seek real or – as is more often the case – fictive vengeance, what they desire is to recover their self-esteem. You have picked a vast subject, my friend, and one that is as dear to novelists as to their readers, a fact that suggests that people fascinated by crime and punishment are legion. From the beginning of time, the world has been governed by the universal law of an eye for an eye, a tooth for a tooth. Whether this is meant to compensate for the shortcomings of human systems of justice or is believed to be God's will, it is an endless cycle. It leads to wars between nations. What can I tell you that you don't already know? If any of my patients were potential murderers, their motives would be too complex to be reduced to some literary cliché such as: "For a Spaniard there is nothing sweeter than revenge." '[28]

He had walked up to his desk, and was leaning over it, drumming his fingers on a medical dictionary. Victor understood that the interview was over.

They crossed the waiting room, watched by the patients, who followed them with their eyes. Victor wanted to be clear in his mind about the painting above the fireplace, and he pointed to it.

'Is that a Gauthier?'

'No, it's by Jaubert, a minor artist. I'm not terribly keen on it, but it's a souvenir of my distant days in Lyon, when I studied under Professor Jardin. I'm the third on the left – the beanpole with the goatee. It was a long time ago now.'

'The Medical Faculty there is reputed to be one of the best.'

'Indeed. If you are interested, you should come to the Sâlpetrière. I lecture there in the amphitheatre on a Wednesday afternoon. You can keep me abreast of your research.'

In the carriage on the way back to Rue des Saints-Pères, the word *Lyon* occupied Victor's thoughts. *Lyon*. Everything was linked to that name, even the animal that had killed Pôpeche. Yet what was the psychiatrist's involvement in this affair? Was it a mere coincidence that he had lived in Lyon? It couldn't be. Aubertot's name appearing alongside Charmansat's on the note found in Gaston Molina's shirt clearly implicated him. He only had to find out how. Victor decided to abandon logic and follow his intuition.

He felt besieged by a flurry of contradictory ideas. As he turned to look out of the window, he noticed a sign that read: *Bill stickers will be prosecuted. Bylaw of 29 July 1881.* Beneath it was a Grasset advertisement for L. Marquet ink. The ornate black lettering reminded him of the big black cat associated with Rodolphe Salis's cabaret. Suddenly he remembered where he had seen Aubertot: at Le Chat-Noir, the day before Noémi Gerfleur's body was discovered.

'I caught a glimpse of the fellow Louis Dolbreuse was talking to – was it Aubertot? Except the name wasn't Aubertot.

No, I must be mistaken. What would a big shot from the Sâlpetrière be doing at a place like Le Chat-Noir? Although he did say he dabbled in journalism . . .'

He remembered seeing a few copies of *L'Écho de Paris* in the waiting room, the journal Dolbreuse had mentioned after his tête-à-tête with this Aubertot who was not Aubertot. What was the name of the man he'd been introduced to? He needed to speak to Dolbreuse, but he didn't know his address. If he asked Tasha, she would immediately accuse him of jealousy. He had better ask Eudoxie Allard. It would mean having to put up with her advances, but he considered the game was worth the candle. She had given him her card and he seemed to recall slipping it into the letter tray where he kept his papers. He must act quickly, though. Aubertot might also suddenly remember having met him at Le Chat-Noir. He got out of the cab at Quai Malaquais.

The bookshop was deserted. Victor was about to go upstairs when he heard the drone of voices at the back of the shop. He crept over quietly. Jojo and Iris were sitting side by side next to the glass cabinet where Kenji kept the books and other objects he brought back from his trips abroad. They were leafing through a volume bound in gold and red that contained risqué illustrations. Standing on tiptoe, Victor was able to read the title of the book upside down: *Dangerous Liaisons*. The choice of book and the behaviour of the two young people suggested an intimacy he felt was inappropriate. How could an educated young lady jeopardise her reputation with a mere clerk in a bookshop!

'Who gave you permission to leave your post?' he barked, so ferociously that Jojo nearly fell on the floor.

Iris stood up calmly.

'What have we done to deserve such a display of bad manners, Captain?' she asked merrily.

Victor realised that his outburst had been completely unwarranted.

'Forgive us, Captain,' she continued in the same unruffled tone, 'we were sailing at a few cables from the coast and as the lookout reported no giant squid or squalls in the offing, we retired to the poop deck. Did we do something wrong, my Admiral?'

Irritated by this impudent mockery, Victor snapped rudely at Joseph.

'Did you hear me? What are we paying you for? Get back to your post!'

He looked sternly at Iris and muttered: 'Is Kenji here?'

'No, he went to see a customer.'

'There's another good reason why you should not be here alone. In your godfather's absence it falls to me to look after you.'

'I was in pleasant company.'

'That is precisely the problem. Be careful not to cross the line, Mademoiselle.'

Aware of how ridiculous he must appear, he turned on his heel and walked over to the stairs, trying his best to ignore Joseph's grumbling.

'Back to your post! Back to your post! He's never at his post! The ship could be sinking and he wouldn't even know it! And what about liberty! And equality! Liberty, equality, fraternity, my eye! They might be carved on our monuments, but not everybody enjoys them in equal measure. A fellow would be lucky to receive any sort of justice in this place!'

Victor rummaged furiously through the letter tray, but stopped suddenly, troubled by a tune that was coming from behind him. He turned around. Iris was nodding her head in time to the music and swinging a chain. On the end of it hung the watch Victor had given Kenji for his birthday two years earlier.

> *London Bridge is falling down,*
> *falling down, falling down . . .*

'It's pretty, isn't it? It plays this tune I grew up with every hour. It belonged to your father, then your mother and then it passed down to you.'

'I . . . but . . .'

'How unfortunate! A detective without a clue! Did you never wonder what happened to the Aunt Gloria whom Daphné visited three afternoons a week?'

'How do you know about that?'

His hands were trembling and he pushed them into his pockets. He could see his mother leaning towards him, feel her lips brushing his brow, hear her whispering goodbye before she left him in Kenji's charge. He remembered, too, the letters he received at his boarding school in Richmond with tedious passages concerning the fragile health of a relative who lived in Hampshire: a Miss Gloria Dulwich.

'She died soon after I moved to France, sometime in 1879, shortly after the death of my mother,' he said softly, without waiting for a reply. 'Kenji told me about it.'

'No doubt he didn't go into any detail.'

'What is this all about?'

'When I was little I lived in a pretty cottage not far from Winchester. My nanny, whom I adored, was called Gloria. She was from Dulwich, near London, and was very proud of having visited The Crystal Palace which, you are doubtless aware, was built with materials left over from the first Universal Exhibition in 1851.'

'Gloria Dulwich,' he repeated in a faltering voice.

'Three times a week, a beautiful lady visited and showered me with love and treats. But what gave me most pleasure was her watch. I used to put it up to my ear and imagine that the fairies were ringing their little bells inside it just for me. When I was four years old the beautiful lady suddenly stopped coming. Gloria held me tight and told me that my mother was dead, but that I shouldn't cry because she had gone to the angels. After that an elegant gentleman with slanting eyes came into my life, declaring that he was my godfather. The little fairies watched over me and I have never felt unloved. When Gloria went to join my mother, Kenji sent me to Dawson's Boarding School in London under the name of Abbot. I suppose he wished to conceal my origins.'

Victor stared at her in dazed astonishment.

'She's taking you in, my dear Legris!'

But the voice of another, more sardonic, Victor said: 'What a chump! He looks like a carp standing there with his mouth open.'

'Are you trying to tell me that you are my . . .'

'I apologise if this feels like melodrama. I meant to break the news to you more gently, but your moralising tone just now infuriated me. I am happy to have a brother and for you to be him, but I am tired of being chaperoned. First Mrs Dawson, then Mademoiselle Bontemps, then Kenji, and now you.'

'How can you be sure that Daphné was your . . .'

'I found the proof in two sealed envelopes hidden beneath my father's mattress. Do you know what was in them?'

'No,' Victor replied, stunned by the girl's inappropriate behaviour. 'I would never have allowed myself go through Kenji's personal belongings.'

'I am far more devious than you. When I set myself a goal I reach it. The envelopes contain my birth certificate, a photograph of Daphné holding me in her arms and my baptism certificate according to the rites of the Anglican Church.'

He found himself staring straight into the girl's face. She was deadly serious. He must adjust himself to the idea that Kenji and his mother had been lovers. Without averting her gaze, she continued.

'It is simple. Daphné made Kenji promise not to say anything for fear of a scandal and out of respect for you, since you were old enough to judge her behaviour. You were fourteen when I was born. If we were to examine our mother's life closely, we would discover that she disappeared for four months in 1874 – the time needed to carry her pregnancy to full

246

term. She wanted to protect you. Imagine how much Kenji must have loved her to keep this a secret for so long . . . After the stupid coach accident that killed his beloved, he was obliged to hide his grief and resign himself to lying . . . by omission. My godfather! I played the game, and, believe it or not, I shall miss it.'

'He sacrificed you for a child who wasn't even his . . . How he must have hated me!'

'That's not true. He has a deep affection for you.'

'And for you!'

'Of course, though we have always lived apart. It was hard for him. He has suffered with his secret and he needs to be comforted. As far as I am concerned, I am delighted to have a brother, although I would have preferred him to be a little less possessive and puritanical. Speaking of which, Joseph and I were doing nothing wrong. I find him charming. You should try to be a little more flexible, Victor. Am I wrong in thinking Tasha might disapprove of your sleuthing activities vis-à-vis a certain young girl in red?'

'What do you know about it?'

'I'm not blind, and Kenji's anxiety, your interrogation of me and my sudden move here to Rue des Saints-Pères confirmed my suspicions. And I read the newspapers too. Poor Élisa, she wanted a passionate love affair. I hope you find whoever did this to her. Nobody but you knows that I know.'

He felt utterly confused and incredulous. His head spun with the effort of trying to make sense of Iris's words. His mother and Kenji . . . The idea was grotesque. The girl was making it up! What had triggered their conversation? Oh yes, the watch.

'Did Kenji show you the watch . . .'

'No. He leaves it on his bedside table every night, and this morning I took it. When I wound it up it played that tune . . .'

Iris was smiling through her tears. Overcome, Victor rushed outside.

He walked very briskly down Rue des Saints-Pères in an attempt to absorb these revelations. When he reached the corner of Rue Jacob he realised he had forgotten his coat; the feeling that his brain was close to boiling point was intensified by a sudden burst of sunlight that warmed the air. He turned back, mulling over his gnawing resentment. Kenji had kept the truth from him all this time! If he had known sooner, would he have reacted positively? He couldn't say for sure. He was torn between his admiration for his adoptive father's stoicism and a cold rage at his oriental insistence on conforming to strict codes of honour. But then his newfound affection for this deceptively fragile sister of his, who had made plain her feelings for him, won him over. He knew he must talk to Kenji. It was a positive, crucial decision and one that would help allay his doubts. And yet he dreaded such a conversation, because the thought of it made him feel like the defenceless, frightened little boy he had been in Sloane Square.

'What should I say to him? Let's shake on it and start afresh?'

He felt irritated by his own weakness. The voice of a man with a hint of an English accent echoed in his head:

'My love. I have found him. You'll understand. You must . . . follow your instinct. You can be reborn if you break the chain.'

Why had he remembered these words now? They had been

spoken in a trance by an English medium called Numa Winner[29] he had met the year before. Had Daphné really spoken to him through this man? Had she been trying to tell him about her secret love for Kenji? Whether she had or not, he could use it to break through Kenji's shell and make him confess, for despite his pragmatism he believed in the spirits of the dead and messages from beyond the grave.

Joseph was leaning against the counter, his arms behind his back, like the martyred St Sebastian. Victor coughed, shifted some books around and smoothed out a magazine with the flat of his hand. No response. St Sebastian held his pose.

'I really am sorry, Joseph. I apologise.'

The assistant stiffened, his face sullen.

'Well, I am not going to go down on my knees! I was wrong, I admit it!'

'You ordered me to return to my post and here I am,' retorted Joseph.

'Oh for goodness' sake, let it go now! Where is Mademoiselle Iris?'

'She's still upstairs.'

'She likes you a lot.'

'And I suppose that comes as a surprise.'

'Not in the slightest. I'm sure you are a perfect gentleman. She needs . . . looking after.'

Joseph relaxed, trying to conceal his pleasure.

'She need have no fear. I am a gentleman. But what about the case, Boss?'

The case! It had gone clean out of his head, and he would gladly have put off thinking about it, but he needed to act quickly before Inspector Lecacheur discovered the trail leading from Noémi Gerfleur to Iris via Corymbe Bontemps, Élisa and Gaston.

'I need to check something important. If Monsieur Mori isn't back by five o'clock, ask Mademoiselle Iris to cover for you, go to the pawnshop and tail Charmansat. I shall be back before closing time.'

'Yes, sir, Boss!' cried the beaming Joseph, standing to attention, his arms straight by his side.

A skinny maid showed Victor to the drawing room. He gave her a friendly smile that sent her scurrying away. He stood waiting amidst a profusion of house plants that eclipsed the mahogany furniture and velvet armchairs. A bearskin rug draped over a chaise longue brought a smile to his lips: Antonin Clusel had been right, Fifi Bas-Rhin had, it seemed, managed to seduce a grand duke. A silvery glint caught his eye. He was intrigued to see a cane lying on the bearskin. He immediately recognised the jade handle carved in the shape of a horse's head with inlaid peridots for eyes: It was Kenji's! He was about to beat a hasty retreat when Eudoxie wafted in, wearing a pink silk negligee.

'My favourite bookseller! What a fool that girl is — she didn't even bother giving me your name!'

He stooped to kiss her hand and glancing towards the bedroom door, which was ajar, glimpsed a mauve silk cravat and a black pinstriped frock coat. There was no doubting they were Kenji's. Victor imagined an extraordinary scenario. He would pretend to be shocked and rush to the bed, declaring that the daughter of this wicked man in a state of undress was in need of her father's help. By the time he had regained his composure, the cane had disappeared and Eudoxie was making a show of polishing the leaves of a rubber plant with her negligée.

'Servants aren't what they used to be. What can I do for you?' she asked, walking over to close the bedroom door.

'I want to find Louis Dolbreuse. I was under the impression you were close friends when we met the other night at Le Moulin-Rouge. I imagined . . .'

'That you might drive him out from between my sheets?'

'That you might be able to give me his address. He suggested I might be interested in writing for an editor he knows at *L'Écho de Paris,* and I wanted to tell him that I am.'

'Oh! Is that all! I thought you might be concerned about my fidelity!'

'My dear Eudoxie, I would not be so presumptuous as to interfere in the complexities of your intimate relationships,' replied Victor, pretending to be fascinated by the cane that was hidden behind the rubber plant.

'Just as well, you naughty boy, for there are some secrets that should never be revealed.'

She placed herself between him and the plant, baring her neck and forcing him to step back.

'I'm willing to please you . . . and to give you that address. Here it is. I rely upon you to be discreet. Louis is a charming man, but a little hot-tempered.'

'Have no fear. Neither he nor anyone else will get wind of your . . . secret.'

She looked at him a trifle anxiously and rang for the maid.

The clamour of traffic on Rue de Rivoli penetrated the fog of his thoughts. No sooner had Iris's confidences revealed an unknown side to Kenji's personality – that of doting father and brilliant schemer – than this image was replaced by that of a shameless womaniser. Who was the true Kenji?

After all, it is partly because of me that he has avoided a formal relationship. It is strange how none of his conquests have anything in common with Daphné . . .

The sound of the cannon blasting in the Jardin du Palais Royal reminded him that it was midday and he was hungry.

Tasha wiped her hands on her smock and stared at the painting before her. It would be best to give up now. She stepped back from the easel. After weeks of effort, this was the disastrous result. She smeared red paint over the tousled figure of a cancan dancer, ripped the canvas off the frame and rolled it up tightly before cramming it into the rubbish bin.

The emphatic gesture calmed her. She was clear in her mind how she would proceed; there were many different approaches but what mattered most were language and style. She crouched on the floor, her chin resting on her knees.

'Yes, painting is a synthesis of all that you have experienced, loved and learnt, which is then transformed into an individual body of work. I should go back to copying the old masters. The best way to discover myself is through them. A few months working at the Louvre would do me good.'

When Victor appeared she leapt to her feet and seized a folder of drawings, which she threw on the bed.

'I have to deliver these to the newspaper before four o'clock. Did you want to talk?'

Victor nodded his head.

'I felt like chatting to you for a moment, Tasha.'

He noticed her drawn look and her pale complexion. He could tell she hadn't been eating properly. She turned away, snatching up her hat so vehemently that the marguerites quivered.

'Do you intend to go out in that?' he asked, pointing to her painted-smeared smock.

'I was about to get changed.'

He noticed that the canvas that had been so important to her was no longer on the easel. He walked over to her, smiling, and registered the uncertainty of her expression, which he understood as an appeal not to mention it. He felt like telling her that he often sensed her despair even when she did not tell him about it, that he could tell she was feeling her way and was held back by self-doubt, and that she had probably forgotten how easy and good it was just to let go. But he did not. Instead he held her in his arms.

'Some men may desire another woman or just for a change a sophisticated seductress,' he murmured. 'But I would go crazy without you. Having you near helps me live in this world, which I find so absurd at times. One thing is certain: I am the only one who really understands you, so trust me: come along, let's make love to each other and take all the time we want.'

She stood for a moment leaning against his chest and then pushed him slowly towards the alcove. Her smock slipped down, exposing her naked body. She remained silent, her head tilted back, her eyes almost closed. She let out a tiny squeal of impatience as he undressed hurriedly. He kissed her throat and her breath quickened. She stared at him through her eyelashes with an expression almost of pain. He laid her down gently. The faint tremor of the bed became a harmonious swaying. They were oblivious to the thunder and the hailstones battering the windowpanes.

Later she said: 'Victor, be careful, it isn't a game. Have you thought about me?'

The rain drummed down on the roof. Victor didn't respond. She waited for a moment.

'Victor, I'm talking to you.'

He sat up and looked at her gravely.

'Has Joseph been talking?'

'Joseph? No! Be wary of us women, my love, we have a sixth sense. In the past, when men left us to go to war we were witches.'

'I'm in no danger, believe me, and I have no intention of going off on any crusades.'

'I'm glad to hear it, darling.'

'Women!' he exclaimed, laughing. 'You'll be the death of us!'

'Don't joke about it, I . . .'

She stopped and began chewing her thumbnail. He had the impression that her words were the beginning of something far more difficult to express. He nestled his head in her auburn hair and pretended to fall asleep.

Joseph was enduring what seemed like an interminable journey on an omnibus, sitting opposite an old lady stuffing herself with marzipan, and bitterly regretting not having partaken of Germaine's roast veal and macaroni with Iris. The apple he had eaten perched like a perfect gentleman on his ladder that morning had not been very big. He sighed, proud to be fulfilling a mission worthy of Monsieur Lecoq, and tried to stop his stomach from rumbling.

Charmansat had taken an omnibus as far as Rue Étienne-Marcel and then caught another headed for Montmartre. The nausea Joseph began to feel as he contemplated the rolls of fat on the back of the man's neck beneath his cropped hair was accentuated by the jolting of the omnibus and the old woman's incessant chewing. He decided to concentrate on the people to his left. A man was reading a newspaper beside a young girl, who sat looking out of the window, her elbows placed on the mahogany armrests. Joseph's malaise grew as he witnessed the surreptitious brushing of the man's trousered leg against the girl's stockinged one. Although both parties seemed unaware of the other's existence, everything pointed to a secret complicity between them, and when the man rose to ring the bell the young girl quickly did likewise. Her seat was immediately occupied by a woman wearing a hat with a veil who held a fidgeting child on her lap.

His head reeling from the rattle of the windowpanes, the

toing and froing of the conductor and the sound of the driver's whip, Joseph dozed, groaning each time the toddler gave him a kick. He woke with a start. The back of Charmansat's neck had disappeared! He turned round in time to see him step off, and just managed to jump off the vehicle himself before it turned into Boulevard Rochechouart.

Joseph stayed close to Charmansat, threading his way along Rue de Steinkerque and into Place Saint-Pierre, where he regretted not being able to buy a bag of *frites* at a stall called The Frites Palace. His stomach rumbling, he walked beside a fence where a row of embroiderers had set up shop. His quarry had begun the ascent of the steps of Rue Foyatier.

Joseph had the impression he was following a monkey as he watched the ease with which the little man climbed the ten flights of steps overlooked by a rotunda ornamented with Florentine arches – the new reservoir on the hill. The sky turned dark and a shower of rain obliged Jojo to turn up his collar. He took no notice of the colossal scaffolding beneath which the votive church of the Sacré-Coeur was growing up like some gargantuan mushroom, but glanced now and then at the fenced off thicket on the side of the hill where a monumental staircase was planned. His only concern was not to be spotted by his prey, or by the murderous thieves he imagined were hiding behind every bush. Euphrosine had read aloud to him from the newspapers about the bloody crimes that occurred in this place after sundown. He had duly cut out the articles and kept them in his notebook for future use in his novels, but he had no desire to put their veracity to the test in person!

He was relieved, then, to leave behind the tangle of dried

shrubs on his right and pursue Charmansat up Rue Gabrielle and into Place du Tertre. At that time of the evening and in such weather, the restaurants offering food, music and dance attracted only a handful of inveterate drinkers. The sky had cleared by the time they reached Rue Mont-Clenis, and Charmansat took advantage of the break in the weather to stand under a washerwoman's awning, push up the brim of his bowler and wipe his brow with his handkerchief. Joseph was obliged to hide behind a section of wall. He felt as though he had been transported to a foreign land, where everything seemed unfamiliar, as though in an oriental fairy story. In the damp gloom, the winding streets with their jagged paving stones looked like stairways cut into the hillsides of a trompe l'œil stage set; six-storey buildings stood next to small shacks with thatched or tin roofs; painters carrying their materials, their easels slung over their shoulders, walked past him, and ragged urchins ran around the courtyards shrieking. His reverie was interrupted as Charmansat moved off again, like a puppet operated by invisible strings. He left Rue du Mont-Cenis, which wound on down towards the flats of Saint-Ouen and Saint-Denis, disappearing into the dusk that echoed with the sound of train whistles, and took a left into Rue Saint-Vincent. Joseph hurried past the corner of Rue des Saules, where the previously named Cabaret des Assassins was now called A Ma Campagne. The last rays of sunlight chased out by the encroaching darkness gave the neighbourhood a surreal atmosphere.

'Where is that rascal taking me? Has he seen me? We seem to be going round in circles!' Joseph muttered as Charmansat turned left again into Rue Girardon. He just managed to glimpse the intersection where Rue Lepic climbed steeply to the windmill at the top of the hill, before plunging into the undergrowth. He found himself in the middle of a village full of lean-tos made from planks of wood filched from the building sites and separated from one another by shrubs and tiny patches of grass. The place was swarming with animals: hens clucking, flea-bitten dogs scratching, rutting toms proclaiming their desire for scrawny she-cats. Virginia creeper grew up the broken, lopsided windowpanes of the shacks, which were clad in cardboard painted with tar, and bristling with makeshift chimney pots – artists' studios, labourers' cottages and brigands' dens.

Charmansat slipped down an alleyway covered in graffiti. Joseph hesitated to follow him, fearing he might be noticed. All of a sudden, he felt a hand on his shoulder and he stifled a scream. It was only an old man in rags with a mop of yellow hair asking for money, who received five coins from a reluctant Joseph.

'Thank you, kind gentleman, you're a good sort. Two sous for bread and three for liquor and the world can continue on its merry way. What are you standing here for? Have you come to see Yellow Melanie?'

'Yellow Melanie?'

'The trollop with the ague who lives down that alleyway. The one your friend went to see.'

To the old man's astonishment Joseph suddenly dived back into the undergrowth. Charmansat was coming back, apparently satisfied at having been given an audience. With a blank look on his face, he continued walking until he reached the winding Rue Caulaincourt where, to the immense relief of his pursuer, normal life resumed its course.

Charmansat stopped and leant against a lamp post. What are you doing now, you rogue? Joseph thought as he hid behind a cart parked next to the pavement. A man wearing a check jacket and a sombrero walked out of number 32 and into a wine bar. He swigged back a glass at the counter while Charmansat, who had hidden in a doorway, waited. In no apparent hurry, the drinker re-emerged and strolled down Rue Caulaincourt. At the corner of Rue Lepic, Charmansat, who was halfway across the road, collided with a passer-by. Joseph, pressed flat against a wall, recognised the man he had followed to the Roman arenas, whom Charmansat had met with in the Église Saint-Étienne-du-Mont. The two men exchanged a few words and went their separate ways. The same dilemma presented itself. Which one should he follow? He decided to stay with Charmansat. He hurtled down Rue de l'Orient, where he caught sight of the bowler and the sombrero again. But his luck soon ran out. Two drunken women burst out of a cheap eating-house next to which a man selling chestnuts had set up his stall. The women hurled insults and struggled, and in their bellicose rage knocked over the brazier. The hot coals, perforated pan and sizzling chestnuts went crashing to the pavement, and the poor stall owner went down on his hands and knees to retrieve his property from underneath the feet of the people attempting to separate the two furies. Caught up in the commotion, Joseph lost sight of his two targets.

'That's done it! Back to square one. Never mind, I've more than enough to report back to the Boss. He'll be happy with me.'

He retraced his steps, deciding to collect some more information on the way. He entered the bar where the man in the check jacket and sombrero had gone to slake his thirst, and ordered a glass of Mariani wine. The photograph of a young drummer boy in uniform pinned behind the counter gave him an idea of how to broach his subject.

'Is that you?' he asked the landlord whose face was lined with wrinkles and who was busy dusting off a row of bottles on a shelf.

'Yes, that's me all right. June 1870 – a proud, eager recruit. That didn't last long. Two months later I was in the battle of Reichstoffen. There are experiences in life we'd prefer not to have had, eh? I kept the drum, in memory of my comrades who never came back.'

'What a strange coincidence. I'm looking for the bugler in my regiment. We met by chance last month. You see I play the trumpet, and he promised to try to get me a job at a local dancehall. I know he lives around here, but I can't for the life of me remember his address.'

'What's his name?'

'Well, in the barracks we called him Pignouf.'

'Describe him. You never know.'

'He wears a sombrero – an eccentric-looking chap.'

'There's no lack of them up here in Montmartre. Anyone would think all the lunatics in the world had decided to congregate here. If that's all you can tell me about him you won't get very far,' said the landlord, a deep furrow creasing his brow.

'Hold on a minute, I've remembered something else: he wears a jacket with a grey and beige check!'

'Oh, I know him! He's a poet, apparently. I find poets . . .
Well, they're all penniless. But this fellow is an exception. He
pays and I respect a customer who pays. So you want me to tell
you here he lives do you? *Nicht Möglich*[30] as the Germans say.
I'm not in the business of telling; I just listen to what people tell
me, and believe you me I've heard a lot of drunken confessions
in my time. However, you're in luck because I happen to know
where your poet works. Go to Le Chat-Noir – a little bird tells
me you'll catch him there.'

Joseph was thankful to catch a yellow omnibus with a red
interior from Rue Damrémont via Rue Caulaincourt all the way
to Rue des Saints-Pères. His legs were especially grateful for the
rest and he told himself that the three mile journey would give
him ample time to prepare the report he would give the Boss the
next day. He did his best to concentrate, but within a few
minutes a wave of tiredness had swept over him, his eyes closed
and the other passengers became a blur. Victor's face was
replaced by that of Iris, and before long he had joined the young
girl in the land of dreams.

CHAPTER 13

Tuesday 24 November

THE lights were blazing in the Temps Perdu, which shone like a beacon through the rain that had cast a gloom over the early morning. The waves of bargemen and mattress makers from Quai Malaquais arriving at the bar took no notice of the fellow in the frock coat and sodden felt hat who sat dripping next to the stove. Victor had leapt out of bed at six o'clock after a fitful sleep plagued by bad dreams, and slipped quietly out of the studio on Rue Fontaine to meet Joseph at the bistro. Two coffees drunk in quick succession had failed to help him clarify his thoughts. The different elements of the case had become entwined in his imagination with Iris's revelations, like two jigsaw puzzles hopelessly jumbled together. The figures of Prosper Charmansat, Doctor Aubertot, Grégoire Mercier and Noémi Gerfleur reached out to other ghostly shadows. He felt a migraine coming on, and had visions of his last dream: a mass of snakes spilling through a crack in a wall writhed over his body and transformed into the thick, ebony and copper coils of Iris and Tasha's hair.

Joseph's arrival interrupted his reverie.

'Well, Boss, talk about a soaking! The only part of me that's dry is my throat. You don't mind moving your things so I can warm myself?'

The landlady, a plump busybody of a woman with a

crumpled dish cloth tucked into her waist, served him a bowl of milky coffee and three slices of bread and butter.

'Why, I know your mother! There's a woman who's worth her salt, bringing up a glutton like you all on her own! Let me know if you need any extra!'

When she had moved away, Joseph muttered between his teeth as he tucked in with gusto, 'I wonder what Maman has been saying about me? What is it, Boss? You've got a sad mug this morning.'

'A little more respect, please, Joseph.'

'What I meant to say is you look tired and peaky this morning. I'm showing concern!'

'I had a bad night. Did you tail him?'

'Did I! Talk about an expedition! My legs are killing me. I'm dead beat. That Charmansat dragged me all the way to Montmartre! We went up the hill and through a maze of streets with hovels worse than the ones at Cours de Miracles. I arrived home at Rue Visconti so late I went to bed without any dinner so as not to wake up Maman and . . .'

'Spare me the details.'

'The Boss *is* in a mood this morning,' Joseph muttered under his breath before continuing.

'. . . and finally my man posted himself outside number 32, Rue Caulaincourt where he waited for . . .'

'Did you say 32 Rue Caulaincourt?' Victor interrupted, perking up.

'Yes.'

'That's the address I was given yesterday! The man who lives there is Louis Dolbreuse.'

'I was unable to discover his identity, but I know he works at Le Chat-Noir.'

'Dolbreuse,' repeated Victor, stirring his teaspoon in his empty cup. 'What part could he play in all this? He knows Aubertot.'

'Is that the Aubertot from Cour Manon? The doctor you traced to the Salpêtrière?'

'He has another name. Dolbreuse used it when he introduced him to me at Le Chat-Noir. Joseph, we're nearly there. Our murderer has connections to the medical world. He threw acid in Élisa's face and strangled Noémi with a piece of gauze.'

'Do you fancy Aubertot as the killer? I'd put my money on Charmansat. He's a shady character.'

'We can only allay our doubts by cornering our suspects and forcing them to give themselves away before there are any more victims. Here's what I think we should do . . .'

By the time Victor arrived at the bookshop, Joseph had had time to open up and sell a limited edition of *Money* – volume eighteen in the *Rougon-Macquart* series – to an admirer of Zola. Kenji looked up from where he was working at his desk and said good morning to Victor, who was frantically leafing through his notebook, his hat still on. He clapped his hand to his forehead.

'Jojo, I've just remembered! You must go and deliver a copy of Ronsard's *Loves* to Salomé de Flavignol straight away, it's urgent.'

'Shall I take a cab?'

Kenji peered over his glasses.

'That boy will ruin us.'

Victor slipped his assistant a banknote and whispered: 'Buy a rose for Tasha too.'

Victor leant on Molière's bust, taking advantage of the empty shop to look at his adoptive father sitting there hunched over his desk.

'Why are you staring at me like that? Are you testing out your powers as a fakir?' murmured Kenji, who disliked being the object of such intense scrutiny.

'Do you believe in life after death?'

'Is this the moment for such a discussion?'

'"My love. I have found him. You'll understand. You must . . . follow your instinct."'

'What has come over you? Are you feverish, perhaps?'

Kenji had put down his pen and swivelled round in his chair.

'You haven't forgotten Madame de Brix's English medium, Numa Winner, have you? I came across him when I was investigating the disappearance of Odette de Valois. Those were his words to me, or rather the words of my deceased mother, relayed to me through him.'

'You're talking nonsense. The man hoodwinked you.'

'I thought so too, at the time. Now I'm not so sure. Answer me truthfully. Did my mother find love with you?'

Had Victor not known Kenji for so long, he would probably have taken his apparent impassiveness at face value. But his sudden pallor and the half-gesture of loosening his tie spoke louder than if he had visibly winced.

'And what if it were so?' Kenji replied defiantly.

'I would be overjoyed.'

'Really?'

'No less than if I were to learn that your daughter is . . . my half-sister.'

This time Kenji was unable to contain his emotion. He pushed back his chair and began pacing up and down between the fireplace and the shop counter.

'She knows and she couldn't stop herself from telling you,' he concluded, gesturing with his chin to the floor above.

'Well!' Victor exclaimed, his expression neutral, 'supposing my mother really did send me a message from the hereafter, you must admit it was rather cryptic. And yet I often think of it. When you confessed to me that you were Iris's father, naturally I noticed a certain resemblance, and . . .'

He stopped mid-sentence at the sound of footsteps on the stair. It was Germaine looking furious, her bun half-undone.

'I'm a slave to no man!' she screeched, waving a packet of meat at them. 'This is a republic and if the food I make isn't good enough for Your Highnesses, I shan't hesitate to go elsewhere and you can go and poison yourselves in some cheap eating-house like Duval's!'

'Come now, Germaine, calm yourself,' breathed Victor, glancing anxiously towards the street.

'I've had enough, Monsieur Legris! You're too fussy!'

'Fussy? Me? Germaine!'

'Don't play the innocent with me. You dine out at the first opportunity! But it's not about you this time. What I'm trying to say is . . . It's your guest, Monsieur Mori.'

'How has Mademoiselle Iris offended you?' Kenji enquired, articulating each syllable.

'Little Miss Fusspot! The defender of lambs! She won't eat them, she says, on account of their being killed too young. Why, she all but called me a cannibal! And yesterday it was the veal she took issue with, and before that the chicken! I was up at the crack of dawn to buy carrots, turnips and onions at the market like a good slave and what do I get in return? A grilling!'

'You're right. It is unacceptable behaviour. I shall plead your case to Iris. In the meantime I suggest you punish her by giving her boiled eggs, and I promise I shall have second helpings of your . . .'

'Of my lamb *Navarin*,' Germaine finished his sentence for him, her voice distinctly mellowed. 'Oh, Monsieur Mori! If it weren't for you, I'd have long since given in my no—'

'Navarre! That's the name I was trying to remember!' exclaimed Victor, dashing through the door.

'You see! It's just like I said, he dines out at the first opportunity!' cried Germaine.

'Where is he off to now, the blighter,' Kenji groaned, furious at being deserted again. 'Just when we were finally going to have a serious conversation.'

'About what?'

He turned round. Germaine was stomping past Iris, who stood at the bottom of the stairs, an enigmatic smile on her face.

Joseph flattened himself against the wall of Le Chat-Noir in an attempt to shelter from the rainstorm. He was relieved to see Victor arrive with an umbrella.

'Sorry I'm so late. Was Tasha at home?'

'Yes, Boss, she was very pleased with the rose.'

Finally their knocking paid off and Bel-Ami, the guard, dressed in a grey smock and holding a feather duster inched open the door warily.

'What do you want?'

'I am a journalist. I've been commissioned to write an article about some of the artists who perform here.'

'We're cleaning; you'll have to come back this evening,' the man muttered, and began to close the door.

'But surely this evening you'll be much too busy for interviews.'

The door swung open.

'Do you want to interview me?'

'Naturally,' Victor assured him.

'Well, in that case, come in, but you'll have to excuse the mess. Last night there was a hell of a rumpus. Some of the gentlemen took it into their heads to play bullfighting and grabbed some wretch off the street. They wrapped him in a towel and took him to the guard's room where they made him sing along . . .'

'Is the uniform you wear to greet your customers genuine?'

'An authentic Swiss Church costume: the cane has a solid silver handle and the halberd cost a fortune.'

'You must cut a dashing figure. I'll wager you dream of treading the boards!' declared Joseph, following Victor's lead.

Bel-Ami struck a pose.

'I am not without talent, or so I've been told. My rendering of "Wilting Flowers" by Monsieur Paul Henrion makes the ladies weep. He began to wail:

> *Poor flowers, that wilt as the day doth end*
> *We two shall be joined for ever my friend*
> *For your dear face . . .*

Joseph's timely fit of coughing and request for a glass of water successfully ended the recital. Bel-Ami cleared his own throat and was about to finish the couplet when Victor tapped him on the shoulder.

'Bravo! Dolbreuse was right. What a marvellous voice you have!'

'Did Monsieur Dolbreuse mention me to you?'

'Yes, and he's not the only one! Oh, by the way, what time will he be here?'

'He didn't turn up yesterday, even though Monsieur Salis made it clear at the beginning that if he wants to become known he must show his face regularly.'

'At the beginning?'

'Monsieur Dolbreuse has only been coming here to recite his poems since late summer. But he's unreliable, and at this rate he's going to lose his place. Poets are ten a penny up here in Montmartre.'

'You appear to know everybody. I'd also like to interview a man called Navarre. I believe he is a writer too.'

'Yes. He spends a lot of time at 16 Rue du Croissant, at the offices of *L'Écho de Paris*.'

'What a mine of information! We shall come back this evening.'

'Monsieur! You didn't tell me the name of your newspaper!'

'*Le Passe-partout!*' cried Joseph.

Rue du Croissant was less busy at this time of day than at dawn. Gigantic rolls of white paper protected by oilcloths stood in the doorways waiting to be turned into printed pages. Joseph's hearty breakfast was now a distant memory, and he would gladly have gobbled up a whole plate of croissants or a couple of apples or even some *frites*, but Victor would not spare him the time. Just as they were approaching number 16, where the offices of *L'Écho de Paris* were located, a fair-haired young man with a monocle and a cigar charged past them.

'Alceste, Alcibiade, Alcide!' Victor muttered to himself and then cried out, 'Alcide Bonvoisin!'

The young man stopped dead in his tracks.

'Monsieur . . . ?'

'Victor Legris, we exchanged a few words at Le Moulin-Rouge. Would you mind awfully if I . . .'

'Yes! I remember you. Wait for me here in reception. I'll be five minutes.'

The fair-haired young man hurried to the end of a corridor that had a large window with a sign above it saying 'Cashier' and hurried back again wearing a look of contentment.

'Forgive me. My column nearly went by the board and with it my dinner. Now I have enough in my pocket to pay my landlady. Who dares maintain that the muse of letters does not feed a man? How might I assist you?'

'Tell me what you know about a fellow named Navarre.'

'Not a lot, except that he is mad keen on literature and writes articles about everything except medicine, despite lecturing at the Salpêtrière.'

'Does *L'Écho de Paris* have an archive?'

'Yes, I'll show you where it is.'

He led them to a room full of glass-fronted cabinets containing bulky volumes bound in green cloth that were presided over by an elderly, melancholy man in a peaked cap.

'Tell Herbert what you want and if he can he will be only too happy to help. Goodbye!'

'Much obliged,' replied Victor.

'November 1886,' Joseph announced to the archivist, who scratched his chin forlornly.

Victor and Joseph exchanged disappointed looks.

'In that case, perhaps we could take a look at the year 1887.'

The old man bounded with extraordinary agility over to one of the cabinets and climbed to the top of a rolling ladder in order to reach the volume. Joseph offered to help him, but the old fellow only relinquished the tome in order to set it down on a lectern.

'You're in luck. We have a few copies of *L'Éclair*. Don't put spittle on your finger when you turn the pages,' the old man stipulated, returning to his desk.

Standing side by side, they scoured the back issues.

'Boss, I think we've drawn a blank.'

'There!'

Victor pointed to a headline and, bending over, murmured: '14 January 1887 . . .'

Joseph continued reading under his breath:

'Yesterday saw the close of the hearing marking the end of the jewel trial, the two unfortunate protagonists of which were cleared of all charges of colluding with the fraudulent Baroness de Saint-Meslin. The following is a summary of events . . .'

They became engrossed in their reading.

On 15 November 1886, an elegantly dressed lady in a veiled hat went to Les Asphodèles, a private clinic run by Doctor Aubertot, the well-known psychiatrist, situated some twenty miles from Lyon. The lady explained that her husband, Baron Saint-Meslin, was suffering from a nervous disorder and that the eminent Professor Jardin of the Faculty of Medicine at Lyon had advised her to seek his help. She produced a letter of recommendation stating that the Baron was suffering from persecution mania and believed people were trying to steal his possessions. Doctor Aubertot assured her he would be able to treat the patient. In order for her husband not to suspect anything, the Baroness implored the doctor to receive him in person. She paid him three months in advance.

The following day she walked into a jewellery store in Place Bellecour. She informed the manager, Monsieur Prosper Charmansat, that she wished to make her sister-in-law a wedding present of a set of diamonds. She urged the jeweller to accompany her to her house with a collection so that her husband, who was confined to bed, might help her choose. The jeweller agreed. They arrived at an opulent residence surrounded by parkland. The Baroness ordered the maid to inform the master of their arrival, and asked the jeweller to give her the briefcase containing the diamonds. She invited him to take a seat and said she would call for him when it came to discussing a price. Prosper Charmansat did as he was told. On her way out the Baroness bumped into Doctor Aubertot. She informed him that her husband was in the next room and that she preferred to leave in case he had an attack. She promised to deliver all the necessary papers for his confinement the following day. Tired of waiting, Prosper Charmansat left the room. When the man he assumed to be the Baron, but who was in fact Doctor Aubertot, blocked his way and refused to tell him where the diamonds were, the jeweller grew angry. Doctor Aubertot signalled to a male nurse, who restrained Charmansat, taking him to be Baron Saint-Meslin, gave him a cold shower, then put him in a straitjacket and locked him in a padded cell.

It took more than three weeks for the police to unravel the plot, during which time Monsieur Prosper Charmansat remained incarcerated. The Baroness and the jewels have yet to be traced.

'What an incredible story, Boss! I can just picture it: the

mysterious Baroness behind her veil, Prosper Charmansat trussed up and desperate, and the Doctor austere and . . .'

'Yes, but this is real life, Joseph, and if we don't get a move on dear old Herbert is going to start looking daggers at us!'

They avoided the old man's baleful glances. Out on the pavement of Rue du Croissant, they stood for a moment, stunned. A sudden downpour roused them, and Victor swiftly put up his umbrella.

'One thing is sure; this is a case of revenge. But who is taking revenge on whom? Charmansat on Aubertot? Or vice versa?'

'It might seem strange, Boss, but I think those two are as thick as thieves. I wouldn't be surprised if Aubertot was the man I followed who met Charmansat at Saint-Étienne-du-Mont and then in Rue Caulaincourt again yesterday!'

'Yes, your description fits,' agreed Victor.

'And what's more I followed him down Rue de Navarre, near the Roman arenas and Rue Monge, so maybe that's where he got the idea for his nom de plume.'

'Joseph! You're getting quite good at this.'

'I know, Boss, I never cease to amaze myself. Are our two chaps in cahoots or is someone else pulling the strings? As for Noémi Gerfleur, her goose is cooked: exit one Baroness Saint-Meslin, and Élisa who was unfortunate enough to have a thief for a mother.'

'Yes, but where does Louis Dolbreuse fit into all this?'

'Nowhere yet, Boss. But I'm keeping him up my sleeve, because yesterday the other two were after him. Where to first?'

'The pawnshop is nearest to here.'

'That's just what I was going to suggest. If we're lucky, we'll catch him coming out for his lunch break.'

'. . . and we can grab a bite ourselves,' added Joseph, ever hopeful.

A stream of clerks and office workers filed down Rue des Franc-Bourgeois, but the tubby, bearded fellow was not among them. Victor collared a stooped young man with bushy eyebrows.

'I must have missed one of your colleagues, Prosper Charmansat . . .'

'I'm not surprised. He's ill.'

'Since when?'

'Since this morning. I'd be telling a lie if I said I missed him. People like that make you wish the plague still existed.'

'Why? Is he an unpleasant sort?'

'Worse than that, he takes himself seriously,' replied the young man, whose shoulders looked as if he were bearing the weight of the whole world upon them. 'There are times when he behaves as though he owned all the rubbish these poor people come here and dump on us. Oh, and it's thanks to him, too, that the wheel was invented. Well, all I can say is with well-oiled cogs like him, the machine of state will never cease to turn,' he declared, spitting in the gutter.

Victor and Joseph looked at one another and hailed a cab in unison.

The ex-jeweller was not at home. They ran after their cab and shouted to the driver to take them to Rue Monge. Victor left the famished Joseph in the carriage and went to knock on Aubertot's door. The mute valet he had met on Saturday gave him a pained look.

'Monsieur is not at home,' he said through gritted teeth.

Victor produced a coin from his pocket, and by his customary sleight of hand transferred it to that of the servant, whose mouth, forming an O as if he were about to emit a smoke ring, miraculously began to move.

'A messenger delivered a note to Monsieur while he was in the middle of lunch and Monsieur left for the Salpêtrière immediately.'

The servant snapped his jaw shut, exhausted after such a long communication.

Nobody on Mazarin or Lassay Wings could boast having received a visit from Doctor Aubertot that morning. Victor cursed the ill-fortune that had sent him on so many wild goose chases in one day. Joseph, as wet as he was hungry, found it hard to keep up. He swore never again to go off on a case, however exciting, without enjoying a hearty meal first.

'Hey! I'm getting wet here under this so-called umbrella.'

'What are you complaining about now?'

'Nothing, I'm just talking to myself.'

They walked alongside the Chapelle Saint-Louis, which looked like an animal crouching beneath the overcast sky. A tiny hunched figure stirred near the entrance and a voice cried out:

'Help! A ghost!'

Victor looked at Joseph and passed him the umbrella.

A woman as thin as a reed with a halo of white hair clutched his arm.

'I came to listen to the music of God. I was floating up with the angels when I saw him,' she breathed. 'He's in there, waiting.'

Victor recognised the little old lady from Cour Manon, who only a few days before had been recalling her first kiss. She looked back at the chapel and, regaining her composure, spoke in a barely audible voice.

'I saw him, I saw him, he's come back, the sly devil, and he's dancing like a pendulum, right, left, ding, dong, ding, dong, black as a ghost under a red moon. I know who is; he's come for Zélie Bastien.'

Fear in the eyes of another, even an old lady lapsed into second childhood, strikes at the heart. Joseph gulped. The sinister Cours des Comptes[31] took the place of the squat shape of Chapelle Saint-Louis and suddenly his appetite had vanished.

'Please don't leave me alone,' begged Madame Bastien, looking like a terrified child who has seen a wolf. Her knees buckled and she propped herself up against a sculpture depicting Cain and Abel, which Victor would not have wished to encounter in any forest. He motioned to Joseph.

'Stay with her. I'm going to see what it is.'

As he entered the icy interior of the building, he had the impression of walking into a cave where a wild beast has its lair. The gloom was mitigated by the sputtering flames that cast a yellow light on to the figures of the paintings hung round the walls – copies or imitations of the old masters – that flickered briefly to life as though animated by a desire to exist in three dimensions. He recalled the terrifying English gothic horror novels he had read, from Mary Shelley's *Frankenstein*, which Kenji had given him one summer when he was thirteen, to Robert Louis Stevenson's *The Strange Case of Doctor Jekyll and Mr Hyde*, which he had devoured when it first came out in 1885.

His steps echoed as he walked into each of the side chapels. When he reached the third he saw something. He moved between the rows of prayer benches.

'Are you all right, Boss?' Joseph called.

'Yes,' he replied.

His voice sounded as if it were coming out of an organ pipe and the noise bounced off the walls of the nave. The waning daylight filtering through the stained-glass windows depicting saints gazing up at azure skies mingled with the encroaching darkness and cast terrible shadows. Victor paused. He felt his legs turn to jelly. On one of the walls a huge, black shadow was swinging. He turned round slowly.

Terrified, he tried to calm his wildly beating heart. He stumbled and grabbed hold of the rail round the altar.

'Get out! Get out!' a voice whispered inside his head.

He had seen many corpses, but this one was different.

The body was suspended from the pulpit by a rope round its neck. One end of it had been tied in a double loop and was lying under the dais. The man's feet were dangling some eight inches above the tiled floor. In front of the corpse a chair lay knocked over.

Victor found a candle and put the chair upright. Doctor

Aubertot would be giving no more consultations. His head was bare and his face stained with the blood that had poured from his nose and ears. There was some severe bruising beneath his left ear.

Victor's first instinct was to call for help, and yet there was something about the corpse that intrigued him. It was the expression. He had never dealt with a hanging before, but he couldn't help feeling this one had a staged quality about it. There was no swollen tongue sticking out of the corpse's mouth and the half-open eyes stared at him from an ashen face. He lowered the candle. A pool of red was spreading across the floor.

All of a sudden a cackling laugh rang out from behind a pillar.

Victor jumped out of his skin. In the gloom he made out a screwed up face and a bulging neck. It was a woman, a wretched woman with goitre who was pointing her finger at him and shaking with laughter that seemed more like sobbing. He moved back, horrified, and ran out into the fresh air where he stood for a long time letting the rain run down his face.

The hospital attendant hurrying in the direction of the main building tried without success to avoid the stranger running towards him waving his arms. Victor seized the poor man by the wrists and ordered him to go and cut down the body hanging in the Chapelle Saint-Louis. Panting, he hurried back to Joseph, who was only too relieved to be delivered from Madame Bastien's lamentations.

'Anyone would think you were being chased by demons, Boss!'

'Aubertot has been murdered! There's not a moment to lose!'

Joseph, astonished, and still clutching the umbrella he had closed in order to be able to move faster, set off behind Victor in the direction of Boulevard de l'Hôpital.

The widow Galipot was blocking their way. Sprawled across the bottom step, she was brandishing an empty bottle and railing against the bastards who had stolen her drink. Unruffled by her haranguing cries of 'fools!' and 'rascals!' they managed to climb over her and up the stairs.

'On the left, Boss!'

Victor was about to push against the door when it flew open. A man in a sombrero, wearing a check jacket, knocked Joseph off his feet and leapt down the stairwell.

'Dolbreuse!' roared Victor.

'Stop him!' shouted Joseph at the top of his voice.

There was a high-pitched shriek and the words: 'Your dough, you imbecile!' rang out, followed by the dull thud of a hard object coming down on someone's head, and then a general commotion. Joseph went downstairs to find out what was going on, and Victor searched the apartment, ending up in the bedroom, where he found a man hanging from the window latch by a piece of gauze. It was Charmansat. Victor rushed forward, hoisted up the wretched man, who was twisting about frantically, and managed to untie him, but failed to stop him from falling.

'If he isn't already done for, that might have finished him off,' he murmured, kneeling beside the ex-jeweller who lay in a heap.

Charmansat was in a sorry state. He sat up with difficulty, choking and spitting, his hand clasping his side. Victor helped remove his waistcoat and his ripped shirt. He was astonished to see that the man's chest, which was protected by a leather breast plate, had only suffered a surface wound. Had it not been for this unusual corset, the knife attack would have proved fatal.

'It's a souvenir from the psychiatric hospital,' Charmansat breathed, grimacing. 'I strained my back struggling when they put me in that cell. This contraption keeps the vertebrae in place.'

'It saved your life.'

Victor laid him out on the bed and placed a pillow under his neck. He had brought him a carafe of water and a glass when Joseph appeared.

'That drunkard has good reflexes! She knocked Dolbreuse out cold with her bottle. The neighbours are bringing him round and they've gone to fetch the police.'

'Lock the door. There are a few points that need clearing up.'

'Do you think he's in any state to talk, Boss?' said Joseph, pointing at Charmansat, who was sipping some water.

'Are you able to speak?' asked Victor.

The ex-jeweller felt his throat and nodded.

'Was it you who murdered Élisa, Noémi, Gaston and Basile?'

'No, as God is my judge,' whispered Charmansat.

His voice was hoarse and his breathing short and laboured. He complained of pains in his neck and jaw.

'Why did Dolbreuse try to kill you?'

'Because the doctor and I were about to . . .'

He drank another sip of water.

'. . . eliminate him and make it look like a suicide. We planned to force him to confess to his crimes. He's the murderer.'

'But he was one step ahead. He turned the tables on you. He tried to hang you, and in the doctor's case he succeeded . . .'

'Is Aubertot . . . ?'

Charmansat sat bolt upright, his face white as a sheet. His strangled voice took on a steely tone.

'The swine!'

'You hate the man. But who is he? Did he play some part in the affair that ended in a trial on 14 January 1887?'

'You couldn't know. The newspapers never reported what happened next. The doctor and I lost everything. Everything! His patients stopped coming because he was blamed for not having notified the prefecture about my confinement. And as for me . . . my fiancée broke off our engagement because I was suspected of having defrauded the insurance company. The fact that I was a victim didn't save me from the vile calumny . . .'

He closed his eyes and continued to relate his story, punctuated by sighs.

'After our release, Aubertot and I decided to join forces.'

'You didn't hate him then.'

'He was as much a victim as I. And when I realised that I became his ally. We wanted revenge. We wanted to find the

Baroness. We pooled the little information we had. The carriage that had taken me to Aubertot's was green – a four-seater with a coat of arms still on the door. I had glimpsed a coach hire number on the back when I got out. The coachman was young and dark-skinned, possibly of Mediterranean origin. Aubertot made a tour of all the depots in and around Lyon. He traced the coach. It had been hired on 14 November 1886 by a man named Carnot, who had left a deposit that was returned to him on 17 November. This Carnot . . . he gave us a hard time but we finally located him. He was a hospital attendant on Professor Jardin's ward. Only as it turned out . . . we were too late.'

'Too late for what?' exclaimed Joseph.

He had been sentenced to five years for insulting and attacking a policeman a week after the jewels went missing. We continued our investigations. Carnot had worked at the hospital by day and played the trumpet in a Lyon nightclub – La Taverne des Jacobins. His lover was a singer, Léontine Fourchon. She vanished shortly before his arrest. We needed to be certain. I went to visit Carnot in prison. We met in the visiting room without exchanging a word. I recognised the Baroness's coachman and accomplice immediately and he recognised me.'

'Why didn't you go to the police?'

Charmansat laughed out loud, triggering a coughing fit.

'We reckoned that when the villain was released the first thing he'd do would be to look for Léontine – who we supposed had cheated him too. Who better to lead us to her? We decided to sit and wait. If it hadn't been for the doctor, I don't know how

I would have survived. He took me under his wing. We moved to Paris. He procured a post for me at the pawnshop and in the meantime he started a new career under Professor Charcot. He sold Les Asphodèles and opened his practice on Rue Monge. I've been his patient all these years. A few months before Carnot's release from prison the doctor hired a private detective who followed our man to Montmartre. Carnot was definitely an artistic type. He was a poet who recited his work at Le Chat-Noir under the pseudonym . . .'

'Louis Dolbreuse,' whispered Joseph, who was taking notes.

'So the doctor also assumed the identity of Navarre, a man with literary interests, and got to know Carnot. From then on we never let him out of our sight. One of us was constantly on his tail. That's how we discovered that his revenge included killing Léontine's daughter, Élisa. He paid Gaston Molina, a ruffian he had met in prison, to seduce the girl and deliver her to him. He killed the two of them and then unmasked Léontine, who was masquerading in her faded finery as Noémi Gerfleur. He strangled her.'

'And also killed Basile Popêche, a troublesome witness . . . But you stood by and did nothing to prevent these murders. And you dare to swear your innocence before God!' cried Joseph.

'You considered yourselves cunning, but Dolbreuse outwitted you,' added Victor. 'He murdered his former lover and her daughter according to a well-thought-out plan intended to throw suspicion on to you and Aubertot. He outwitted me too . . .'

'He outwitted all of us, Boss!'

There was a loud knock at the door. Charmansat opened his watery eyes with a look of profound weariness.

'The doctor is dead. He won't be able to look after me any more. What will become of me? Is there no justice?' he snivelled to Victor, his expression lifeless.

CHAPTER 14

Sunday 6 December

JOSEPH sat at his packing-case desk, staring at the bundle of manuscript pages. Euphrosine was pottering about in the kitchen; he could make out her every movement. She was rinsing the dishes, removing an iron ring from the cooker to put the coffee pot on it, talking to herself: 'If only money grew on trees!' She went heavily over to the stone sink to empty the greasy water into it, dragging her leg and then letting herself sink on to a stool, groaning: 'What will become of us if I can't work any more! Oh, the cross I have to bear!'

Since he had finished dinner, Joseph had not been able to write a single word. He imagined his mother, head resting on her chest, eyes closed, pale; at the end of her tether. He had to act. He must. He was going to become someone; he wanted it so much! And he had also boasted about it to Monsieur Legris, to Valentine, and to Marcel Bichonnier.

'How I bragged! Mademoiselle Iris is right: people who talk don't act; their life dissipates in words and they persuade themselves that reeling off words is an achievement in itself. I've put it off for too long. I'm going to take myself in hand and launch in.'

He was already imagining the day on which he bought a newspaper and saw his work published:

THE STRANGE AFFAIR AT COLUMBINES
By Joseph Pignot

What a beautiful dream! He would go tomorrow to *Le Passe-partout* and submit his serial. And if *Le Passe-partout* turned him down, he would plead his cause with all the Parisian papers. Whatever it took, he must succeed in getting it published. Who knows, perhaps one day his name would figure alongside those of Xavier de Maistre, Washington Irving and Tolstoy in guides to popular literature.

Oh, yes. His mother would no longer be a slave to her cart.

He took up his pen, and threw himself feverishly into his work. Without pausing to search for the perfect phrase, racing to finish his prologue so that the dream could become reality, he dashed off:

The clock was chiming ten o'clock as a Brougham driven by a liveried coachman drove up to the villa named 'The Columbines'. It skirted a fountain and drew up in front of the steps of a small manor house. A woman, her face hidden behind a veil, stepped out of the carriage, hurried up the steps and pulled the bell. A lady's maid showed her into the drawing room. When she was alone, the woman looked at herself in the large looking glass, and then turned her attention to the picture of a medical professor performing an operation that hung over the fireplace.

'Hmm! Elegantly attired, proud bearing, vicuña wool coat, expensive jewellery! Young or old? Damned veil, but what does it matter, this smells like nobility,' murmured Dr Eusèbe Rambuteau, leaning towards a two-way mirror that allowed him to spy on his visitors without them knowing.

No thread of grey could yet be seen in his thick dark hair or his jet-black beard frizzled in the old-fashioned style . . .

Feeling pleased with the word 'frizzled' that he had found by rifling through the dictionary, Joseph smiled at the photograph of his father.

'You're right, Papa, "nothing succeeds like success".'[32]

Wednesday 16 December

Bundled in a cape with military-style trimming, Inspector Lecacheur strode purposefully into the bookshop and removed his fur toque. He had to wait for several customers to pay for their purchases before Victor greeted him. Iris was helping Joseph untangle himself from the string used to tie up parcels of gilt-edged books to be offered as gifts. Meanwhile Kenji was moving among the shelves, anxious to satisfy a bespectacled lady whose son was keen on adventure novels. He glanced furtively at the newcomer and saw a resemblance to Jules Verne's Michel Strogoff; this provoked in him a sudden flutter of emotion at the memory of Eudoxie Allard's gentle curves as she lay naked on a white bearskin rug. The spirited Fifi Bas-Rhin, last heard of in the royal suite of the Hôtel Continental in the arms of a Muscovite prince, owner of an estate near Nijni-Novgorod! Her farewell present had pride of place beside the telephone, a wonderful typewriter, the Lambert, an extremely original invention, that Eudoxie had shown him how to use during unforgettable evenings during which instruction led seamlessly to practical demonstration:

'It's all done by touch, my dear Kenji, but that should present no problems for you. You merely have to touch the character plate and it oscillates gently, producing the impression . . . "No revolving parts but still it writes." Isn't that absolutely true?'

Kenji had literally fallen in love with the Lambert, and no one was allowed to touch its eighty-four keys. It was the height of modernity: all you had to do was change the plate and the Lambert typed in different languages: it was polyglot and had a leather case. Kenji sighed with satisfaction and showed the bespectacled lady the large in-quarto volume of *The Robinsons of Guiana* by Louis Boussenard.

'I see you are very busy, because of Christmas I suppose,' observed the inspector, smoothing his dark moustache. 'Can I offer you a lozenge?'

'No thank you,' replied Victor. 'So you succeeded in giving up tobacco?'

'Yes, for several months, but now I'm addicted to the astringent flavour of the lozenges; unfortunately one dependence has been replaced by another . . . Have you managed to get hold of an original edition of *Manon Lescaut*?'

'Not yet sadly!'

'But, dear chap, you are a specialist on Abbé Prévost, are you not? . . . The Salpêtrière holds no more secrets for you than Le Moulin-Rouge, Killer's Crossing or the environs of the River Bièvre, all places you have been over with a fine-tooth comb . . . Can we go and discuss this somewhere more private?'

Reluctantly, Victor led him into the back office, where the inspector looked attentively at Kenji's collections. He sensed that the bookseller was nervous and took pleasure in fuelling his discomfort. Shaking his box of lozenges like a rattle, he leant against the cabinet and stared at Victor.

'Although this is not an official visit, and our conversation can not be admitted into the file on Élisa and Léontine Fourchon, don't think that I am taken in. I can't prove your involvement in this business, but everywhere the case leads me – the boarding school at Saint-Mandé, or Grégoire Mercier's house, to name but two places – I come up against your shadow. When they arrested Louis Dolbreuse and Prosper Charmansat, whom should my colleagues stumble upon? Upon you, Monsieur Legris. And don't think either that I am persuaded for one moment by the confused explanations of your assistant Joseph, who, let's just say, has a vivid imagination. He dared to make out that although he knew Prosper through the pawnshop, you and he were walking past his home by chance when you were alerted by shouting! If I decide yet again not to call you as a witness at this trial, it's only because I am grateful that you saved Charmansat's life and put a stop to the murders perpetrated by Dolbreuse. So I will keep quiet about Dolbreuse's explanation that he misled you, setting you off on a false trail by means of a note that he wrote himself and placed with Gaston Molina's belongings under cover of fetching a forgotten hat at Le Moulin-Rouge. The literary extracts left beside Noémi Gerfleur's body were intended to perform the same purpose for the police. Had you not put a stop to him,

Dolbreuse would have sent a confession to the press, in Charmansat's name, revealing that Aubertot and he were the culprits and that after killing the doctor Prosper preferred to take his own life rather than face justice . . . You see there's not much that I don't know, in spite of the fact that several people, including the headmistress of the Bontemps Boarding School, the goatherd and our ex-jeweller, seem to be hit by temporary amnesia whenever your name is mentioned.'

The inspector felt the need to suck on some more lozenges. Victor, a little red in the face, said nothing and seemed fascinated by the state of his fingernails.

'I have come to disturb you because I am missing a piece of evidence that I suspect you of holding. You see, I already have the necessary proof to convict Louis Dolbreuse, or rather Louis Carnot, Léontine Fourchon's lover and Madame de Saint-Meslin's coachman, who was so in love with her that he couldn't forgive her for trampling over his feelings to avoid sharing the spoils of their larceny. That's right, Monsieur Legris; all these crimes had only one motive, betrayed love: when you see what these feelings can lead to you can understand why I prefer celibacy. But returning to the case in point, even though I hold many trump cards, I just can't help wanting more. So, without you having to say a single word, I would ask you, if you are indeed in possession of it, as I think you are, to place by the door of this room the second shoe belonging to Élisa – or rather to Iris Mori . . . oh yes, I am well-informed, the stutterings of Grégoire Mercier, the simpering of Corymbe Bontemps were no match for the temptations of the jingling stuff, which never fails to deliver up information. I shall therefore now lose myself in reading *Journal des Voyages* and when I have recovered the shoe I shall leave your bookshop without any fuss . . .'

A few minutes later, Inspector Lecacheur addressed an amiable greeting to everyone in the bookshop and went back out to brave the biting cold. The right pocket of his cape, now curiously misshapen, would long remain impregnated with the smell of goat. Victor let out a sigh and hurried over to help Kenji, who was teetering under a pile of books by Jules Verne and Alexandre Dumas.

Joseph clutched *Le Passe-partout*, not daring to open it, although the temptation was overwhelming. He resisted. Supposing it was not there? The weather was becoming bitter. He sheltered under the awning of the packaging shop opposite the bookshop, and watched Inspector Lecacheur leave. Slowly, he unfolded the daily, lingering over the page layout. Suddenly his hands trembled. It was so unbelievable that he remained rooted to the spot, his lips moving as he read:

We are happy to announce to the many readers of *Le Passe-partout* that we are introducing a new serial entitled:

THE STRANGE AFFAIR AT COLUMBINES

from the pen of promising author, Joseph Pignot. In a mystery that will keep you on the edge of your seat, the action takes place at Paris and Lyon, in the most diverse milieux. *The Strange Affair at Columbines*, the first episode of which appears in this edition, is tipped for great success.

'Papa, Papa, do you see this? That's your son's name there!' murmured Joseph in a quavering voice.

Kenji took a step back and contemplated the picture he had just hung in the alcove of his bedroom: *The Rooftops of Paris at Dawn.* He had kept it for more than eighteen months in his solid oak chest, so that he could put off telling Tasha and Victor that he had bought it at her exhibition at Le Soleil D'Or. What had he been worried about? That Victor would misunderstand his intentions and be jealous? That Tasha would imagine . . . No, the time for all that had passed. He would never again let the fear of what people might say dictate his conduct – that way of doing things had already cost him too much suffering and difficulty. From now on, he would live his life without pretence. He experienced a moment of absolute happiness as he took in the jumble of roofs and gutters lit by a yellow light. How beautifully she had rendered it all! How good it was to be able to drink it in, to see the sun rise over the city, to dream of all that a new day promised! And what joy to finally be free of the burden of the secrets that had been gnawing away at him! Iris and Victor knew the truth, and there had been neither tears nor recrimination. Each time he looked at the picture, he would experience the same gratitude at the way life had turned out. He was proud to think that soon everyone would know Iris was his daughter.

Joseph also knew the truth, but it was not Kenji who had told him. Iris had jumped the gun during one of the English lessons she gave Joseph in the back office. Her pupil had been so surprised that he had finally succeeded in pronouncing 'father' correctly, which linguistic prowess had been rewarded by an unforgettable kiss on the cheek.

How many times had Joseph dreamed of nonchalantly tossing the newspaper containing his published serial on to the counter and mentioning casually to Victor as he climbed his ladder:

'Take a look at page four. I think you'll find a piece by someone you know quite well.'

But the scene so often replayed in his mind now had a different protagonist, because all his thoughts were taken over by a charming young girl.

Taking advantage of having to sort a range of dead stock, he led Iris down to the basement and without a word held out the copy of *Le Passe-partout* to her. She scanned the page, flabbergasted, then said in a husky voice: 'It's your name. It's you!'

'I hope you don't mind that I have found a publisher?'

'Of course not, it's brilliant, Joseph!'

'Yes, it's a bit easier to read when it's printed,' he said as if that was the only thing that mattered to him.

'When did you write it?'

'In my spare time – during lunchtime, at night, after work. It was child's play – I wrote about the things I had experienced and then added a bit of imagination . . .You don't have to read it, of course! I know you're not very fond of literature.'

'Oh, but I . . . Yes, I am, you're mistaken!'

'I wanted you to be the first to know, because now I don't have to worry about my future. Writing pays well, you know.'

'Won't we see each other any more? Are you going to leave?'

'No, I have a future now, but I can't only live by my pen. I need other work as well until . . . And I still have to master English.'

'So you're staying – I'm so happy! Do you know what? I could type your next manuscript on Father's typewriter. Without him knowing, obviously.'

'Of course, I . . . Bother! Listen, there are customers. Wait a little bit before you come up,' murmured Joseph.

She touched his hand. He recoiled as if she had burned him, hurried to the door, flew up the stairs then froze when he reached the shop. Those voices! If only the ground could swallow him up . . .

This is the last straw, he told himself wandering along the shelves, filled with the absurd hope that he was invisible.

He spotted Kenji and guessed from his unctuous manner that he was struggling valiantly to remain courteous. Opposite him, in the manner of Juno reigning at Jupiter's right hand, stood the Comtesse Olympe de Salignac flanked by Raphaëlle de Gouveline and the Maltese lap dog that was her constant companion. As for Monsieur Legris, he seemed to be fascinated by Molière's thin moustache.

'Delighted, Madame, it's such a long time since we've seen you.'

'I've been otherwise engaged, Monsieur Mori. I'm going to be a great-aunt. My niece Valentine is awaiting a happy event, due in the summer.'

'Splendid, splendid, we can no longer say that France is

failing to populate itself. And how is Madame de Brix?'
enquired Kenji, clearing his throat discreetly.

'She couldn't be doing better; she has almost recovered. Do
you know that she has found a fourth suitor? She met him at
Lamalou-les-Bains, a retired colonel. They are to be wed in
February. Naturally it will be a very simple ceremony, at her
age . . . No maids of honour or veil. We have chosen a dress of
silver grey and a white lace hat embellished with a very delicate
sprig of orange blossom.'

'Splendid, splendid,' repeated Kenji, beating a strategic
retreat behind the counter.

'Indeed, Monsieur Mori. She has charged me with ordering
the complete works of Claire de Chandeneux. I hope you have
them,' she concluded in a tone that brooked no refusal.

'Claire de Chandeneux . . . Claire de Chandeneux . . . Uh . . .
I . . .' stammered Kenji, throwing a desperate look at Joseph,
who stepped valiantly into the breech.

'That's lucky, Boss. I put all her books aside in the bilge
section when we were doing the stock take. They're in the
stockroom. I'll run down and fetch them.'

Relieved, Kenji gave a sigh of relief and deigned to smile at
Joseph, who had just won himself an ally.

Raphaëlle de Gouveline had nonchalantly gone over to
Victor.

'Monsieur Legris,' she murmured out of the corner of her
mouth, 'would you by any chance have a copy of *The Damned*?
I like keep up to date, and everyone is carping about that book!
And, while you're at it, could you add in *Nana* and *The Kill*?
I'm behind with my reading. Could you make me up a gift

parcel, but out of sight of Olympe?' She pointed her chin meaningfully in the direction of the Comtesse de Salignac. 'Oh, I almost forgot, I would also like *Madame Bovary* and *The Vatard Sisters*[33] – I've heard it's a very interesting novel of manners, if you understand what I mean.'

'Perfectly, Madame de Gouveline, perfectly.'

'We have identical views on the spice of life, don't we, Monsieur Legris?'

She gave him a conspiratorial wink and rejoined the Comtesse, who was examining the books brought by Joseph.

'Have them all delivered to me,' ordered the Comtesse. 'Claire de Chandeneux departed this world too early, depriving Catholic literature of its most ardent exponent.'

'Oh yes! Claire de Chandeneux!' agreed Raphaëlle de Gouveline. 'You finally have her complete works, dear Olympe! I adore her chaste, sentimental stories; they have none of the vulgarity of masculine writing. Monsieur Mori, I shall immediately buy *The Brambles on the Road* and *Val-Régis the Great* for my long winter evenings. And it's lucky there are two of them; I'll be able to lend them to Mathilde de Flavignol and her friend Helga Becker who are both still immobilised after their terrible bicycle collision.'

Monday 21 December

'Madame Pignot, I have one! I was lucky – they're fighting over them!' yelled Madame Ballu, brandishing *Le Passe-partout*. 'But have you lost your mind? You shouldn't have got up with that

297

knee of yours; it's bigger than an ostrich egg! Dr Reynaud's going to tick you off and, as for your son, he'll tick me off. Does it hurt?'

'My dear Madame Ballu, it's like having a piston thumping away in my leg.'

'You must get back into bed under the warmth of your eiderdown and take your soothing remedy, otherwise I won't read to you. Do you remember where we were?'

'Yes, Baroness de Saint-Pourçain left in a hurry, begging Dr Rambuteau not to frighten her poor husband, lest he have a fit right there in the drawing room.'

'Right, time for Bedfordshire. Prop yourself against the pillow, there, that's good. I'll pour us some juice, settle myself down and reread you the last sentence, because it's so beautiful:'

Dr Rambuteau nodded gravely. He understood. She was an adorable little woman, very unlucky in marriage; she did not deserve such a fate . . .

'That's exactly like me, I didn't deserve that my Ballu should rise to heaven because . . .'

'Read!'

'All right, all right.'

Felix Charenton twisted in his seat, unable to bear it any more. He had pins and needles in his calves. The sofa was extremely uncomfortable. He rose and began to pace up and down the drawing room, looking several times at his watch. The family confabulation was dragging on interminably.

'At this rate, I could be hanging about here until evening! But what on earth are they doing, for the Lord's sake?'

He felt an overpowering desire to smoke a cigarette.

'Very well observed, don't you think? Just like my Ballu, when he had been reading his newspaper too long and he . . .'

'Continue reading!'

'Oh, you, you're hooked!'

Unable to restrain himself he gently opened the door and found himself face to face with a man who looked at him strangely. Adjusting his pince-nez, he noticed the Légion d'Honneur on the man's lapel and deduced that here was the Baron of Saint-Pourçain, not so ill after all. He cleared his throat.

'Are the jewels to your liking?'

'Of course, my friend, of course.'

'Have you chosen the set of rubies or the set of emeralds? It's late and I'm hungry.'

'That's just like my Joseph; he has a good appetite, you know,' remarked Euphrosine.

Madame Ballu's face softened. She continued:

'Do you wear braces?' asked the man with the Légion d'Honneur.

Felix Charenton opened his mouth without knowing what to say. It was true: the Baron was completely deranged.

'If you wear braces, you'll have to get used to doing without them, and the same goes for laces,' continued the man with the Légion d'Honneur. 'Let's go, quietly now.'

He spoke in a neutral tone, staring at a point just over Felix Charenton's shoulder. Felix turned round and saw surging out of a hidden entrance a heavy-set individual dressed in white.

'My jewels! Where are the jewels? God Almighty! You're mad! Let me go!'

Restrained by the heavy-set fellow, he thrashed about and bucked, in the grip of a terrible panic that twisted his guts.

'Help! Help me! Stop thief!'

Dr Rambuteau had heard enough to convince him to administer his new patient a radical treatment.

'Nurse, shower him.'

'To be continued . . . Oh, misery. We'll have to wait until tomorrow to find out what happens. It's so well written you can really believe in it. Apparently Felix Charenton is based on an actual person, and he's had a relapse. It's not surprising, he was pushed over the edge, poor man. He was sent to the asylum because he completely lost his mind! All those cold showers would be enough to addle anyone's brain!'

'Well, yes, but it wouldn't do Joseph any harm to shave once in a while; it's a question of cleanliness. He's letting himself go.

Don't you think there's a strange smell in here? Good Lord, what's that stink?'

A strange, rangy fellow stood at the door to the bedroom, a bowl in his hands.

'Excuse me, are you Madame Pignot?'

'Yes, that's me, but what do you want? It's normal to knock before entering.'

'Your son sent me, a nice young man. I went to see him at the bookshop to discuss the death of my cousin, Basile Popêche. Monsieur Pignot told me you were suffering with your joints, so I didn't hang about. I went straight off to find Pulchérie.'

'Pulchérie? Who on earth's that?'

'A lovely little goat who's just had a kid and who I nourish on rosemary, so that her milk is healing for rheumatics. I've brought you a bowl. You have to drink it all down right to the last drop. I'll bring you some every day. It will sort you out in no time at all.'

'I'd like some too!' cried Madame Ballu.

At lunchtime Victor did not want to annoy Germaine, so he forced himself to sit down with Kenji and Iris and eat the goose sweetbreads with turnip. Conversation was limited to the sales made that morning and the drop in temperature, and other subjects less sensitive than the sudden increase in the size of the family. Then Victor took his leave, and went through the apartment to exit by the outside staircase. He came across Madame Ballu and stopped to speak to her, struck by her worried expression.

'Oh, it's nothing, Monsieur Legris, it's just that I'm worried about Euphrosine. I've just come from her and her knee is very painful – her old rheumatism playing up again; she won't be able to pull her cart any more. She's lucky to have such a devoted son. Joseph goes home each lunchtime to prepare her a meal. When I'm old and decrepit there'll be no one to look after me, seeing as how that imbecile Ballu kicked the bucket before we'd had time to make an heir . . .'

'You've got plenty of time to work it out – you're the youngest of all of us!' said Victor, continuing down the stairs.

'You say that, you say that, but I have my aches and pains and they're not all in the mind!'

Tasha's wrist was becoming stiff, so she laid her paintbrush to one side and stepped back to study Nicolas Poussin's *Moses Saved from the Waters*, hanging in the Louvre, which she was trying to reproduce. She pressed her finger on a yellow drape of her painting to accentuate a fold. She was quite pleased with her work. Thanks to Victor she was now associated with the Natanson brothers and had visited La Revue Blanche to attend the first exhibition of a very young artist, Édouard Vuillard. Through him she had met a painter from Bordeaux, Odile Redon, whose strange compositions she had admired and whose advice she thought about constantly. According to him, art should be the servant of the unconscious mind, should strive to reproduce the interior world of the artist, putting the logic of the visible to the service of the invisible. Redon had encouraged her to distance herself from the impressionists, whom he reproached for simply letting nature speak for itself, and to study the old masters, whose work was continued by Ingres, Delacroix, then Gustave Moreau and even Degas. She had spent time in the halls of the Louvre dedicated to French painting and had discovered an affinity with the severe charm and tempered gravity of Poussin.

Inspired by *The Childhood of Bacchus* she had sketched a female nude, which had much impressed Victor by the modernity of the pose, and was now launched on an entire canvas.

'That figure of the women bent over the baby in its basket is very touching. Could you not undress her a little?'

Victor was standing behind Tasha, leaning eagerly towards the easel. She threatened him with her paintbrush.

'I forebade you to come!'

'What were you afraid of? That I would encounter one of your many admirers? Is the abominable Laumier anywhere near?'

'No need to worry about him. Since Gauguin left for Tahiti in April, Laumier is inconsolable and never leaves his studio.'

'No doubt he's churning out another pictorial theory. So what was it you were afraid of?'

'That you would distract me. For once I am half-satisfied with what I have done . . . I think I'm on to something. I think I've opened the door to one of those secret chambers of the mind Kenji is so keen on. That woman, that child in the water, I'm going to transpose them to modern times, to a wash-house perhaps, and paint them in my own way. No doubt it's a little too impressionistic for Redon . . .'

'Redon? Who's that?'

'. . . but too bad; I'm sensitive to the interplay of light. I'll reduce the depth, that will make it more dreamlike and symbolic than my previous works, while at the same time remaining true to life. A blend of styles. What do you think?'

'I'm happy that you have found your own way. I think I have also found mine and that gives me confidence. I'm going to dedicate my photographs to children at work, not for the aesthetic effect, but to bear witness to a reality that amongst many other things will contribute to a deeper understanding of the society in which we live.'

'That's wonderful, Victor! We must celebrate that!'

'I've already planned it. My furniture has been delivered. This evening I am moving in officially to my bachelor apartment. I am inviting you to dinner at Le Grand Hôtel. Afterwards if you have nothing better in mind, we can spend a chaste evening by the fire discussing painting and photography . . .'

'And you can also tell me all about the thrilling investigation you have been involved in, unintentionally, I am sure . . .'

The caretaker in charge of guarding the new gallery of French artists in the Denon Pavilion turned away as he passed a couple whose loving embrace was really rather shocking. The nudity displayed on the canvases surrounding him prompted him to hurry into the next gallery, where the sight of Charles Le Brun's *Battles of Alexander the Great* restored his equilibrium.

PARISIAN NIGHTLIFE IN THE
1890S

THE 1890s saw the heyday of the *cafés-concert* and night-clubs, which embodied all the modernity and daring of *belle-époque* Paris. There were many such venues, to which both Parisians and visitors to the city flocked in the evening, mostly concentrated in and around Montmartre, the hub of artistic life in the city.

Founded in 1881 by Rudolph Salis, Le Chat-Noir, the first-ever cabaret, began life as an informal artistic salon. Artists, musicians and writers were invited to Salis's home to discuss their ideas and perform their work, amongst them Claude Debussy, Paul Verlaine, Erik Satie, Aristide Bruant and Caran d'Ache. It quickly became a fashionable nightspot, where the bohemian world rubbed shoulders with the aristocracy and bourgeoisie. The cabaret gave rise to a journal also called Le Chat-Noir, with contributions from Salis's regulars. It was successfully published on a weekly basis for over ten years.

Aristide Bruant, immortalised in a poster by Toulouse-Lautrec, went on to open his own cabaret, Le Mirliton, which became the home of satire and was particularly famous for Bruant's songs in which he made fun of the upper class members of his clientele.

Perhaps the place that most symbolises the Paris of that era is the greatest *café-concert* of them all, Le Moulin-Rouge, whose *fin-de-siècle* incarnation lives on in the art of Toulouse-Lautrec. Built in 1889 by Joseph Oller, it still stands today on Boulevard de Clichy in the neighbourhood of Pigalle. It was famed for its spectacular music hall, which included many different kinds of entertainer, including the extraordinary Pétomane who, amongst other tricks, could fart the tune of *La Marsellaise* at will. But it is as the home of the cancan for which Le Moulin-Rouge is best known. The dance had first emerged in dance halls much earlier in the nineteenth century and was originally performed by men, and then by courtesans during the Second Empire. Yet it was at Le Moulin-Rouge with a chorus line made up of professional dancers that the cancan took on the form by which it is still known today. Respectable members of society would come along to be shocked at the flying splits and extraordinary high kicks of legendary dancers such as La Goulue, Jane Avril and Nini Pattes en l'Air. And the tradition continues to this day at Le Moulin-Rouge, where visitors can still see regular performances of the outrageous cancan.

NOTES

[1] This catastrophe left forty-four people dead and more than a hundred injured.

[2] Situated on the left bank up until 1957 on the site now occupied by the Jussieu Campus of the University of Paris.

[3] Now called Gare d'Austerlitz.

[4] The river that used to cross the fifth and thirteenth arrondissements of Paris. Today it is channelled underground.

[5] Le Carrefour des Écrasés – the crossroads at Rue Montmartre and Boulevard Poissonnière.

[6] The Salon des Indépendents was founded in 1884 by Georges Seurat and welcomed the work of all artists, in contrast to the Salon des Beaux-Arts, which had very strict admission policies.

[7] Her real name was Louise Weber (1869–1929).

[8] On 15 March 1891, every region of France aligned its time with Paris, which became the official time of the country.

[9] In 1891, during a May Day demonstration in the little town of Fourmies in the Upper Loire, soldiers fired on a crowd, killing nine people.

[10] (1602–1674). A Japanese representative painter of the early Edo Period, most famous for his folding screens and hanging scrolls.

[11] See *The Père-Lachaise Mystery*, Gallic Books.

[12] Drinking fountains scattered throughout Paris, fifty of which

were donated to the city by British philanthropist Sir Richard Wallace in 1872.

[13] Song by Maurice Marc.

[14] See *Murder on the Eiffel Tower* and *The Père-Lachaise Mystery*, Gallic Books.

[15] French journalist (1833–1902), who was a theatre critic and the author of a number of novels.

[16] Her real name was Lucienne Beuze. Her nickname means literally 'drainage grille'.

[17] A popular figure of the Latin Quarter during the 1890s. He was a bohemian and autodidact, who supported himself doing odd jobs, and became the right-hand man of the poet Verlaine, selling off his mementoes of the poet after Verlaine's death in 1896.

[18] A drinker of liquefied ether, a nineteenth-century practice that fell out of favour when the gas was reclassified as a poison.

[19] A language constructed by a German Roman Catholic priest, Johann Martin Schleyer, in 1879–1880, after he dreamt that God wanted him to create an international language.

[20] French painter (1864–1951), known for his lithographs, etchings and watercolours.

[21] A singer whose real name was Léon Fourneau; his name was first 'latinised' to Fornax, and then made to sound Russian by inversing the letters: Xanrof.

[22] Play (and novel) by Alphonse Daudet.

[23] See *The Père-Lachaise Mystery*, op. cit.

[24] Georges-Louis Leclerc, Comte de Buffon, naturalist and biologist who had a profound influence on the work of later naturalists, including Charles Darwin.

[25] French writer (1829–1890). She contributed to the *Journal de la Jeunesse* and the *Bibliothèque rose*.

[26] Xavier de Montepin, 1881. Jules Mary, 1886.

[27] The policeman hero of the novels of Émile Gaboriau.

[28] Alain-René Lesage (1668–1747): *Le Diable Boiteux*.

[29] See *The Père-Lachaise Mystery*, op. cit.

[30] Impossible. (Author's note.)

[31] See *The Père-Lachaise Mystery*, op. cit.

[32] Alexandre Dumas the elder: *Ange Pitou* (1851).

[33] Novel by Karl-Joris Huysmans (1879).